the further adventures of

SHERLOCK HOLMES

THE GIANT RAT OF SUMATRA

THE GIANT RAT OF SUMATRA

RICHARD L. BOYER

TITAN BOOKS

THE FURTHER ADVENTURES OF SHERLOCK HOLMES:
THE GIANT RAT OF SUMATRA
ISBN: 9781848568600

Published by
Titan Books
A division of Titan Publishing Group Ltd
144 Southwark St
London
SE1 0UP

First edition: March 2011
10 9 8 7 6 5 4 3 2 1

Names, places and incidents are either products of the author's
imagination or used fictitiously. Any resemblance to actual persons, living
or dead (except for satirical purposes), is entirely coincidental.

Visit our website:
www.titanbooks.com

What did you think of this book? We love to hear from our
readers. Please email us at: readerfeedback@titanemail.com,
or write to us at the above address. To receive advance information,
news, competitions, and exclusive Titan offers online, please register
as a member by clicking the 'sign up' button on our website:
www.titanbooks.com

A CIP catalogue record for this title is available from the British Library.

Printed in the USA.

Author's Note

When your eyes pass over these words, dear reader, I shall be many years in my grave. For a multitude of considerations, some of which will become apparent in the pages that follow, it is necessary to withhold publication of this narrative until after the passing of the people named therein. Accordingly, this manuscript shall lie in the strongbox of Barclay's Bank, Oxford Street Branch, London, until the year 1975, a round figure I choose arbitrarily with the assurance that, by then, the people who could be injured or offended by what follows shall have long since turned to dust. This I do ordain as a condition and procedure of my last will and testament, to be so carried out by its executor or his appointees.

John H. Watson, MD
London, 1912

One

THE TATTOOED SAILOR

The summer of 1894 was hot and dry and without noteworthy cases or events, save for the mysterious disappearance of Miss Alice Allistair which threw the Kingdom into shock and sorrow. On a mid-summer holiday to India with her chaperone, she was abducted from a Bombay market without a trace.

Her father, Lord Allistair (whose name was, during the last half of the previous century, upon the tongue and in the mind of every British subject), secretly summoned Sherlock Holmes to his assistance. But weeks passed, and still no word arrived from the East as to the fate of his daughter. Early September found my companion restless, bored, and morose. A trip to Bombay, and a handsome fee paid by his Lordship were in the offing, but still Holmes paced and fretted, fretted and paced, and muttered interminably.

I must here inject the observation, based upon long experience, that for all the excitement of living with the world's most renowned consulting detective, life with Sherlock Holmes had its drawbacks. He kept odd hours, was often moody and uncommunicative and was, in his personal habits, untidy to the point of slovenliness.

It was early evening of 15 September of the year mentioned when, glancing at Holmes sunk in thought on the divan, I could bear the silence and oppressiveness of our flat no longer. Our quarters reeked of stale smoke and chemical fumes, and Holmes' insular behaviour and despondent attitude did nothing to relieve the situation. I rose and went over to the bow window, opened it, and allowed the balmy summer breeze to enter — dispelling the fumes and boosting my spirits.

'Lovely evening, Holmes. Perhaps you would care to join me for a walk?'

'I think not, Watson. I have enough to occupy myself for the present.'

'The Bradley forgeries, or the Allistair case?'

'Both. The first is unimportant, and easy: if the clerk has a limp, he's guilty. I expect a solution at any moment. The other, more serious one I am powerless to attack without evidence.'

He gazed at the wall, and sank deeper into thought.

I returned to the window. The sky was the brilliant copper colour of the dying sun, fading to dark blue towards the horizon. The faint babble of pedestrians wafted upwards to my ears. Peering down, I could see the sheen of top hats and the lilt of parasols as the couples passed beneath. Their laughter enticed me. Where had they been? Where were they going? More directly: why were we imprisoned in our drab flat, away from it all?

'I say, Holmes, just a short jaunt — enough to stretch the legs and mind, would be — *hullo*, what's this?'

Holmes shot a glance towards the open window. 'Well, Watson, what is it?'

The clatter of hooves and a pair of wildly veering carriage lamps had drawn my eye. In the fading light I could barely see the driver standing in his box and flailing at the horses with the utmost savagery.

'It appears to be a drunken cabbie. Poor beasts.'

'Hardly a drunken cabbie. I'll wager it's an *ambulance*.'

He rose from the divan and joined me at the window. To my utter amazement the vehicle, dashing past the street lamps below, showed itself indeed to be an ambulance; the markings on its side were unmistakable.

'You astound me, Holmes! How could you tell it was an ambulance?'

'One can observe with one's ears as well as one's eyes. The ambulance, for obvious reasons, has a longer chassis than the four-wheeler cab. A hospital carriage, bouncing over cobblestones, reveals itself by a curious deep rumbling in its timbers which the four-wheeler lacks. This particular sound is also emitted by lorries and dray carts, but given the hour and the vehicle's speed, we are left with the ambulance.'

'Bravo!' I cried.

'But only half the puzzle it seems,' said Holmes, as he leaned further out of the window and swept his eyes anxiously over the horizon.

'I have a strong suspicion that in addition to the misfortune in this neighbourhood, there is occurring at this very moment elsewhere in London a catastrophe of great magnitude, perhaps a large fire, that we shall no doubt read about in tomorrow's newspapers.'

This stream of inferences so stunned me that I remained speechless. Holmes observed the puzzled expression on my face.

'Come now, Watson, you're a medical man and know ambulances: was there anything amiss?'

'No,' I replied after some thought, 'except that some unfortunate –'

'Tut, man! Not anything else?'

I shook my head.

'Let me enquire then, how it happens that you were unable to determine the vehicle's identity until you saw the markings on the door?'

Once again, as in so many instances during my long association with my friend, I felt embarrassment at having overlooked the obvious.

'The bell. There was no *bell*!'

'Precisely. The warning bell carried by our ambulances was not sounded. This explains both the erratic path of the carriage – attempts made by the driver to avoid running down pedestrians – and the rather frenzied behaviour of the driver himself, both interpreted by you as being brought about by an excess of drink.'

Holmes continued to scan the horizon and the streets below. He charged his pipe and, between staccato puffs of smoke, muttered to himself.

'Of course there is always the question as to *why* the bell wasn't sounded...'

'A new driver...'

'No. The man's skill in handling the team and avoiding people shows that he is quite experienced. The walk that you mentioned earlier has suddenly taken on a new attraction. Let us be off.'

'Of course it's obvious,' he remarked as we scurried down the staircase, 'that the ambulance was bound from St Thomas' Hospital.'

'Hah! I'm afraid you're wrong there, old fellow; you seem to slip a bit, Holmes, if you don't mind my saying so,' I said with some smugness. 'Here I shall use your own methods against you. You seem to overlook Charing Cross which, although situated in the same general direction as St Thomas', is considerably closer. Logic decrees therefore, that the wagon came from there, since all possible haste was necessary.'

'Excellent, Watson! Really, you quite outdo yourself!'

I was deeply flattered, for Holmes was not a man to shower praise about willy-nilly.

'It is a pity you are mistaken,' he added.

'What makes you so sure?' I retorted, somewhat piqued.

'Once again, you have failed to observe completely. Did you see how the driver plied his whip?'

'He was quite zealous.'

'So much so in fact that you cried "poor beasts". Did you also observe the horses themselves as they passed beneath the street lamps? Their flanks were frothed with sweat. These two observations together force us to conclude that the horses had come from the *direction* of Charing Cross Hospital, yet a much greater distance. The point of departure was therefore St Thomas'.'

Once explained, the conclusion seemed simple.

'But you have done well in using logic, Watson, because we see that the *illogical* has happened: instead of coming from the nearest hospital, the ambulance has come across town. That is interesting. Also the want of a bell arouses our curiosity. Perhaps we can fit these two pieces together. We know the driver did not neglect to ring the bell – he is too experienced for such an oversight. What does this leave us with?'

We were walking south down Baker Street towards Portman Square, but engrossed as I was in the puzzle the evening's beauty escaped me. I plied my brain to the questions Holmes had raised.

'The bell was then either broken or missing,' I suggested.

'*Exactly!* Which indicates that this particular ambulance, being ill-equipped, was not intended for use. It was, then, dragged out of the repair shop at a moment's notice, and from the wrong hospital at that. Does this suggest anything to you?'

'Of course – all of the regular carriages were engaged!'

'Ah! But engaged for what purpose? Obviously they have hurried to the scene of some terrible calamity. I'm quite certain it is a fire. Why a fire? Well, what else could it be? Flood? Certainly not; the river is normal and we're in want of rain. Earthquake? Preposterous. Mass murder? In America perhaps, but never here. No, it is a fire that has occurred, and I –'

'What is it?'

I observed on Holmes' face the look of eagerness that told me of a new development at hand.

'See that crowd there by the kerbside? There's our ambulance too. I just saw Lestrade making his way into the centre of it, and I fear that this personal tragedy may have sinister overtones. Come on, hurry up! We want to arrive before the police make a total ruin of things.'

We fought our way through the knot of curious pedestrians. Arriving towards the middle of it, I could hear Lestrade's gravelly voice barking orders to subordinates and onlookers alike. In the gaslight, that was partially blocked by the crowd, I could see a dark form sprawled in the gutter.

It was obvious that Lestrade viewed Holmes' presence with a mixture of relief and annoyance.

'It beats me, Mr Holmes,' he remarked, 'how you seem to materialize on the spot when there's been murder done.'

'Murder,' said Holmes, visibly quickening. 'Watson, our evening stroll grows more engrossing by the minute. With your permission, Lestrade, I should like to examine the corpse.'

When the crowd of onlookers was sufficiently dispersed, the three of us were at liberty to examine the body in detail. The victim was a middle-aged, powerfully-built man with thick, dark hair and beard and a swarthy complexion. The man appeared to be diving headlong into the street; his feet remained strewn on the kerb – his head and shoulders shoved forward into the paving stones. A pool of blood had collected on the pavement beneath the open waistcoat and blouse which Lestrade drew back. The cause of death was immediately apparent. A horrid gash, extending up the trunk from the waist to the left shoulder, and terminating in a series of smaller slashes, had brought a quick and brutal end to the victim. The wounds were so vast and grotesque that, despite my medical experience, I was shocked and repelled in the extreme.

'Not a pretty sight, if I may say so,' said Lestrade. 'But then murder never is, no matter the method.'

'From these tattoos on his arms and chest and from the look of his clothes, he appears to have been a seafaring man,' observed Holmes. 'Has the body been moved?'

'Not to our knowledge,' returned Lestrade. 'The constable who discovered him is Roberts – a good man mind you – but for the life of him he's unable to track down one witness to this affair. The crowd drew him to the discovery. But as to what occurred, we are unable to locate one shopkeeper, resident, or passer-by who can give us the slightest account.'

'That is odd, considering it is a natural evening to be outdoors. There are many people on the streets tonight. Given the nature of the wounds and the physique of the deceased, one must assume there was a struggle, at least an outcry. It is very singular that the event failed to draw anyone's attention.'

Here my companion paused and looked, not without remorse, at the body sprawled beneath him in the gutter.

'Of course, since we have no living witnesses to aid us in our enquiry, then the dead man must tell the story.'

Holmes then proceeded to examine the body to the minutest detail. He skipped nothing, examining his clothing, particularly the shirtcuffs and pockets, the torn waistcoat and ripped shirt, the boots, the tattooed chest (butchered though it was), and concluded by thrusting his nose into the dead man's whiskers and sniffing vigorously. The next instant he was gone, pacing up and down the street and puffing furiously at his pipe, glancing in all directions.

Having become accustomed to this sort of behaviour on the part of my companion, I fell into conversation with Lestrade, remarking how strange it was that no excitement had been aroused during the murder, and how odd it was that not a mark of identification, nor any personal possessions for that matter, was found on the body. The attendants having placed the body on a litter, I watched Lestrade conversing with several correspondents who had been waiting at the edge of the crowd. I was thus engaged when I heard Holmes calling to us.

'Up here, Watson, Lestrade. Come up, this may interest you!'

Looking up past the glare of the street lamps, we caught sight of Holmes' angular face peering from the rooftop directly above.

'Take the second door there – the plain one, not the storekeeper's.'

Leaving two constables to dispatch the ambulance, we clambered up the narrow and dingy staircase which led unobtrusively from the street. At the first landing we found Holmes waiting for us. He led us up another flight of stairs and then through a narrow door of crude wood.

'This is the stairway that leads to the roof. Lestrade, if you've your dark lantern, now's the time it would be helpful.'

We found ourselves on a flat rooftop with a facade about three feet high on the Baker Street side, in front. Holmes, having taken the lantern from Lestrade, walked to a corner of the roof and let the beam fall upon a crumpled handkerchief.

'There's a piece of evidence for you, Lestrade. Perhaps you can smell the chloroform from here.'

'Yes, so it is…' mused the detective, somewhat chagrined at Holmes' astuteness. 'But how the devil did you seize on *this* place?'

'Logic, my friend. Consider this: a large, muscular man in the prime of life has been brutally murdered with a dagger. The body is discovered on a busy London thoroughfare. Yet, in spite of these two things, no one seems to have witnessed the deed. To explain this, we must either assume that our citizens are deaf, dumb, and blind, or we must seek a more rational explanation: that the man was murdered *elsewhere* and his remains deposited on the kerbside. But *how* deposited? A passing carriage would be a means, but it would be noisy and conspicuous. The absence of alternative explanations has led us to this rooftop where, as you can see, the evidence suggests the murder was committed.'

To make his point, Holmes pointed to the facade top overlooking the street. It was splashed profusely with blood.

'But why the chloroform,' I asked, 'if the deed were done with a dagger?'

'The man was drugged into unconsciousness beforehand – hence the silence of the deed. The murderers, and I believe there were more than one, then waited from this vantage point until the street below was temporarily vacant, whereupon they hurled the body down into the street, then fled down the ladder which overhangs the rear of the building.

'It's my guess, Lestrade, that your men will find several broken ribs on the corpse to substantiate my theory.'

'Well, Holmes,' said I, as we descended the stairway, 'things seem a bit clearer now, don't they?'

'On the contrary, Watson. What was cloudy at the outset is now murky. What before was merely unexplainable now becomes incoherent: *mad*. This latest discovery only lifts the curtain on what promises to be the most intricate and diabolical case we've handled in some time.

'Let me ask you, my dear fellow,' he continued, 'hasn't this rooftop killing raised some questions in your mind? Remember that just as the physician seeks the extraordinary, the unique, in making his diagnosis – so does the detective seek the illogical, the grotesque in guiding himself to the source of the crime. What *irrationality* have we indirectly witnessed?'

'That the man needn't have been stabbed – the chloroform or the fall would surely have killed him.'

'Yes, there's that. But hasn't it occurred to either of you that the criminals, once having committed the crime, were placing themselves in jeopardy by *throwing the corpse down into the street for public display?*'

'Your point is well-taken,' admitted Lestrade. 'In fact, the oddity has just occurred to me. The usual preoccupation of the murderer is *concealing* the body.'

'But these killers have deliberately set the law after themselves and made their escape perilous by "giving up" the body rather than disposing of it.'

'Perhaps they wish the killing publicized to serve as a warning.'

'I agree, at least for the present.'

Lestrade and I followed him to the rear of the building, where Holmes examined the wrought-iron fire ladder and the pavement under it. The examination yielded nothing except a shred of dark blue wool which Holmes plucked from a projecting ladder bolt.

'Here's a piece of good fortune,' he said turning it round in his fingers under the lantern beam. 'At first guess I'd say it was from a Norwich mill, but closer examination is necessary to make certain.'

Holmes was interrupted from his reveries by a great commotion in the street. The sound of police whistles and tramping boots brought us to the front of the building on the run. There we spied several constables waving their arms.

'Are they still on the roof?' cried one. 'Fetch a calling trumpet, will you? I – no *there* he is! Inspector Lestrade! We're wanted on the docks quick as a wink if you please, sir!'

'The fire is a large one then?' asked my companion.

'Frightful! And spreading fast. I –' Lestrade stopped in mid-sentence.

'But how came you to hear of it? I myself was just notified by police wire. I heard no one mention it.'

'Do you mind if we tag along?' asked Holmes, avoiding the detective's question.

'Well, I suppose there's no harm in it. I say, Mulvaney, is there room in that wagon? Very well, can you handle three more? That's a good fellow. Come on then, but mind, stay out of the way…'

We swung aboard and settled ourselves on the benches of the open wagon amidst a dozen bobbies, who could talk of nothing except the great fire on the docks. I assumed they were exaggerating the calamity. But thirty minutes later, when I saw the eastern sky aglow and the Thames a ribbon of gold, I knew it was worse than any of us had feared.

The first indication of the fire's size was the traffic. Roads were clogged to overflowing; children ran shouting in all directions; barking dogs scurried in front of carriages and between flying hooves. Horses reared and cried. A steady stream of the curious flowed towards the waterfront – only to be met by terrified residents fleeing the area. And the glow in the sky grew larger, brighter, with each passing minute.

'The weather we've had hasn't helped, you may be sure,' said Holmes out of the corner of his mouth, his eyes glued to the sky.

Countless times we were mired in a sea of people and vehicles. But fortunately, the bell on our police wagon *was* in working order, and it sang out mightily until my ears throbbed and ached.

'Stand to there! Give way for the police! You! Mind your reins I say!' shouted the driver, a burly fellow, obviously an expert. He handled the four sets of reins, and the eager animals they led to, with admirable skill. We dashed around corners at dizzying speeds. We clattered through alleyways. We flew along the streets. Above the pounding of the hooves and thunder of the wheels, I could hear the furious panting of our horses – a sound like a thousand giant bellows.

Presently I saw a ball of fire loom up behind a building, and knew we were nearing the scene. At the same instant, there shot forth from a side street a fire engine, trailing plumes of oily smoke and drawn by six magnificent horses in glistening livery. We fell in behind, and the two vehicles raised a terrific din!

Onwards we flew, the crowds parted, and cheered us as we passed.

At Preston Road we turned south, and continued until we were well within the Isle of Dogs. Here were the great wharves and quays: the maw that fed the Empire. Here too lived the working folk who took their livelihood from the maritime industries: sailors, pilots, stevedores, shipwrights, riggers… and, of course, tavern-keepers.

We sped out from between two huge warehouses, and a great and terrible panorama met my eyes.

To call it a fire would be an injustice. A slice of Hell, fetched up and planted on the river bank, would be a better description. The awesome power, the horror of it! Great fireballs leapt into the sky. Horrendous showers of sparks and glowing debris spewed upwards and drifted down to start new fires.

Three buildings were ablaze, and several more would shortly follow. They were huge. One giant in the centre seemed to be the source of the inferno. Even as I watched, a hole broke through in the roof and a pillar of flame, perhaps two hundred feet tall, erupted from the structure like a slender, malignant toadstool – its rounded head bursting outwards in a giant red ball. The flames lighted the ground for hundreds of yards around. A sea of faces, eyes upturned, surrounded us. Children in their innocence raced to and fro, shouting in the din. To them, it was merely an event to break the summer's tedium – they were blissfully unaware of the destruction being wrought.

Our van pulled up close to the blazing buildings. I jumped down, my face stinging from the heat. I could scarcely breathe. All around me firemen scurried and shouted. Three immense engines stood in a line, working furiously. The teams, despite their training, reared and pranced in the firelight, sending huge, grotesque shadows dancing over the pavement. The scene repeated itself endlessly into the distance: fire engines pumping and belching smoke, frantic teams being led away and tethered, men pushing hose carts, carrying ladders while their officers shouted orders through trumpets. Above it all rose the tremendous roaring, crashing din.

The one factor in the firemen's favour was the nearness of the Thames: drafting hoses were lowered over the quays into the limitless supply of river water. An enormous steam-driven 'fire-float' was brought up alongside the docks and from its squat, barge-shaped hull spouted a stream so powerful that it shattered the wooden walls of the buildings to reach the flames within. Nearby, knots of men struggled as close as they dared and raised their hoses – but they were as pathetic as mice attacking a lion, and the streams of water entering the windows had little, if any effect. Hearing a commotion behind me, I was surprised to see a coal wagon approaching. I watched the curious irony of the firefighters feeding the flames at the base of the engines.

Police formed a cordon to hold back the crowd, and I saw Lestrade barking orders. Seeing him thus engaged prodded me into a painful realization. Cursing myself for idleness, I dashed from Holmes' side and sped to the nearest constable.

'I'm a physician – where are the injured?' I cried and, having received his directions, fought my way to the rear of a brick building where, sheltered from the heat and din, a crude nursing station had been set up. At once I grew optimistic: there were very few casualties. Most of the people were suffering only from minor burns. Looking past them, I could see the reason for our 'ill-equipped' ambulance of an hour earlier. Long lines of the carriages stood nearby in readiness, the horses stamping their feet with impatience. To my amazement, they weren't needed. The severely injured had already been taken away, and I busied myself with cleaning and bandaging the 'walking wounded'. Thank God, I thought to myself, that the buildings are mostly warehouses, which accounts for the few casualties. I was distracted though, by a sight and sound I shall never forget – and all my relief and optimism vanished in an instant.

There came to my ears a wailing sound, and I rose in search of it. In a dark corner alcove of the old building, huddled in a worn shawl, was a woman who clasped to her breast a tiny bundle. She looked up at me with a face that was not a face, and shrieked in a voice that was not a voice. She tore at herself in the agony of her grief – her face a shambles of torn skin and tears.

'Abbie! My Abbie!' she screamed, and fought off those who tried to calm her. Finally the attendants succeeded in placing the blanket-wrapped bundle in a carriage. The crazed mother clambered after, and amidst the dreadful sound of grief the sad procession departed.

It was some time before I could bring myself to return to my work. Seeing death almost daily, a physician becomes inured to most of it. The passing of an old man or hopelessly sick woman, these are part of the doctor's work and world. He recognizes them as natural.

But the snatching of a young life – the taking of a child who was perhaps two hours earlier laughing, sitting on her mother's knee with her evening sweet – the transformation of this creature into a tiny mute bundle... this kind of death smites us with full force if even for the hundredth, the *thousandth* time. Pray God the day shall never come when I can accept it.

After several hours of tending minor wounds, I made my way, exhausted, back to Holmes and Lestrade. Although the fire had spread considerably, the huge plumes of flame had vanished. Instead there was a great glowing at ground level and the heat issuing forth had become yet more intense. The firemen had wisely given up on the big buildings and concentrated their efforts on saving neighbouring ones. The fire was now contained, and the din and excitement were abating, save for occasional tremendous crashes as walls and roofs collapsed. But still the great engines worked, and still the bands of men sallied back and forth, often carrying a fallen comrade. Wearied and depressed, Holmes and

I arrived at Baker Street shortly before midnight. The roar of the fire, clatter of engines, and the horrific grieving of the mother still rang in my ears.

We sat for some time in silence. In a voice made dull by sadness, I related to him the incident of the dead child. He was deeply touched, and let out a slow sigh.

'There is so much suffering in the world, Watson, and it is no accident, I can assure you, that most of it falls upon the poor.'

'Certainly this is an evening we won't soon forget,' said I. 'I am exhausted, and yet I'm certain I cannot sleep.'

'I confess I feel the same tension. Let us have some whisky then, and we'll talk about the earlier occurrence.'

So saying, he poured two glasses, reclined on the divan with his pipe, and assumed a far-away expression.

'It seems safe to conclude,' he said at last, 'that the man was a sailor...'

'I'd certainly say so, from his clothes and appearance –'

'... recently arrived in London from Borneo or thereabouts... and was, at the time of his murder, coming to see me.'

'What!'

'I must say his death touches me more now, knowing he was seeking my assistance...'

'How are you sure of this?' I asked.

'At this stage it's pure conjecture, but let us reconstruct the chain of events. As I have stated, the man was in or near Borneo not longer than six or eight weeks ago. This is revealed simply and unequivocally by a recent tattoo on his right wrist. It is Malayan in origin, and appears to be about two months old. Figuring on a sea voyage of about the same length of time, we know he had not been long in London. Fetch *The Times*. Let us see if by chance there has been an arrival from that corner of the globe recently.'

Whilst I rummaged for the paper, Holmes curled up on the divan, drawing on his pipe.

'There are three within the last fortnight. The *Yarmouth Castle* arrived on Tuesday last from Foocnow...'

Holmes shook his head with impatience.

'The barque *Rangoon* put in the day before last, bound from Hong Kong...'

'And the last?' he queried.

'The packet-trader *Matilda Briggs* – by Jove! – put in this afternoon, from *Batavia*!'

'That's our sailor's vessel! I see by scanning these back issues that there's been no other ship from there in two weeks. Our dead friend arrived this afternoon then. He must have had something of the utmost urgency to tell me. It is a pity that his lips are sealed for ever.'

'How do you know he was bound here?'

'Picture this in your mind, Watson: a sailor arrives in port after a sea voyage of many weeks. What is the natural thing for him to do?'

'Go on a fling, I should imagine.'

'It would seem so. But this fellow is a queer bird. He is not grogging down in Limehouse – no, he's up in the West End, in Baker street. Why? I don't wish to appear vain, my friend, but you know as well as I that I enjoy a considerable reputation in this city, and not only in the more proper circles.'

'That is certainly true.'

'It is entirely possible that one of my shadier acquaintances down on the docks referred the man to me. Also, I have what I think may be evidence to support this.'

Holmes took pen and paper and drew the following marks:

'Do these marks suggest anything to you?' he enquired.

'Absolutely not – mere hen scratchings.'

'The police think so too, no doubt. I found them on the man's right shirtcuff, evidence, by the bye, that he was left-handed. He'd drawn them on with rough crayon of the type oftentimes carried by seamen. Like most sailors, he was accustomed to representing numbers with vertical strokes. Hence, we derive the numbers 2–2–1, or, if you please, 221B Baker Street.'

'Extraordinary!' I exclaimed.

'Not really. The man obviously didn't bother to write down the name of the street: he could remember that easily enough. But he wanted to be sure of our number.'

'Poor chap.'

'He was dogged and ambushed one street away from his destination, which suggests that those who murdered him know of me. Otherwise why would they murder him here and not down by the docks?'

'They feared he would reveal his secret to you, and therefore did away with him.'

'But not before removing all of his identification. Yet the throwing down of the body seems to have been done to serve as a warning to other confederates who would hear of this man's death. I fear it is a dark and vile conspiracy we are confronting, Watson: a band that will stop at nothing to protect its secrets. As tangled as the problem appears however, there is a thread that runs through it. We know that the problem is international; it is not confined to London but has roots either on board the *Matilda Briggs* or even in the Orient. Bearing in mind the man's tattoo, and the *Briggs'* port of departure, we see that Malaya keeps reappearing. Did you observe closely the wounds on the victim's body?'

'They were severe in the extreme.'

'Was there nothing unusual about them?'

'They were different from ordinary knife wounds, but I am at a loss as to exactly *how* they were different. I vaguely remember having seen similar wounds before…'

'In Afghanistan, perhaps?'

I jumped clear of my chair in amazement.

'Holmes!'

'Don't be alarmed, I made a hazard and it proved correct. Afghanistan would have been the most likely place for you to have seen such wounds but not as likely as the Malayan archipelago. The instrument used on our sailor, if I'm not mistaken, is of Malayan origin. The *kris dagger,* as it is most often referred to, is a double-edged combat weapon with a serpentine blade, which is, as you have seen, capable of inflicting the most ferocious of wounds.'

There was a pause as I collected my thoughts.

'You think then that he was killed by a Malay?' I asked finally.

'That is uncertain. I believe that the crew of the *Matilda Briggs* may be of some help to us in this matter. I'm afraid you will breakfast alone tomorrow, Watson; I shall be down at the riverside at an early hour. Who knows? Perhaps in some dingy lane or noisy grog-shop I'll find a piece of this puzzle. Did you notice the moon on our return? There's a halo around it; there'll be rain before dawn, which will aid the firemen. Get to sleep, you're pale as a ghost. Goodnight, Watson.'

I bade my companion likewise and, as I prepared to enter my bedchamber, could not help but wonder at the way in which a lovely autumn evening had been so suddenly transformed into a night of destruction, mystery, and havoc.

What Boatswain Sampson Had to Tell

I was awakened next morning by a blast of thunder and rain lashing at the window panes. Upon dressing and entering the parlour I saw the remnants of Holmes' hasty breakfast. I rang for my own and, while waiting, chanced to see the *Morning Post* strewn in front of the fireplace. My eyes fell immediately on the following story:

WAREHOUSE FIRE CLAIMS 7 LIVES

Preston Rd, 15 Sept.: A fire of horrendous proportions last evening claimed the lives of seven citizens. The conflagration, which purportedly began in the maritime shipping warehouse of G. A. McNulty & Sons in Preston Road at approximately 6:00 P.M., raged until 3:30 A.M. this morning when it was finally extinguished by the 2nd and 4th fire brigades. A list of the dead follows in the next column.

The cause of the fire has not been established. Police have not ruled out the possibility of arson, and have requested the assistance of Scotland Yard.

All the victims were trapped in adjacent buildings. The total number of buildings destroyed is eight: five residential buildings and three commercial properties, including the previously mentioned one belonging to Mr McNulty.

The article continued in greater detail, but it made me so heavy-hearted that I deferred and went on to the next page. Relief was not in sight, however, for no sooner had I turned the page than my eyes fell upon the following piece:

BAKER STREET MURDER

London, 15 Sept.: The mutilated body of Raymond Jenard, Able Seaman of the cargo vessel *Matilda Briggs,* was discovered on the kerbside opposite Curray's, the clothier, of 157 Baker Street. The cause of death was a series of stab wounds.

Inspector Lestrade, of the Paddington District Station, has informed the *Post* that the deed appears to have been a street murder with robbery as the motive, since no valuables, nor identification of any sort, was found on the body.

Identification was made possible only by the assistance of Mr John Sampson, boatswain of the *Matilda Briggs* and a friend of the deceased.

Mr Jenard, who left no family, resided at 22 Preston Road, and was considered an honest and kind fellow by the shipmates who knew him well.

I was in the midst of my breakfast, which Mrs Hudson had brought up, when I heard a tread upon the stair. A moment later the door opened, and there stood before me a wizened old sailor, his hoary beard partially obscuring a wrinkled, ruddy face. The eyes however, shone with a merry twinkle, as if the old man were delighted at my surprise.

'I beg your pardon –' I said abruptly as I put down my cup.

'Mr 'olmes in, mate?' he rasped.

'No he isn't,' I replied with some indignation, 'and I'll thank you to knock when you come to a stranger's doorway, sir. Furthermore, you're ruining Mr Holmes' carpet.'

His oilskin, glistening with rain, was dripping on the rug that was given to my colleague by the Shah of Persia for recovering the famous Delak Tiara. I knew Holmes wouldn't be pleased. The strange, bent old man stood wheezing before me, swaying slightly as if on a ship's deck at sea.

'Kindly state your business, sir,' I said in a clipped tone, 'and be off if you please; I am very busy this morning.'

This was not true, of course, but I wanted to be rid of him. Something in his stark manner unsettled me.

''ey mate – got a dram o' rum for a cold old man?'

'Certainly not! Now if you'll not state your business –'

'It's the murder. I've come,' and, saying this, he shuffled over until he stood directly over me, '… to tell about the murder, don't you see…'

I stared up at him with incredulity. He then bent his face down to mine and said, in a low coarse whisper: 'You see, mate… I'm the one what *done* it!'

I sprang from my chair and, in a flash, had flung open the drawer to Holmes' side table. I had clasped the revolver handle when the cry of a familiar voice stopped me.

'Whoa, Watson! I fancy a joke can go too far!'

Turning round, I observed the old salt transformed as Holmes removed the false whiskers and putty.

'This is indeed one of my better efforts,' he said chuckling to himself. 'If my closest friend cannot recognize me so close, I am assured that the denizens of the East End were deceived as well. Ah Watson, a touch of brandy doesn't seem so outrageous after all, for I am chilled to the marrow.'

'Really, Holmes! It's a bit early in the day for pranks of this nature. I seem to have quite lost my appetite.' Indeed, I was still reeling slightly from the encounter.

'Then in all sincerity, I must apologize. I did not intend to make you the object of ridicule, nor to give you a fright.'

His apologetic tone had a remarkable effect upon my recovery, and I managed to finish my somewhat chilled breakfast while Holmes removed the remnants of his masquerade, lighted his pipe, and settled himself before the crackling fireplace. Outside, the storm raged on; the rain fell in great sheets, and thunder burst incessantly above us.

'Well, Watson, I see you've had a glance at the *Post*. Was there anything about the two news items, the fire and the murder, that caught your attention?'

I replied in the negative.

'Isn't it curious,' he pursued, 'that our sailor Jenard resided in one of the buildings that was destroyed by the fire?'

'I seem to have missed that,' said I, examining the paper again, 'but it's a coincidence certainly.'

'I fear not. I think rather that the two tragedies of last night are in some way bound together. You realize, of course, that the *Post* is in error.'

'You mean as to the motive for the murder?'

'Obviously on that count. But I am referring to the fire. The article states that it began in McNulty's warehouse. By reading the article carefully, one sees that this could not have been so. The article is a self-contradiction of sorts.'

I joined Holmes before the fireplace and, paper in hand, applied myself to discovering the discrepancy that he had found so obvious.

Before long, however, my train of thought was broken by the appearance of Mrs Hudson.

'Mr Holmes, sir,' she said, 'there's a gentleman downstairs to see you.'

'Did he give you his card?' asked my companion.

'No, sir. But he did mention his name.'

'Yes?'

'Mr John Sampson.'

'Show him up immediately,' said he, his face full of eagerness. 'Quick, Watson, stir up the fire while I pour a glass for our visitor. This is an extremely fortunate turn of events, for, if I'm not mistaken, here is a man who can shed much light on these calamities.'

I busied myself with the tongs and bellows, and lighted a cigarette in anticipation of the arrival of Boatswain Sampson. His tread on the stair was slow and heavy.

Although John Sampson undoubtedly possessed the build and carriage of a boatswain, it was indeed a pale, harrowed man who appeared in our doorway. He was large, no older than thirty, with blue eyes and great curls of blond hair. Were it not for his temporary condition, I would suppose him to be a man of great strength and vitality. His countenance had a frank and honest look; he appeared a fellow who would grant favours and make friends. On the other hand, I fancied it would be imprudent to make an enemy of him.

For the present, however, he was visibly shaken, and seemed to weave before us in a fit of anxiety.

Holmes diagnosed the man's state as quickly as I did, and led him to a chair.

'Pray sit down before the fire, Mr Sampson, and warm yourself. This is my fellow boarder and friend Doctor John Watson. You may tell him anything you wish to tell me.'

The boatswain gave me a firm handshake and settled himself before the fire. Before long, the fire's warmth and the brandy worked their magic, and a touch of healthy colour sprang upon his cheeks.

'Mr Holmes and Doctor Watson,' he began in a shaken voice, 'as you may have read in today's papers, I am the bos'n on the merchant vessel *Matilda Briggs*. It was I who identified the body of my unlucky shipmate Raymond Jenard late last night –'

'Indeed, we've been reading about it.'

'I had intended to go to the police today, but early this morning I was knocked up by a Mr Josiah Griggs, who strongly recommended I pay you a visit, Mr Holmes.'

'This man is a friend?' I asked.

'No, sir. In fact, I'd never laid eyes on him. He just stands there at my doorway, dripping wet, and says, "Mr Sampson, if it's advice and help you'll need, and you don't wish all of London to know about it, Sherlock Holmes is the man for you." He seemed a trusty fellow, and one who'd bumped around the world a bit, if you know what I mean. So I took his advice, and here I am.'

'Good. Now let us hear your story,' said Holmes.

'First of all, you may wonder how I came to be at the city morgue last night at so late an hour. As you might guess, I was one of the many spectators at the dock fire last evening, for I live nearby, as most men of my calling do. While watching the flames, I suppose it must have been after two in the morning, I overheard several constables discussing a mysterious murder that had taken place earlier. When I heard them describe the victim, my suspicions became aroused, for reasons which will soon become clear to you. I asked the constables if the man were tattooed, and when they answered yes, I rushed over immediately in a cab. Sad to say, my suspicions were right.

'What first set me thinking was the fact that Jenard's own dwellings were ablaze – but he was not in the ring of onlookers, though I searched for him. But there is something else, something deep and terrible I fear, that had made me uneasy about Jenard's safety for some time…'

At this point Sampson paused, as if he were too embarrassed to continue. Holmes said nothing, but remained settled in his chair, eyelids halfway closed in scrutiny, his fingertips pressed lightly together.

'Now, Mr Holmes, I know you may think it strange that I suspected foul play from the beginning —'

Holmes nodded slightly.

'Were not the tale so strange, the circumstances so mystifying, I would tell you all without the slightest hesitation…'

'Then do so,' urged my companion. 'I have found over the years that the only way to arrive at a solution to any problem is for my client to tell all, having complete trust in me and my colleague. You appear a bit shaken, but otherwise in sound health. I shan't think you daft if you relate to me the entire history of the past few months, omitting nothing.'

Heartened by these words, Sampson leaned forward and began his tale:

'I have been aboard the *Matilda Briggs* four years. I signed on directly out of the mercantile service. This is my first position, and I've been happy with it up until the past few weeks. Naturally, I don't want to give notice, but recent events may force me to.

'The *Matilda Briggs* makes a fairly regular run between London and Batavia. We haul freight and, now and then, passengers as well. There has never been a mishap aboard her, and nothing amiss until this last voyage. We'd loaded up in Batavia in the middle of July and were set to put out. We were delayed, however, by the arrival of Mr Ripley, a missionary from the interior, who sought passage to London. This is often the way with cargo vessels, since any loss in time is offset by passage fees. Mr Ripley seemed pleasant enough, and no doubt paid Captain McGuinness handsomely for passage for the three of them —'

'*Three* of them?'

'Yes, sir, he arrived with two companions. His friend Mr Jones, who apparently had been a sailor, and his man Wangi, a horrible wretch he brought with him from the interior. An ugly, heathen devil with a hump on his back…

'Well, shortly after they came aboard, the three of them: Reverend Ripley, his friend Jones, and our Captain McGuinness had a long gam in the cabin. Afterwards, the first of the queer things occurs: the Captain calls us aft and announces that, as of that time forward, Mr Jones is First Mate, replacing Armstrong. We were dumbstruck by this, since Armstrong's the finest mate in the packet trade. But the Captain's word is law, as you gentlemen may know. So there we were, stuck with the situation, you might say.

'But we got off all right, sailing with the tide that evening. There was a fresh wind up, and we fairly boomed along. It was mighty pleasant, except that Captain McGuinness seemed out of sorts, as if some strong spell were upon him. This was most unusual for him, such a pleasant man as he is.

'We soon entered the Straits of Sunda, and it was here that the second strange episode took place. Directly we left the straits behind us, Captain McGuinness gives the order to change course. Instead of proceeding along the usual route, which would take the *Briggs* just under the tip of India and Ceylon, he took the ship northwards. We were then running along the coast of Sumatra. When I enquired as to the reason for this change in plans, the Captain brushed me off. "Oh, Johnny," says he, "the Reverend Ripley has a final bit of business to transact before we make for England. He must make a quick stopover on the coast to visit his mission." Informed it would only take a day or so, and realizing it was for the good of the church, we obeyed willingly enough – though some of the crew were mad as hornets about it, they being in a rush to get home…'

The boatswain paused to sip his brandy and light the cigarette I'd offered him, then continued.

'A day and a half later, the *Briggs* eased into a deep inlet halfway up the Sumatran coast. We dropped anchor in the sheltered lagoon. It was lovely enough: the inlet was fringed with palm trees and wide beaches, and the water was so blue and clear it hurt your eyes to look at it. We all stayed aboard whilst Ripley and Jones went ashore in the jolly boat. We frittered away the time on deck till they returned, which was at sunset. But rather than hoist anchor and be on our way, the Captain, with the passengers on each side of him, calls his petty officers aft.

'"See here, men," he says, "our good passenger, Reverend Ripley, thanks you for your kind patience. We will sail with the tide tomorrow morning and resume our usual course. In the meantime, Mr Ripley has been kind enough to provide you and the crew with a treat." So saying, the three of them hoisted a keg from the after hold. "Roll it forward, men," shouts Mr Ripley, "and let each have his full share!"

'Well, we all thought it was bully, and raised a cheer for Mr Ripley and the Captain. I was whooping as loud as the rest, but noticed that Captain McGuinness looked anything but happy. Indeed, he seemed more worried than ever. This, and the fact that doling out rum is a strange custom for a reverend, should have set me thinking. But I was lost in the moment, as they say. Jones and I rolled the cask forward and what a carrying on there was that night! I've never been much for drink on account of my upbringing, Mr Holmes, and was also aware of my duties as boatswain. But Mr Ripley, seeing I wasn't pitching in with the others, came forward to set me at ease.

'"Don't worry, lad," he says to me, "there's nothing in this calm inlet can harm your ship. The three of us shall stand the watch tonight, so have your fun." Of course, I must ask the Captain and he weakly gave in, saying we should all indulge the reverend in his kindness. So I joined in the merrymaking, and a real ripper of a party it was too. Considering the potency of the rum, and the amount of it, it wasn't long before the crew was senseless in the foc'sle – many of them unable even to find their bunks.'

Here the boatswain paused for another sip.

'I had turned in ahead of the others. The only one to beat me turning flukes was Jenard, who I saw was fast asleep. By and by – it was very late – I was awakened. I sat up in my bunk. Save for the drunken snoring of the crew, the ship was quiet. But then I heard it: the clanking of the aft windlass. The noise stopped, and I heard a distant thumping upon the deck.

'"Sampson!" A hoarse whisper cried, "Sampson, are ye about?"

'It was Jenard. I answered that I was indeed awake, and was curious to know who'd been turning the windlass.

'"Let's be topside," says I, "and see what's what."

We made our way in the darkness of the foc'sle through the clots of men, lying where they had fallen in the stupor, and scurried up the forehatch. We'd heard stories of the Indian Ocean pirates you may be sure, but Jenard was a good fellow in a fight, and I've never considered myself a pushover. He was in the lead, and he'd no sooner popped his head up and looked aft when he ducked it down, saying: "Something queer's up, Johnny, we'd better lay low."

'Now I've never been a fellow to sneak about ferret-like, and considering my position as bos'n, it was my duty to render assistance if the ship were in any difficulty. So I led Jenard up the forehatch. It was a fair night, but black as pitch owing to a new moon. It was then that we spied a knot of men on the quarterdeck, leaning over the taffrail. A lighted lantern was all that made them visible, and we could scarcely hear their voices. As we reached the main hatches, we could see it was our Captain McGuinness, Reverend Ripley, and his two companions.

They were talking excitedly in hushed tones, and were peering sharp out into the darkness.

'It was obvious they were waiting for a boat of some sort, and it was also clear they wanted none of the crew to know about their rendezvous. But curiosity had got the best of us, so Jenard and I slipped over the gunwale as quiet as cats. Our feet on the main channels, we crouched behind the deadeyes and shrouds. From where we hid, we could look out across the water, and had a clear view of the men on deck as well.

'By and by, we saw a light twinkling far off on the water and drawing closer every minute. It excited the men a great deal, the evil Wangi especially, who fairly danced and spouted gibberish until he was hushed by a blow across the face from the Reverend Ripley. The light on the water was extinguished, and in its place, a triangular sail appeared. As it drew closer, we could see it was a lateen rig – a native boat, and swarming with the heathen devils!'

Sampson paused for another sip, and I observed that Holmes' face bore a look of rapt attention as he leaned forward in his chair.

'The boat, a sleek dhow trader, came up alongside, not forty feet from us, but, owing to the darkness of the night, we were invisible. The crew was a wicked lot, clad in white robes and turbans, their dark faces gleaming in the lantern light, and daggers in their sashes. A dozen of their number swarmed aboard the *Briggs*, then busied themselves rigging a jury derrick to the mizzen. I again heard the windlass turning and the clinking of the heavy pawls as they fell into place. It was then that Jenard and I noticed a large crate lashed to the deck of the native boat. It was a full yard high and deep, and the length of a man. It was of the stoutest timber and must have been of considerable weight, since the windlass was required to hoist it, by means of the heavy tackle, on to the deck of the *Briggs*. It was then lowered into the after hold, through the hatch on the quarterdeck. Throughout the entire proceedings, hardly a word was spoken by anyone, and the utmost care was taken to maintain silence. Having watched these strange events, and the manner in which they were executed, I was firmly convinced that our once-honest Captain was engaged in smuggling. It may surprise you, gentlemen, but such activities are not at all uncommon, especially in the far reaches of the world. As the heathen crew was making ready to sail off, Jenard and I returned to the foc'sle.

'"Jenard," says I, after crawling into my bunk, "I think it the best thing if we don't breathe a word of this to anyone. There's not much we can do in the middle of the Indian Ocean now, is there? When we reach London, I'll notify the authorities." He agreed wholeheartedly, and, thinking the matter ended, we turned in.'

John Sampson paused again, and the anxiety which Holmes had laid to rest welled up in him once again.

'It's here that the fantastic part of my tale begins,' he said nervously. 'Two nights after our episode, I was enjoying my evening pipe on the foredeck, as is my custom, when Jenard sought me out.

'"Johnny," he pleaded, "may I have a word with ye?" His eyes shone as if with fever, and despite his deep tan, I could see the pallor in his face. I begged him to tell me all that troubled him.

'"Johnny," he cried, all a-quiver, "would ye think me daft if I told you that I've seen a *monster rat?*"'

At these words, Holmes started visibly. In disbelief, we exchanged a quick glance. Holmes grew yet more attentive, leaning forward on the very edge of his chair. John Sampson continued his tale.

'So shocked was I at hearing this exclamation that I asked my shipmate to sit down and repeat it.

'"A *rat,* Johnny," he said. "A rat as big as all Creation!"

'Upon hearing these words, I naturally supposed the poor fellow to be ill. I advised him to get out of the sun, and was about to summon assistance, but he was so strong in his manner, Mr Holmes, and such a close friend, that this action seemed a betrayal. Seeing that nobody was within earshot, I asked him to tell me how he came about seeing this creature.

'He explained that he had observed Jones entering the after hold, which is below the officers' quarters, and reserved solely for their use, with a large bundle of food. Curious, he had followed the mate and seen him enter the stern locker. As the door swung open, he'd caught a glimpse of what he claimed was a monster rat.

'"I saw its face I tell you, peering out from the crate. It was a rat's face, Johnny, as big as a keg!"

'Sitting there on the foredeck in the lovely evening, I felt that his tale was incredible. The *Matilda Briggs* had resumed her normal course and the morale of the crew, owing to the generosity of Reverend Ripley, couldn't have been higher. How strange then, to think of this ungodly monster less than fifty yards from where I lay and smoked my pipe! Yet he insisted that the creature was on board, and in so earnest a fashion that I felt bound to verify his story.

'That night, we concealed ourselves in the aft passageway shortly after midnight. At this time of course, the crew is either on duty topside or secured in the foc'sle, and since it is always dark below decks even with the paraffin lamps, concealing ourselves amongst the cargo was no problem.

'Presently, Jones appeared bearing a large bundle, which we supposed to be food. We watched intently as he unlocked the stout door that led to the hold and entered. He did not close the door after him, but paused to light a lamp. It was then, Mr Holmes and Doctor Watson, when the lamplight filled the little hold, that I beheld the face of the giant rat.'

John Sampson's manner became earnest, persuasive, as if he were eager to convince us of the validity of his amazing tale.

'It *was* a rat, gentlemen. Of that I am sure. I've been at sea long enough to know a rat when I see one. But its size! It had upright, roundish ears, a twitching, rodent snout –'

'You saw the entire animal?'

'No, Mr Holmes, only the head, which peered out through a hole cut in the crate. A brief glimpse of the monster was all we were allowed, for the next instant Jones closed the door, and we made our way back to the foc'sle, full of fear and wonder.'

'Is it not possible,' I enquired, 'that this "monster" could have been a puppet contrivance fashioned from animal fur?'

'No, sir, of that I'm sure. It was not a puppet, nor the trick of a magic lantern. It was a live, breathing animal, for we heard it snort, and saw the eyes roll, the teeth gnash in a most horrible fashion! It was the most fearsome and repulsive object I have ever looked upon, for a rat is surely the lowest of God's creatures... but a rat the size of a calf!

'Of course,' the boatswain continued, 'it wasn't very long before others of the crew had seen it also, and within two days the entire crew was paralysed with fear. No one would venture even into the aft passage, but clung tightly to the foc'sle except when on duty. Every rat on board was searched out and flung overboard, lest they somehow breed with the monster and overrun the ship. Never have I seen a body of grown men so gripped in terror. I cannot describe the relief we all felt when we made port yesterday. To a man, we cleared the ship, and most won't venture back, even though we've not been paid. There has been no talk of the monster on the docks, for fear of being ridiculed, or thought insane.'

'The Captain McGuinness, the Reverend Ripley and the two other passengers, are they on board the *Matilda Briggs*?'

The boatswain's face darkened.

'The main purpose of my visit this morning, Mr Holmes, is that I was informed by Mr Josiah Griggs that you might be of assistance in tracking down the killers of my friend. I have come in hopes that you will accompany me to the *Matilda Briggs*, for I am convinced that the people you have named are at least in part responsible for his murder.'

'And you have decided not to leave the matter solely in your own hands. Mr Sampson, I see that you have brains as well as stature, for such an approach would be unwise, even dangerous. Now let me ask you a question: did the *Matilda Briggs* stop at Gravesend?'

'No, sir.'

'Thank you, you've been most helpful. Now we had best start for Limehouse. Come, Watson, with Sampson here we should be able to gain access to the ship without delay.'

We were met on the stairway, however, by Inspector Lestrade and two constables.

'Mr John Sampson,' said the inspector gravely. 'In the name of the Queen, I arrest you in connection with the murder of Raymond Jenard. It is my duty to inform you that anything you say may be used in evidence against you.'

Sampson said nothing as the iron bracelets were put on, but the look of astonishment and outrage revealed his emotions.

'Mr Holmes, is there nothing you can do?'

'I'm afraid not at present, Mr Sampson. I advise you to co-operate, and rest assured that both my companion and I shall be working night and day to clear you of this charge and secure your release. Lestrade, after you have delivered your prisoner, I would be obliged if you would secure a warrant and accompany us to the merchant ship *Matilda Briggs,* moored in Blackwall Reach.'

'There's a fine bit of English justice,' I said bitterly, as Holmes and I waited for Lestrade's return. 'I must say, Holmes, I am surprised at your callous behaviour towards your client. The man comes to us, pours out his soul with the deepest trust and confidence, and at the end of this tale is hauled away to Clink Street. It's appalling.'

'I am in total agreement, Watson, were it not for one fact: John Sampson is best off behind bars for the time being. I fear his life is in grave danger, and can think of no safer place for him than in one of Her Majesty's lockups. It was, in fact, with deep misgivings that Josiah Griggs recommended that he make the journey across town to our flat.'

'Who the devil is Josiah Griggs?'

'Josiah Griggs, my friend, is the elderly, rather uncouth sailor who unwisely tried to fool my fellow lodger. Now then, here's Lestrade in a four-wheeler; fasten your oilskin, Watson, for the weather, I fear, has grown worse.'

Three

THE SHIP OF DEATH

'I'm sure you're aware, Holmes,' remarked Lestrade as he settled nervously into the cushions of our carriage, drawing on the double-claro Havana cigar that Holmes had given him, 'that we can't hold Sampson for ever. He was taken merely in connection with the murder, not charged as having committed it.'

'Have you taken anyone else into custody? No? Then I pray that this excursion to Limehouse will put us on a new scent. What is your impression of the tale that Watson and I have related to you?'

The inspector was shaken by a fit of laughter so intense that he all but choked on his cigar.

'I must admit that my curiosity is pricked,' said he whimsically, 'but certainly it's without foundation. An amazing cover story, if you ask me.'

'Nevertheless, one we can easily verify or repudiate; surely we shall track down other members of the crew. Let me ask you, gentlemen, does this tale bring any others to mind?'

Holmes sat with a twinkle in his eye, but the rest of his features bore a grave expression.

'Ah, yes!' exclaimed Lestrade at last. 'Five years ago, in eighty-nine.'

'You mean the Baskerville business?' I interjected.

'The very same, Watson. Now if ever a tale had foundation, that one had, and yet to the casual listener it was merely diabolical nonsense.'

'But the animal you shot to death on the Grimpen Moor that night was still a hound,' said Lestrade. 'A huge beast, but a genuine one. The mere thought of a rat any bigger than a house cat is incredible. Yet this man Sampson claims to have seem a rat as large as a calf. Impossible!'

'And yet the islands that comprise the Javanese archipelago contain some very interesting fauna,' my companion continued. 'As a matter of fact, according to Charles Darwin, insular animal populations, being cut off from the rest of their species, tend towards freakishness – especially insofar as *size* is concerned. The giant land tortoises of the Galapagos figure prominently in *The Voyage of the Beagle*. And Kodiak Island, in the Aleutian Sea, is the home of the largest bear on earth. On the diminutive side, we have our miniature ponies of the Shetland Isles…'

Lestrade knit his brow.

'I'm an amateur student of zoology, but I *am* aware that the islands of Java contain two unique species: one is a rare rhinoceros the size of a spaniel dog, the other is a gigantic lizard, named Komodo after the island it inhabits. Is it not possible, gentlemen, that the interior of one of these primeval specks of land plays host to a race of monster rodents?'

The mention of the Devon tragedies of four years ago, and the speculation around Sampson's weird tale set my nerves on edge. Glancing out the carriage window, I could see coaches dashing through puddles and driving over the shiny paving stones. Working men in raincoats scurried about their business, slick with water and raw with chill. Though the hour was before noon, it was dark. It was hard to see, yet I could tell by the gradual decline of the neighbourhoods that we were on East Commercial Road, and approaching the Isle of Dogs for the second time in four and twenty hours. I lighted a cigarette and, for diversion, asked Holmes to explain the contradiction that he had found in the two *Morning Post* articles.

'You see, gentlemen,' he explained, 'it is natural for most people to assume that the fire began in McNulty's warehouse for two reasons. First, fires often begin in warehouses in the early evening: a departing stevedore is careless with his pipe. He leaves a spark behind which goes unnoticed in the empty building. Secondly, this type of building, being large and airy, burns more fiercely, hence people assume the fire started on the premises.

'But in this case, the fact that seven people perished in the blaze is remarkable as well as tragic. I discovered this morning that all the seven dwelt in the residence at 22 Preston Road, the same residence as Jenard's. Considering the hour of the fire's inception, it is incredible to think that the blaze erupted in the neighbouring warehouse. The inhabitants were obviously awake and alert at such an hour, most probably at their evening meal. Had the fire begun in an adjacent building, they would have been sufficiently forewarned to escape to the street.

'If, on the other hand, the blaze began in their own building on a lower floor, escape would be much more difficult. And yet, it would probably have been possible. What then, made escape impossible for these unfortunate victims? It was, in all probability, a combination of two things: a fire in the same building on a lower floor, and secondly, a fire that spread upward and outward with incredible speed and energy –'

'You are inferring then that the blaze was unnatural?' enquired Lestrade, leaning eagerly forward.

'I've no doubt of it. The blaze started in Jenard's quarters, and some substance, probably paraffin, was used to ensure a thorough job.'

'Have you any idea what it was the arsonist wished to destroy?' I asked.

'If we had the answer to that question, we would be on the verge of a solution to the murder of Raymond Jenard, and perhaps the key to the puzzle of the *Matilda Briggs*' fantastic voyage. It is clear that this band of cutthroats gives not a farthing for human life, and they are a desperate lot indeed to sacrifice innocent victims who had obviously played no part in their foul scheme. Watson, I have never been more determined to reach the solution of any problem that has ever been laid before me. I vow to bring them to justice, not only to avenge Raymond Jenard, but for the sake of the seven innocents who by circumstance were swept away, including one in particular – Abbie Welling, aged six.'

A sigh escaped Lestrade's lips at hearing this poignant detail. I again recalled, as I have on innumerable occasions throughout the years, the torn face of the girl's mother as she clutched the tiny bundle in her arms. The revelation that the fire was deliberate sent hot rage coursing though me. I swore an oath of revenge, and knew I spoke for my friends as well, for their faces were full of fury. Truly, there were three grim men who disembarked from their four-wheeler at the banks of Blackwall Reach. Lestrade tugged at my sleeve as we walked towards the water. Looking back, the three of us could see a long plume of grey smoke and steam rising slowly up the river bank – the remnants of the previous night's disaster.

As our investigation with Lestrade was official, there was no delay in obtaining the assistance of Jennings, a customs house inspector who secured a launch for us. We descended the narrow stone stairway that led from the quay, with its gargantuan iron rings and bitts, down to the water's edge. Here we boarded the steam launch of the customs house. It was an open, wooden vessel with a small steam engine aft. It was fired by soft coal evidently, for thick oily smoke rose out of the chimney pipe. It was stationary and silent until we were all seated, then Jennings turned a small valve at the base of the boiler, and the engine took life.

A flip of the flywheel and the steady chuffing and clanging commenced. We cast off, and churned our way into the inscrutable mist beyond. The visibility had not improved; Jennings minded the tiller with great care, and kept our speed down to a crawl. Before long, large masses loomed out at us, and we found ourselves passing under the bows and transoms of sailing ships. Through the mist and rain, their upper spars were barely visible, which added to their ghost-like quality as they swung suddenly at their mooring cables.

Above the clatter of the single-cylinder Jensen engine could be heard the shouts and curses of the sailors as they worked or gambled the time away. More than once from beyond the wooden bulkheads I caught the strains of a concertina. As we passed almost directly under the transom of a large barque I read in gilded letters: *Rangoon,* and recalled that she had arrived just a day before the *Briggs,* bound from Hong Kong.

Jennings again turned the brass valve and the engine's clatter ceased. A low groan of escaping steam and the chuckle of water were the only sounds to be heard. I cannot describe the melancholy I felt at this time. It was as if the engine's chuffing served to drown out the oppressiveness of the rain and fog, and now in utter silence we drifted forth into the grey mist.

'Keep a sharp eye out if you please,' requested Jennings. 'The *Matilda Briggs* lies dead ahead.'

As if upon command, a dark, melancholy shape ghosted into view ahead of our bows. As we drifted closer, the shape became the dark, low hull of a packet trader. Perhaps it was her black hull, or the strange tale of violence that surrounded her, but she bore an aura of dread and foreboding.

Thrice we hailed her, but only the hollow echoes of our own voices responded.

'Jennings, has she her dockside clearance yet?' asked Holmes.

'Not to my knowledge, sir. There's been no preparation for transfer at all, sir. The Captain must apply himself, or send his mate if he's indisposed.'

'And you have seen no one of his ship?' enquired Lestrade.

'No, sir. There has been no sign of life on or about her after the crew went ashore yesterday afternoon.'

'The Captain and officers, do they remain aboard until the clearance is obtained?'

'Usually that is the case. I would be much surprised if she were deserted.'

'We had best board her and see for ourselves. Over yonder, Jennings, the boarding stair.'

The three of us clambered up the frail boarding stairway whilst Jennings minded the painter.

Seldom have I experienced a more ominous feeling than when I swung over the gunwale and planted my feet on the deck of the *Matilda Briggs*. She was a typical threemasted cargo vessel, around two hundred feet in length. What gave me pause was the dead silence, the desolation, of the ship – deserted and swaying at her cable like a waif.

Hawsers creaked and groaned. The water slapped hollowly below us. Meanwhile, Lestrade scurried about, flinging glances over the entire deck. Holmes paced in methodical fashion, his keen eyes roving deliberately round him, taking in everything. Watching them, one had the feeling that the London police detective epitomized energy and thoroughness. Holmes, on the other hand, gave an impression almost of leisure. Yet, one could not help but be aware of the incredible force, the terrible power and energy of the mind that churned behind the keen face.

I drew my waterproof more tightly round me, for the wind and rain brought an unbearable chill. No other vessels were visible through the mist. For all appearances we could have been in mid-Atlantic, and there was a profound feeling of melancholy and desolation.

I paced the deck forward to the hatch that Sampson had described. From there, I looked aft to the quarterdeck. In my mind's eye I tried to picture the same scene in the middle of a tropical night, with scores of Malay tribesmen swarming like insects as they lowered the huge crate to the deck. I remembered the beast, and paused to consider: was it only the weather that caused me to shiver? Was that same monster lurking in its vile den somewhere below these very decks? I felt a hand on my shoulder and turned.

'Whoa, Watson! Did I startle you?'

I was looking into Holmes' face, the rainwater cascading off his cap.

'So you see — Sampson's powers of description are excellent. I might suggest he's got a touch of the poet in him. You were, no doubt, reliving in your mind the strange events of several weeks ago. Here are the very channels in which the pair hid themselves,' said Holmes, leaning over the side. 'In this tangle of rigging, with its shrouds and halyards, great coils of line and pin rails, they were hidden. But mind, what a view they had of the proceedings! Come down here with me, Watson — there — now, see that gaff on the mizzen? That's where the derrick was rigged. A block and tackle could then easily be lowered alongside to receive even a very large parcel.'

We were called from our reveries by the tolling of a bell.

'Halloa! Anyone here?' cried Lestrade as he snapped the lanyard back and forth. He stood at the mainmast. At his waist, the brass ship's bell sang out mournfully.

'I declare, Holmes,' he continued. 'This *is* odd... surely someone must be about. Let's have a look below.'

'Let us proceed then, but with caution,' I warned.

Advancing on to the quarterdeck, we tried the aft companionway but found it bolted from within. Moving forward, we found the main companionway ajar. Sliding back the hatch, Lestrade bounded down, followed by Holmes, who was forced to stoop almost double. I managed to follow without much difficulty, and we found ourselves in some sort of narrow passageway, in almost total darkness. Suddenly Holmes shot back up the hatch. We heard his tread on the deck above. There was a heavy sliding sound, and, as if by miracle, the passageway was flooded with daylight.

'Well now, Mr Holmes,' remarked Lestrade as he returned. 'I had no idea you'd been a sailor.' He winked in my direction. 'Next we'll have you swarming up the ratlines to mind the braces, won't we, Watson?'

'I accept your compliments, Lestrade. I think that the inspection of the *Matilda Briggs* will be a great deal easier with the skylight open. Ha! You see? Look what we have here!'

He directed our attention to a tallow stub stuck on to a bulkhead timber just under the hatchway cover.

'A candle butt. So? I'll wager there are three score aboard this ship,' I ventured.

'A safe wager, too, Watson. Yet even ordinary objects, when used or placed in a certain way, can be suggestive. From what we see before us, we can perhaps put together a chain of events which will prove interesting.'

After noting carefully the position of the candle stub on the timber, Holmes plucked it delicately from its resting place and turned it round in his hand. Taking out his pocket knife and pocket lens, he shredded off a minute curl of the drippings which he scrutinized under the magnifying glass.

'I say, Holmes,' said Lestrade impatiently, 'are you not exaggerating the significance of that bit of candle? There are surely more important matters to investigate.'

'I'm not so sure, Lestrade,' observed my companion. Lestrade waited in exasperated silence, stamping his booted feet against the cold.

'We can say with reasonable certainty,' Holmes said at last, still turning the stub in his fingers, 'that the *Matilda Briggs* has been visited in the last twelve hours by a right-handed man of above average height.'

Lestrade and I stared blankly in amazement.

'Furthermore,' Holmes continued in a monotone, 'he is unfamiliar with the ship, or at least this part of it. He undoubtedly used this very candle in a curious manner, which will I hope clarify his motives for visiting the ship. Also, he came in stealth, and wished his actions kept secret –'

'Holmes! I never –' interjected Lestrade.

'And finally, he was obviously overcome with a tremendous emotional burden – in fact, driven to a frenzy that was unendurable.'

'Dash it, Holmes, enough of this quackery!' demanded Lestrade. 'I *challenge* you to substantiate this outlandish set of deductions. If they make sense, I'll pay for your luncheon!'

Holmes' eyes sparkled. 'Done, Lestrade! Where shall I begin? Ah, yes, the simplest first. The man's height, you see, is elementary. The stub was placed on this timber, not either of the two lower ones. Furthermore, observe how this corner of the chandler's bench sticks out. You see, one must bend over it before reaching up to place the candle – further evidence of the man's height.'

'I suppose that's sensible enough,' growled Lestrade, 'but what about the other theories? How do you know the fellow came in stealth?'

Holmes pointed to a black object projecting from the bulkhead less than a yard from where the stub was found.

'Of course, gentlemen, you know what this is. Quite so: a wrought-iron candle sconce. Although differing slightly in appearance from the ordinary sconce, the caked tallow drippings in the dish and the small pile of spent Lucifers makes its identity obvious.

'Now assuming the man was leaving the *Briggs* with a lighted candle in his hand, what more natural place to deposit the stub than in the sconce? But he did not use the sconce. Why not? Because he did not *see* the sconce. He'd extinguished the candle, you see, before entering the main passageway, and was forced to find his way out in darkness. Obviously, he did not wish to show even a candle light near the main hatch. Hence, he wished his visit kept secret.'

'Remarkable, and yet simple,' I mused.

'We can also see by the sconce's misuse that the man wasn't familiar with the vessel, or at least wasn't a crewman. If this were the case, he would have no doubt felt for the sconce in the darkness, since he would have been aware of its presence.'

"Then explain how it is that the man is right-handed,' demanded Lestrade.

'Very well, sir. Do you both observe how one side of the candle tip is much lower than the other? See how the drippings are clustered too on the opposite side of the depression?'

'Of course I see it,' said the detective. 'It's obvious that the man held the candle tipped to one side –'

'Yes. Now notice how the thumb has left a hollow in the tallow drippings. The hollow points diagonally downward. See how my right thumb nearly matches the hollow, yet switching the stub to my left hand –'

'It runs the opposite way from the thumb mark,' I added. 'It doesn't fit.'

'Of course not. The man held this stub in his right hand, and at a strange angle too – I am hopeful we will find additional signs of the use he put this candle to.'

'Holmes,' said Lestrade, 'I'll admit that you've indulged in a bit of cleverness here. And I'll further admit that what you say makes some little sense. But I'm dashed if I can see how a candle butt can tell you that the visitor was here within the last twelve hours. I'd be right obliged if you would explain this to me. And I'm sure Watson and I would both like to know what determines that the man was on the brink of mental collapse.'

'Have you ever touched molten wax, Watson?'

'Now and then, but I avoid it if possible,' I chuckled.

'Certainly you do. Molten wax is hot and painful. Yet here's a man who allowed wet drippings to *cover his thumb*, and evidently bore this pain without notice. Therefore, something of enormous consequence was occupying his faculties. As for the evidence of elapsed time, I call your attention to this hallmark on the bottom of the stub.'

With this, Holmes then turned the stub upside down to reveal the following hallmark embossed in the wax:

'It's the Broad Arrow,' observed Lestrade, looking at the candle bottom closely.

'Yes, the mark with which government property is identified, from candles to cannon. This is a regulation Navy candle. They may be purchased at most marine supply houses. These candles contain much whale oil, and are highly prized because of their brilliance. I've made a rather thorough study of candle tallows, as Watson can vouch for. Now a candle high in spermaceti is brilliant, but too brittle for use. Therefore, the makers of our navy candles have added a good dose of beeswax. The two blend together remarkably well, and produce a candle that is bright, yet long-burning and durable. Because of the addition of beeswax, this tallow does not dry to brittleness for some time. As you may have observed when I peeled at the drippings with my pocket knife, the tallow parted in a fine curl – it did not flake or chip as the body of the candle would have. Observe too the colour of the drippings: they are of a delicate pale opalescence, not the opaque white of thoroughly dried wax. From these characteristics, I deduce with near certainty that this candle was lighted not more than twelve hours ago. For your edification, Lestrade, I would suggest, once again, that the smallest details are often of the gravest importance. And now, while I contemplate my free lunch, let us proceed to the forecastle.'

Leading an eager companion, and a somewhat irritable Lestrade, Holmes led us down the narrow passageway toward the bows of the *Matilda Briggs*. The odours of tar, hemp, and canvas were much in evidence. The huge oaken timbers creaked and groaned with dismal regularity as the ship rolled slightly in the current of the reach. For some reason, Holmes had departed from his usual detective habits. In the past I had grown used to observing him bent over like a strange old man, searching for footprints or a fallen object. Now, however, he held his head upright and seemed to scan the wooden beams and deckboards above.

Soon the passageway grew dark, and Holmes took Lestrade's dark lantern to lead the way. Far ahead was a dull bluish glow.

'The fore-hatchway,' said Lestrade pointing.

We passed under the hatch, which was bolted with a stout brass rod, and proceeded through a low doorway into a large, triangular room. The room was illuminated almost imperceptibly by a pair of heavy glass 'bullseyes' set in the deck. Several hammocks were slung from the ceiling beams, but most of the crew apparently slept in bunks: the walls were ringed with them, fashioned from heavy timber and set one atop the other. What drew our attention immediately, however, was the untidiness of the compartment in general. While the sailors had evidently borne off their personal possessions before fleeing from the ship, the bunk mattresses and other ship's paraphernalia were strewn about and heaped in corners.

'Certainly not what I would call "shipshape", eh, Watson?'

'I should say not. It looks rather like the shambles of the Lower Form dormitory after the last day of Spring Term. The lads have certainly cleaned out in a rush, as Sampson stated.'

'There is probably an explanation for it,' said Lestrade. 'I'm confident that after we speak with the Captain —'

'Where *is* the Captain?' I asked.

'If he is aboard, we shall no doubt find him directly,' said the detective in his most official tone. Despite his crisp manner, though, I had the feeling he wasn't really quite sure of anything — at least aboard the *Briggs*.

'Watson! Lestrade! Do come here! I believe I have found what I have been searching for —'

We turned and observed Holmes lying on his back in one of the upper berths. He held Lestrade's lantern on his breast, and let the beam illuminate the ceiling timbers of the foc'sle.

The detective and I, placing our feet on the edge of the lower berth, leaned over and, by twisting our necks into an almost impossible position, could observe, in script letters three inches high, the following words done in candle smoke:

'All is stairs and passageways
where the rat sleeps —
his treasure keeps.'

'Well, gentlemen,' enquired Holmes, from the deep recesses of the bunk, 'what do you make of this latest find?'

'It's some sort of poem or riddle,' I speculated, 'and appears incomplete.'

'The man wrote the passage whilst lying in his bunk obviously. I think it's a warning. Notice that a rat is mentioned too,' said Lestrade. 'The question is: why would a man write a warning up on the timbers above his bunk? It's absurd.'

'An excellent point, Lestrade. For whom is the warning intended, and what does it mean? Or does it mean anything? I for one think it means a great deal,' said Holmes as he rolled out of the bunk and lowered his angular body to the floor. 'As you may have noticed, I have been looking for this writing in candle smoke since I examined the stub in the main passageway. It is curious that we find it over the bunk of a crewman. It would be interesting to know which man occupied this bunk…'

'It was Jenard's,' I observed, pointing to a small metal plaque fixed with a spike to the head timber of the berth.

'Excellent, Watson! I must confess I quite overlooked it, being so intent on what my search of the ceiling would reveal.'

'This means Jenard wrote the words,' I suggested.

'Certainly,' agreed Lestrade. 'He perhaps had a dire feeling with regard to his own life, and left this crude cryptogram here to warn others or implicate the party whom he feared.'

'Your conclusions are logical with regard to motive, my friends, but if what we deduce from the candle drippings is true, the message was written within the last twelve hours. At that time, poor Jenard was lying stone dead in the city Morgue, a shocked Sampson identifying his remains.'

Lestrade and I pondered this twist in silence.

'Even assuming the evidence of the candle drippings is inconclusive, it is plain that Jenard, a left-hander, couldn't have written these words.

You remember, Watson, the markings I observed on his shirtcuff?'

I replied in the affirmative, and explained Holmes' previous deduction to Lestrade, who grew still more confused.

'We know that whoever held the candle was right-handed. Furthermore, after lying on the bunk for a few seconds and tracing the message with my own hands – even allowing for my long arms, I can see it would be impossible for the words to be written with the left hand. That hand, you see, is on the inside, and the proximity of the deck would render the task impossible for anyone save a contortionist. I think this chamber has told us all it can, at least for the present. There's nothing to be found in this bunk, nor in the single one yonder, which I assume to be Bos'un Sampson's. Let us then work our way aft and examine the officers' quarters.'

We made our way back through the dark passageway towards the vessel's stern. We passed the main hatch and, after a few steps, saw a faint gleaming which marked the after hatch. Passing under it, we came upon the termination of the main passage, which was marked by a cluster of doors.

'There are the officers' quarters,' remarked Lestrade.

'Yes, but which compartment belongs to which?' I asked. Realizing that our knowledge of maritime life was limited, Holmes sent me up to fetch Jennings.

'These two belong to the mates, or other petty officers,' said Jennings, pointing to the two doors nearest us, one on each side of the passage. 'The Captain's cabin, or main cabin, will be that one, in the centre furthest aft.'

'And if the vessel were to take on passengers?' asked Holmes.

'The passengers would be berthed in either of these two cabins, the two mates doubling up in the other one.'

We tried the doors of the two smaller cabins and found them locked.

Proceeding to the main door, Lestrade rapped sharply. He rapped and hailed alternately, but there was no answer.

Trying out the latch, we were somewhat startled to find the door swung open without effort. I had seen a Captain's cabin only once before, on my return voyage to England aboard the troopship *Orontes*. That fleeting glimpse was during a spell of the enteric fever which had necessitated my leaving Afghanistan, so the recollection was somewhat foggy. However, glancing at the main cabin of the *Matilda Briggs* seemed to bring those distant memories sharply into focus, for the two cabins were similar. A low ceiling, slightly curved and set with heavy beams, several small windows set in the transom, a trim bunk bed and tidy desk, bookshelves laden with maritime tomes, all these could possibly have been found in any sailing ship of the period. Dull greyish light filtered in through the windows and played upon the brass lamp that swung slowly from a chain over the desk.

The compartment was somewhat gloomy, but appeared to be in order; there was none of the untidiness that we had observed in the foc'sle.

'It appears that Captain McGuinness is preparing to take leave but has not yet done so,' observed Holmes, pointing to a fully packed carpet bag near the bed. 'We had best not touch anything here, Lestrade, until we speak with him.'

'He is most likely in the hold, gentlemen. It is often the custom of the Captain and his chief steward to examine the cargo directly before unloading so as to determine pilferage or spoilage. If you wish, I'll go below and hunt him up.'

As Jennings disappeared down a short ladder we seated ourselves and lighted pipes. In apparent disregard of his own suggestion, Holmes plucked a leather-bound volume from the shelf and began to search through it. His close inspection of the volume, which I assumed to be the ship's log, was interrupted only by an occasional grunt of satisfaction or surprise. After a few moments of this examination, he brought the volume over to us.

'See here,' said he, showing us two pages from the log, 'here's evidence enough that all is not well aboard the *Briggs*. Lestrade, I ask you to examine this handwriting – never mind what it says.'

The detective duly scanned the large, well-formed script whilst I looked over his shoulder.

'Nothing too unusual, Holmes.'

'Precisely. It is good handwriting. It was written in May, during the *Briggs'* outward voyage to the Orient. It is a strong hand, with distinction and some flourish. I would say offhand it indicates a person of strong character and generosity. Now, Watson, I'd like you to examine this specimen.'

'It's clear that the mate wrote these passages. The hand is altogether different.'

'Careful, Watson – don't jump to conclusions. Do you see any similarities?'

'Now that you mention it, there is a marked resemblance in the lower case "o"s.'

'Yes,' interjected Lestrade, 'and notice the curious tail on the letter "y" when it completes a word. These could even be the same hand, and yet –'

'– and yet while the one is strong and steady, the later is weak, unsteady, without character,' added Holmes. 'I tell you, Lestrade, one day there will be a complete and legitimate science dealing with handwriting. Few things reveal as much about a person's character or emotional state as his hand. It is clear that James McGuinness wrote both passages, yet the later passage, penned only a few weeks ago, reveals that the Captain was on the verge of cracking under an intolerable strain. The log itself reveals nothing of Sampson's strange tale, if indeed there's truth to it. It is plain we shall have to depend on the Captain himself to – My God!'

Holmes was interrupted by a sound I shall not forget for the rest of my days. It was a scream, or rather a high-pitched, hoarse shriek that rang about the ship like the trumpet of Doomsday.

It lasted for what seemed an eternity, then ceased. We sprang from the cabin, almost tripping over each other in our haste. We had not gone more than a few feet down the passage, when the shriek sounded again – it was pitched still higher, and sounded even more terrifying.

'Down here!' shouted Holmes, and dove down the ladderway into the hold.

The hold was shrouded in total blackness. The three of us groped our way forward frantically. After much difficulty, we succeeded only in working our way into a blind alley. Bales and hogsheads formed high walls on three sides of us.

'We must take our time,' insisted Holmes. 'In my haste, I left the lantern behind. It is quite possible, I fear, to become lost in this labyrinth for days. Listen!'

A low, mumbling sound came faintly to my ears. After several seconds I recognized it to be a human voice. The words were not audible, but their tone suggested profound grief and agony.

Slowly, the three of us crept forward, feeling our way in the darkness towards the sonorous, dirge-like chanting. For it was a chant, and as we drew nearer the sound I recognized the words 'Dear God, Dear God' being repeated.

After some time, I felt a ladder brush against me. Realizing it was the same one by which we had entered the hold, it became clear to me that we had turned the wrong way upon entering. We were now heading aft, and a short distance ahead could be seen a dimly lighted doorway. I heard a metallic click from Holmes' direction, and knew he had drawn his revolver. Lestrade and I followed suit.

'This is no doubt the after hold Sampson mentioned,' said Holmes in a hoarse whisper. 'Let us proceed.'

An instant later the ship took a roll, and, as if to announce our arrival, the thick oaken door ahead of us slowly swung open with a terrible groaning of its massive iron hinges. The chamber within was small, perhaps built for the personal possessions of the Captain. It was not more than fifteen feet on a side, and was low-ceilinged. In the split second that I examined the chamber itself, rather than its contents, I was aware of large iron rings set in the wall timbers, these no doubt used to lash cargo securely. There was another door, quite small, at the far wall of the after hold. It was shut and bolted with a heavy timber.

The dismal chamber was illuminated dully by a candle. The candle was held aloft by Jennings, who stood in the doorway, frozen in terror. His blank gaze was fixed on what lay in the centre of the small room, sprawled in a heap. We entered the room quickly and calmed Jennings, who had ceased his mumbling. Holmes took the candle and examined more closely the corpse on the floor. The man was dressed to go ashore, and from his cap, which lay a few feet from the body, we guessed him to be Captain James McGuinness.

It was only after Lestrade had led the shaken Jennings topside with orders to summon additional men that Holmes leaned over towards me and asked:

'What of these wounds, Watson? Surely I have not come across the likes of this before. See here, all about his chest and throat. What sort of weapon do you suppose −'

'Holmes!' I shouted, rising. 'Let us be off this ship at once!'

'Steady, Watson!' said Holmes as he gripped my shoulder. 'Watson, you're reeling... there, hold on −'

But at that instant a claustic fit came upon me, and I wanted nothing so much as to quit the dungeon-like bowels of the ship and breathe fresh air. Things went dim, and I was half-conscious of fighting my way somehow to the main hatchway, Holmes steadying me all the way. There I sat near the skylight until things came into a sharper focus.

'There, you're feeling better, eh Watson?'

I saw Holmes' eager face peering down into mine, as he steadied me with a firm grip on my shoulder.

'I lost control of myself, Holmes,' I remarked bitterly. 'I am truly sorry to have disappointed you.'

'Think nothing of it, dear fellow. Perhaps it was the closeness of the chamber itself, as well as the contents. Tell me, were you not conscious of a foul stench?'

'Yes, certainly – a heavy animal smell. But as to what upset me –'

'I was going to remark that something upon the corpse set you reeling, and I know you well enough, my friend, to know that you aren't upset by a trifle.'

'Holmes,' I intoned solemnly, 'you asked me what weapon was responsible for the wounds on the victim...'

'Yes, that seems a puzzle. No knife could have –'

'No knife was used. The wounds upon the Captain's throat are teethmarks.'

'You are certain?'

'I am positive. And what makes it all the more shocking and, if you will, mysterious, is the fact that they are no ordinary teeth.'

'How do you mean?'

'The wounds weren't inflicted by fangs, as a large dog or cat would possess. Nor are they tusks, such as wild pigs have. They were, I fear, *incisors* – or, if we can give even the slightest credence to Sampson's tale, the *teethmarks of a giant rat.*'

Four

⌒

RED SCANLON AT THE BINNACLE

Events moved quickly: Jennings was dispatched to the customs house, and within an hour the *Matilda Briggs* was swarming with inspectors and detectives.

A thorough search was made of the entire vessel. The cargo holds were examined, but yielded up nothing save the original cargo, which consisted of copra, raw silk, and small amounts of tea and tin. Holmes, Lestrade and I returned to the murder chamber and again examined the corpse. Despite his outward show of official confidence, Lestrade appeared inwardly shaken and confused. Holmes said nothing during our inspection tour of the after hold, but his face was full of the keenest interest and curiosity.

The Captain's body lay twisted on its side, as if he were trying desperately to escape. His lips curled back in a grotesque grin; his face bore a look of unimaginable horror. He had put up some resistance, as indicated by the condition of his hands and the flecks of blood on the sides of the chamber. The beast, whatever it was, that killed him, undoubtedly possessed great strength and incredible ferocity, for the man's neck was nearly severed. An indication of the animal's size could be roughly gauged from the crate that stood against the far wall. It was of the dimensions Sampson had described: six feet long by three feet high and wide. At one end, a hole a foot in diameter had been cut. It was through this hole apparently that the monster thrust his head. Holmes examined everything with the patience and thoroughness that were his hallmark. The musky odour that lingered in the small room suggested a beast had been quartered there, and recently. Yet no sign of the animal itself was found. The only interesting discovery we found in the after hold was a transom port, or 'lumber hole' as I believe the sailors call it. It was a hatchway cut horizontally through the transom of the ship, and fastened, when not in use, by the small stout door, heavily bolted, that I had observed when first entering the hold. Jennings, who had by this time recovered from his shock, explained to us that this type of hatch facilitates the loading on of long pieces of lumber, even entire logs, that would not fit down the deck hatchways.

'Tell me, Jennings,' enquired Holmes, 'does the *Briggs* generally haul lumber?'

'I believe not, sir,' was the reply. 'To my knowledge, she has not hauled lumber under her present owner.'

'Then this hatchway should not have been used for several years at least. It appears to have fallen into disuse, doesn't it, Watson? Notice the heavy rust on the hinges, and the marks of discoloration on the wooden beams where they have touched the metal. Yet, I would call your attention, gentlemen, to three curious things.'

Holmes swung the door open.

'First, note the ease with which the door swings. This is most odd for a heavy door not often used. Secondly, note the hinge joints: see how the rust, heavy as it is, is broken and chipped along each groove. Finally, through my lens, observe if you can the minute burring of the iron latch where it strikes the plate – and the shiny metal it leaves. Now gentlemen – one of these signs by itself could be accidental. Two could perhaps be coincidence. But the *three* of them together force us to conclude that this hatchway was indeed opened, and opened recently.'

Engrossed, the three of us peered out the small doorway, which was large enough for a man to crawl through. The water seemed surprisingly close, certainly not more than six feet below us. We left the grim cubicle behind and returned down the boarding stair to the launch. Shivering by this time, we huddled on the cushions while Jennings got us underway.

'The question is, why was the portway opened?' said Lestrade, as he smoked in the bow.

'Obviously,' I replied, 'to enable someone, or *something*, to leave the ship unobtrusively.'

'There are many questions that need answering,' remarked Holmes as he lit a cigarette. 'Who was the night-time visitor with the candle? Did he murder Captain McGuinness? If so, how? To all appearances, the man was worried to death by a large beast. A giant rat? It is hardly believable, yet Sampson swears he saw such a creature. Certainly the after hold smelled of an animal. And there is no denying the teethmarks on the corpse. Ah, here we are at the quay. Mind the painter, Lestrade.

'Now, Lestrade, I'll allow you to live up to your reputation as a man of your word. I know of a lively little inn not far from here much frequented by sailors. It serves excellent beer, good boiled beef, and much dockside gossip. You needn't scowl, my friend; the prices are reasonable. Let us be off.'

We left the iron gates of the customs house behind, and began a twenty-minute expedition through the labyrinth of winding streets and dingy lanes of Limehouse. The object of our quest was the Binnacle public house, an ancient, heavy-timbered establishment named after the enormous brass nautical instrument that stands near the doorway. It is located in Robin Hood Lane, and under its swinging, dripping sign we entered, descended four stone steps, and found ourselves in a low, narrow room that seemed to extend for ever in a series of hallways and turns. We were shown to a table by a stout woman who had three mugs of the dark beer in front of us almost before we were seated. The ale was a refreshing bracer after our morning, and the beef and onions were a fine accompaniment.

'But of all the unanswered questions,' pursued Holmes, 'the most unexplainable seems to be the message above Jenard's bunk. It was plainly put there by our night visitor to the *Briggs*. We know the visitor was not of the crew, and the time of the visit was after Jenard's death. Yet, the visitor wishes us to *believe* it *was* Jenard who wrote the message. Why does he wish this, and what does he want us to take from the message?'

'All is stairs and passageways where the rat sleeps —' I chanted.

'… his treasure keeps…' continued Lestrade.

'What's the treasure?' I asked. 'Do you suppose that Captain McGuinness *was* engaged in smuggling?'

'It is certainly possible,' said Holmes. 'The message, though, seems puzzling in another regard. It mentions *stairs* where the rat sleeps… I cannot recall any stairs.'

'True – there were none, only passageways,' I remarked. 'Furthermore, we can see by the author's use of the word *is*, rather than *are*, that he is illiterate.'

Holmes' thin lips curled into a hint of a smile at this observation.

'Yes, Watson, that is cerainly the most logical explanation,' he said, with a curious gleam in his eye.

At that instant our thoughts were interrupted by a great din of shouts and oaths emerging from the parlour bar of the inn. Leaving our table, we wound our way back to the front room of the Binnacle.

There, in the low-ceilinged drinking room was a great commotion: a dozen or so sailors were clustered around one of their number who, soaked with rain, had apparently just entered the establishment. It was some time before the group settled down enough for their conversation to become intelligible. We caught a few phrases with the words 'murder', and '*Matilda Briggs*', from across the crowded room. We drew closer to the group.

'… just before noon, so I heered it,' said the sailor who had just entered. He was very large, with a bushy red beard and bald head. He had shed his overcoat, and stood at the bar, pausing in his narrative to drain the pint in a single gulp and slam the mug down upon the bar as a signal for another. The bartender, although complying with the request, was apparently too slow for him.

'Step to it, Alf, mind you hurry! Red Scanlon is thirsty and, from what I seen this mornin', will have me six or seven more before I leave…'

He received his porter, turned away from the bartender without thought of paying and, aware of his captive audience, demanded tobacco and the best fireside bench before continuing. The knot of men leaned close in eagerness, and bore the look of fear and wonder on their faces, as Red Scanlon, obviously a master storyteller, went on:

'Well, the first I laid eyes on was old Jennings, slinking around the quay he was, and lookin' pale as death. So I says "What's up?" But he don't answer, don't acknowledge, and I sees three glum lookin' gentlemen followin' close behind – coppers most likely. Well, I knows now it's something bad, and most likely to do with the *Briggs* you see, because of…'

At this point, the storyteller paused.

'Because of what?' several in the group demanded.

Scanlon eyed the questioners uneasily; his eyes lost their boldness and appeared to shift slightly. Two men in the group remained silent, as if they were aware of what Scanlon was referring to.

'Well now, Scotty, you wasn't berthed on the *Briggs*, now was you? Then o' course, you don't know... but Winkler, and Thomas here, *they* know –'

The two men indicated shook their heads ever so slightly, as if to convey their wish to avoid the reference altogether.

'Are you by chance referring to the giant rat of Sumatra?' a clear voice enquired.

The huge sailor lowered his mug and peered uncertainly beyond the group towards the doorway where we stood. Through the dim light of the room, his eyes fixed upon Holmes, leaning nonchalantly against the doorway, for it was he who had asked the question. Scanlon rose and advanced with a catlike silence that was amazing for a man of his stature, and menacing.

'See here, whoever you may be...' he began in a low voice, then hesitated as he inspected the three of us. 'Why, by Jove, it's the three glum gentlemen!'

'I am Inspector Lestrade of Scotland Yard,' began our companion, but he was cut short.

'Now see here, gentlemen,' said Scanlon quickly, 'if it's about that business, me and my mates here want no part of it. We don't know nothin', do we, Thomas? Winkler? No, sir, you see? Now if it's the same to you, good gentlemen, we'll be poppin' off –'

'In the name of the Queen I must ask you to remain,' commanded Lestrade, 'and your two shipmates as well.'

Now the entire group of seamen was staring sullenly at us, and I noticed, not without uneasiness, that one of them had seized the fireplace poker and was holding it firmly across his knees. The lively festivity of the Binnacle had given way to an ominous silence. As I felt the poisonous stares all round me, I realized how far indeed we were from Regent's Park, in distance vertical as well as linear. Lestrade, however, always the policeman, seemed unaware of our true situation, and surged ahead in his most officious manner.

'I would recommend you don't resist,' he said, shaking his finger at Scanlon. 'Your Boatswain Sampson had the good sense to co-operate. Now if you will —'

The men brightened noticeably at the mention of Sampson's name. It was evident, and not surprising, that they held warm affection for him.

'Then you've met Johnny?'

'Yes. Met and arrested him,' continued the detective, blithely unaware that the group had risen and was forming a crude circle around us. 'And I hereby warn you that if you fail to co-operate, you'll all soon be joining him behind bars. Now if —'

'Johnny in the darbies!' cried Scanlon, his face flushed with anger. He turned and addressed his followers. 'Did you hear that? They've taken our Johnny off to jail!'

The outcry served as a sort of general signal to the denizens of the Binnacle. As the circle closed in, I remembered hearing the sounds of scuffing feet and the pushing back of chairs. As I braced myself for the broadside soon to follow, three words caught my ears. They were spoken clearly above the tumult: 'Bully Boy Rasher.'

The circle stopped moving. Scanlon approached Holmes and bent his face close to my companion's.

'What did you say?'

'Bully Boy Rasher,' said Holmes quietly. 'Have you heard of him?'

'You can bet I have — but what of it?'

'I knocked him out in a glove match two years ago, Mr Scanlon. If your intentions are as I perceive, I would prefer an individual settlement rather than a general brawl.'

Before the astonished giant could reply, a squealing, apron-clad figure dashed between the two men. It was Alf, the bartender.

'Mister 'Olmes, sir!' he piped. 'It is you, ain't it? I'm sure if we'd recognized you sooner, sir, there'd ha' been no trouble, such a friend of the working man as you are, sir. I'm sure our good friends here at the *Binnacle* haven't forgotten how you saved Chips Newcombe from the gallows, or cleared the young apprentice Smythe of the burglary charges against him – unjust as they were…'

The mood of the people had changed miraculously; they now gazed with curiosity at this slender, well-dressed man who had acted so nobly on their behalf. Scanlon, half-mollified, inspected the narrow physique of my friend incredulously.

'You beat Bully Boy Rasher, London's top middleweight?'

'Aye, Red, and what a pretty fight it was! At the Cribb Club, was it not, Mr 'Olmes? Such as me aren't allowed there of course, but a pretty fight, so I heard.'

'I might say, Alf,' said Holmes, 'that from appearances, I'd rather face three Rashers than this man before me.'

These words had a most remarkable effect upon Red Scanlon, who unclenched his fists, took two steps backward, and looked at the floor.

'You all should know,' Holmes said in a solemn voice, his eyes sweeping over the entire group, 'that John Sampson was put in jail largely at my unofficial request. To explain this action, I think I need only ask you two questions. First, are you aware of the fate of Raymond Jenard?'

There followed a grim acquiescence.

'Secondly,' pursued Holmes, 'would any one of you wish the same fate to befall John Sampson?'

There was a vehement denial.

'Then I must ask you for your forbearance for a short time, Mr Scanlon. If you would be so kind, I would very much like to ask you and your shipmates some questions concerning the recent voyage of the *Matilda Briggs*.'

The huge man considered a moment, then bade Winkler and Thomas to join us near the fire. He told the rest of the company to 'shove off', which they promptly did.

With gentle prodding from Holmes, he related his personal history and the account of the voyage from departure until the night of the crew's celebration. It was alike in every detail to Sampson's account. Owing to his predilection for strong drink, his memories of that particular evening were somewhat hazy.

'There's not much I 'member, gentlemen, expect that upon 'wakin' I felt that I'd been done over with a capstan bar, and right smartly, too.'

'And none of you was aware of any commotion on deck during the night? Thomas, Winkler?'

They all answered negatively.

'When were you aware of something strange on board?'

'When we first caught sight of Jones sneaking food aft,' replied Winkler. 'Then of course, we saw the rat itself –'

Here Winkler was rebuked by Scanlon and told to hush. Holmes filled in the narrative related by Sampson, however, and the three men grew confident. All had seen the head of the beast; all swore it was of a rat of fearsome size.

'… and alike in every detail to a ship rat,' said Scanlon.

'You have mentioned that Jones took food into the hold where the monster was kept. What did the bundle look like?'

'I can't tell you, sir,' replied Winkler, 'for they were always covered.'

'*They?*'

'Yes, there were always two, both of them covered with cotton cloth. One was thrice the size of the other.'

'That is interesting. What was your impression of the mate Jones?'

'A shirker, sir,' he replied. 'A real laggard, even for an officer.'

'How about Reverend Ripley – did you gain any lasting impressions of him?'

'Now there's a strange one. Didn't seem to me he was much of a parson. Winkler here overheard him rip out a terrible cursin' one day below decks, didn't you, Wink? Cursed the Captain terrible he did!'

Holmes' face sharpened. 'Isn't it odd for a passenger to behave this way towards a ship's captain?'

'O' *course*, sir! But then, there were *many* strange things on the *Briggs* this last one out, weren't there, boys?'

There was an agreement and a brief chuckle as the men pulled at their mugs.

'What does Ripley look like?' asked Holmes.

'A blondish, pale fellow – an indoors man if you know what I mean. And yet...'

'And yet what?' I asked.

'O, I don't reckon it's of any account –'

'Pray tell me, Mr Scanlon: even the smallest details are of great account.'

'I was about to say that frail and retiring as he was, he could be quick and agile on deck when the mood struck. Most often, it was in the form of leaping up to the quarterdeck to watch the petrels.'

'He was fond of them?'

'Quite,' interjected Thomas. 'But he was most keen on the wee creatures, sir.'

'The *wee creatures*?' Lestrade asked in amazement. 'What the devil are the wee creatures?'

'Oh sir, the wee creatures that swim about everywhere. Sometimes in the tropics, they glow like a peat fire – practically read a gazette from the light they give off –'

'I believe, Lestrade, Thomas is referring to various plankton: minute larvae, crustaciae and algae that breed and flourish on the surface of the tropical oceans and prey upon each other.'

'That's it, sir: them's the wee creatures. The Reverend Ripley busied himself by haulin' them aboard with a net he fashioned from cheesecloth and battens. On a calm day, we could see him at the taffrail, trailing the net aft like a ship's log. Queerest thing we'd seen in ages...'

'My dear Thomas – that piece of information is indeed singular – and most welcome. In its own way, it throws considerable light upon the case. Tell me if you can, any of you, what did the Reverend Ripley do with the net and its contents after he hauled it on deck?'

'Oh that's easy, sir – that's the queerest part of all. He would sit on the hatch cover Indian-fashion and dump the net on to the boards. Then he'd watch and poke, and poke and watch as the wee creatures slithered and scratched over each other. All the while, he'd be picking out the choice ones and stuffing them into jars and bottles, which he'd carry down below.'

'Aye, gentlemen,' continued Scanlon, 'and there was more than one of us thought the Reverend must be ailing – calling upon Weiss the cook to brew up his special chowder.'

They laughed heartily – and Holmes almost grinned.

Lestrade grew impatient.

'Enough storytelling. We must find Ripley and his confederates. A thorough search of these neighbourhoods will be undertaken immediately. All roads and railway stations will be closely watched. In the meantime, I assume that you will offer us every assistance possible in the way of information.'

'They've already been most helpful,' remarked Holmes, rising. 'Especially concerning Ripley's pastime with marine fauna. We are looking for three men, together or separate; a nondescript white man, his valet – a Malay named Wangi, and a seafarer named Jones, who is of average stature and appearance. It would seem then, that the most visible is the Malay. I am familiar with several parts of London where such a man might hide, Lestrade, and will be happy to render assistance in that regard. However, there are two major questions still untouched: the whereabouts of the monster rat and the motive behind the multiple murders. Can any of you offer even a partial explanation?'

The three sailors replied in the negative. The only explanation that had occurred to them was that the rat was a fiend, an instrument of the Devil, and had returned to Hell as mysteriously as it had come.

Five

THE HUNTER OR THE HUNTED?

In one of his customary fits of energy, Holmes left the inn directly the interview with the sailors was concluded, leaving us baffled and without the slightest idea of where to go next. Grumbling slightly, Lestrade paid the waiter and summoned a cab. At police headquarters we parted company; I went to my club where I spent a restive afternoon. Returning to our lodgings just before supper time, I heard the sobbing of a woman as I ascended the stairs.

Having prudently knocked, I was immediately shown to a seat beside a middle-aged woman, whose face was all but obscured by the lace handkerchief she held to it.

'John Watson, this is Miss Beryl Haskins, who has been kind enough to drop round for tea and a chat. There, there, Miss Haskins, your tale convinces me more than ever that the responsibility was not, *could not* have been yours...'

'You've no idea, Mr Holmes,' she sniffed, 'how painful it has been to return home alone –'

'I can well imagine.'

'The Allistairs have been so kind, so gracious through it all. Lord knows how much they're suffering. I expected to be turned out –'

'Pshaw! Her Ladyship has spoken most highly of you. You are uppermost in their affections. Now Miss Haskins, I agree with them: a holiday is what you want. Do take the evening train to Brighton. I assure you we'll do our best to resolve this affair as quickly as possible. Now here's your cab just pulled up. Off you go now, and have a pleasant rest. *Au revoir.*'

The lady managed a weak handshake and apology to me and followed Holmes to the door. He returned to his armchair and, without waiting for my obvious questions, launched at once into the explanation.

'As you've no doubt surmised, Miss Haskins is in the employ of Lord Allistair. She has been in his service since 1875 when his daughter Alice was born. The two have been inseparable ever since: Miss Haskins was the little girl's governess and, more recently, had assumed the role of her travelling companion. She was accompanying Alice Allistair on her summer holiday when the girl was abducted. She is now departing for a much-needed rest for she has been, as you have seen, beside herself with remorse.'

'If I recall the newspaper accounts was not the companion – Miss Haskins – detained on a false errand whilst the girl was kidnapped?'

'That is correct: it happened, you'll remember, in a crowded Bombay market place. The girl was forced into a palanquin by two natives and borne off into the throng. No one has seen or heard of her in the ten weeks since...'

'That's a long time to keep a hostage...'

'It is. In fact, it is what worries me night and day. The outlook for her well being is not bright, I'm afraid.'

'But in one sense the great time lapse may be a good sign; perhaps it has taken the abductors this long to get her back into England. If this be true, then she is surely alive, since no one would waste so much time on a corpse.'

'Excellent, Watson! I must say the same thought has occurred to me. However, it's best not to be too optimistic. Remember, pessimists are surprised as often as optimists, but always pleasantly.

'After leaving the two of you at the Binnacle, I set off on a number of jaunts, one which was a call at the Allistair residence in the Bayswater Road. Miss Haskins was not in when I called, so I requested the brief visit that just took place.

'I suppose you think it strange that I should continue on the Allistair case, devoid of evidence as it is, when we have our hands full with the present business —'

'You yourself said it promises to be the most difficult and diabolical one we've handled in quite a while.'

'I've no doubt of it. This morning's events bear that out, surely. Yet the Allistair tragedy has its interesting aspects too. You know me well enough to realize that I generally have sound reasons for what I undertake, and pursuing two lines of enquiry at once may not be as outlandish as it sounds.'

'Have you any theories?'

'Actually, yes. But they are too embryonic at present to warrant discussion. Ah — here's Mrs Hudson with our supper. Despite our hearty lunch, I'm famished. Would you see to the door while I fetch a bottle?'

After our meal, Holmes snuggled into the divan cushions and put a match to the reeking bowl of his clay pipe.

'You see, Watson, as conspicuous as the valet Wangi is, certainly the giant rat, if indeed it is flesh and blood, is extraordinarily visible.'

'Not to say horrifying,' I added.

'I concur. The mere thought of the monster scurrying through alleyways and over rooftops is appalling. And yet there's been no outcry – obviously no one has seen it. It is not aboard the *Briggs*, that much is certain. Has it been destroyed – killed and dumped into the Thames? Or is it caged in some cellar lair, ready to be unleashed upon selected victims, or upon the populace at large?'

'The thought alone gives me chills. When I think of the remains of the Captain –'

'Yes, it is a grisly business. But where is the rat? Whether destroyed or taken away, there is the very real problem of getting the animal off the ship unnoticed – no mean task, for we are already familiar with the method of getting it aboard.'

'In my opinion, Holmes, the rat hasn't been destroyed. All events indicate that Ripley values the beast highly, for whatever nefarious purpose. Otherwise why would he go to the great pains of smuggling it aboard the *Briggs* and caring for it throughout an eight-week voyage?'

'An excellent point. Yet he doesn't value it for circus purposes – that is to say for exposition, since if this were true, he would be anxious to attract publicity.'

'Perhaps the animal has an innate value, perhaps for its fur.'

'If the animal is a rat, Watson, I cannot see any value attached to it. Of course, it most probably is not a true rat. The largest rodent known is the Capabyra, a spaniel-sized aquatic animal that lives in Central and South America. It may be that the animal is heretofore unknown but in any event, it is capable of killing a man and – alive or dead – is no doubt within twenty miles of Blackwall Reach. If the monster is as fearsome and unforgettable as our witnesses have described, it should be difficult to keep concealed. It is my plan to continue the chase tomorrow. To that end, I dispatched two wires today. The answers that will arrive in the morning should be of value. No, Watson, I'll skip my whisky and soda tonight and go directly to bed. Goodnight.'

Next morning I was first to arise and before Holmes had descended into the parlour I had read the following telegrams which Mrs Hudson brought up:

TRAIL ENDS AT BALFOUR LANE AND WHITECHAPEL ROAD
— GREGSON

The above had been posted in London. The other was from Exeter and read:

YOU ARE CORRECT: NO ABSOLUTE PROOF
— MASON-JONES

Holmes was most interested in the first wire, and promptly set up his large Ordnance Survey Map of London and Environs on his marble-topped table, and spent the first half of the morning poring over it. Although he was not a man to lose patience easily, I could tell by occasional sighs and mutterings that the problem was complex, even for his keen faculties. I left him alone.

'I shall stop by and call on Mrs Redding, Holmes, and see how she is recuperating. I'll drop by Mortimer's on my return to pick up my pipe. Do you want anything?'

'Yes, Watson. If you would be so kind, get me four ounces of navy-cut — oh, and while you're at it, if you've the time, stop by the British Railways offices — the one in Oxford Street is closest — and fetch me complete timetables for Bombay and lines eastwards — also a list of depots, offices, and their addresses, will you? That's a good fellow. When you return, I should be most grateful if you would accompany me to the East End again if time allows.'

I performed the errands. Mrs Redding was recovering nicely from her bout of influenza. I bought the tobacco for Holmes and complimented Mortimer on my new pipe stem. I appeared at our quarters shortly before lunchtime, my arms overbrimming with pamphlets, maps, schedules, and office listings. These Holmes took eagerly, and spent another half-hour poring over them, scribbling notes all the while. Finally, he took a black notesheet and printed a lengthy telegram, which began 'HAVE YOU OR YOUR STAFF ANY RECOLLECTION...'

We left the flat, took our lunch at Marcinni's, and proceeded to Whitechapel Road. The intersection of that street and Balfour Lane was nondescript save for its general dinginess and proximity to the river. As there was no policeman or inspector there to meet us (I half-expected there would be), we were left on our own, and Holmes glanced round himself and ambled vaguely about like a dejected urchin. I followed silently, peering into shop windows and through tavern doorways. We proceeded up Balfour Lane, thence in the other direction. We repeated this process in Whitechapel Road. At the end of forty minutes, Holmes leaned against a lamp post, assumed a jaunty air, and asked me if I had any conjectures as to why the trail of Ripley ended at that particular intersection.

'How indeed do we know it does?' I asked.

'Because upon my suggestion Lestrade has employed the rather commendable talents of two of Scotland Yard's most able sleuths.'

'You mean MacDonald and Grimes?'

'Not exactly,' Holmes chuckled. 'I am speaking of Nip and Tuck, who have between them the most successful record in the entire organization.'

'Who?'

'Nip and Tuck are bloodhounds, Watson – the finest I've yet seen. I have no doubt they could give even Toby a run for his money.'

I of course recalled Toby with fondness, the gentle mongrel (now deceased) belonging to Mr Sherman, the Lambeth taxidermist. It was Toby's sharp nose that aided us in the capture of Jonathan Small, the peg-legged jewel thief.

'You see, shortly after we disembarked from the *Briggs*, Lestrade sent for the dogs; they cast Ripley's scent from his bedclothes. Nip and Tuck made a beeline from the quayside to this intersection, whereupon they stopped dumbfounded. Now Watson, what became of our Reverend Ripley? Did he vanish into thin air – dematerialize like a ghost? What is the answer?'

'The answer is simple: he boarded a cab.'

'Ah! That is certainly possible. But why here, instead of at the quayside which the cabs frequent?'

'He no doubt had some business nearby –'

'Yes, Watson! Now it seems we are getting to it. What sort of business?'

'Let me see,' I murmured, running my eyes over the various shop fronts and businesses, 'if it was not the visiting of a friend –'

'Your point is well-taken: it is conceivable that Ripley could have been on a personal visit. If this is the case, our conjectures are difficult. However, let us for argument's sake assume it was a business errand. Do any of the shops catch your fancy?'

'The grocer's to buy food – no, no... the Wheatsheaf public house – no, that would indicate a private meeting – here's one, Holmes, the haberdashery. Perhaps he would want a change of clothing to aid his escape...'

Holmes was growing impatient.

'Really, Watson, every business place can suggest a possibility. The trick is to select that establishment which presents the most *likely* possibility – or series of possibilities – and which will explain the greatest proportion of events. You have stated that Ripley boarded a cab. That is not a bad guess. However, we can see that there is no cab-stand nearby. Furthermore, the intersection is not a lively one; it would be a singular occurrence if a cab happened along just when Ripley would have need of one.'

In a flash, it came to me.

'The livery!'

'Excellent!' beamed my companion. 'Yes, I think that's where we should begin anyway.'

Ballantine's Livery and Smith Shop was a few steps north in Balfour Lane. Underneath the large sign was printed: 'Horses, Carriages, and Wagons to let – Daily or Weekly Rates.' We entered the establishment through a small doorway which led into a narrow hallway, the walls of which were lined with harnesses and horses collars. We could hear the whoosh of blacksmith's bellows, and occasionally the ringing of the hammer. Presently the hallway opened on to a large building set back from the street. Here were housed the stables, wagon yard, and the smithy forge. A wiry man with knotted arms toiled at the forge, while further back, in the shadows, horses of every description stamped and switched their tails contentedly. Upon hearing the nature of Holmes' enquiry, the smith laid his hammer aside and led us back towards the street to where a tiny, cluttered desk stood. From a drawer in the desk he extracted a leather purse, pulled loose the drawstring, and poured gold coins into his calloused palm.

'I don't reckon what place they be from,' said the smithy, 'seeing the funny figures and scribbles on them – but I know enough about metals to recognize gold when I sees it.'

'From India, or perhaps Ceylon,' mused Holmes as he peered into the blacksmith's palm. 'Is it customary for you to demand such a large deposit for your equipment?'

'He weren't renting – he were buying, sir. Bought my stoutest wagon, and a horse to match.'

'Did he leave his name?'

'Oh, no, sir, I didn't think to ask it. He paid for the rig in gold and was off.'

'What time was that?'

'The day before yesterday. It was just before tea – about four. No, I don't have the name, gentlemen. As for his appearance, he looked a gentleman, with a thinnish nose and a fancy bearing. All in all, I would call him an ordinary gentleman.'

'Was there anyone with him?'

'No, sir, he was alone.'

'Was there anything unique about the wagon?'

'Not really. It was similar to the one remaining at the back. A heavy dray wagon with enclosed top and sides, and bolted doorway in the rear.'

We had been returning to the rear building, and now stood near the remaining wagon, which Holmes examined with much interest.

'The wheels, are the rims of similar thickness, with the same type of iron treads?'

'To my mem'ry, sir, they're twins in every respect. I bought the both of 'em from a retired stonemason in Hammersmith. He used them for hauling his tools and rock slabs – they're built like a fortress, as you can see…'

'Lestrade and his crew would do well to have a look at this, Watson. What of the horse – anything special?'

'Twelve-year-old gelding, dappled. He's quite heavy – a perfect match for the wagon I'd say – I'll wager he's some Shire blood in him for the height and weight he carries.'

'Thank you, that is most helpful. Now Watson, let us borrow our noble defenders of justice, Nip and Tuck, if we may, and put them through their paces again.

'While we cannot be absolutely sure it was Ripley who bought the horse and wagon,' pursued Holmes as we made our way towards the quay for the second time in two days, 'we can be reasonably certain. That isn't bad for the present, and Lestrade and his men could spend their time far more foolishly than in looking for the large dapple horse pulling the mate to the mason's wagon.'

'Do you intend to have the hounds follow the wagon?'

'If they could, they would be unlike any hounds in history. To cast a scent from a stable is impossible – but it seems more than likely that Ripley left the *Briggs* more than once – let us see if we can't find another trail.'

It was a twelve-minute walk back to the Quay. The rain had stopped for some time, and the fog lifted enough to enable one to look out across the reach. There the tall ships rode. Some of them were being pushed and pulled about by squat steam tugs belching clouds of oily smoke. Some were moored at the quayside, and derricks and 'donkey' steam engines were busily engaged in the transferring of cargo. The *Matilda Briggs* looked ordinary enough from that distance, except for her deserted appearance. Small groups of onlookers had gathered on the docks, and occasionally one would point and gesticulate in the direction of the silent ship. Word of the murder had spread.

After walking towards the customs house we spied Gregson with two gigantic dogs on long leads. It was my guess they weighed a hundredweight apiece.

'Hello, Mr Holmes, Doctor Watson. It seems the weather is a bit brighter, eh? Still, finding another trail shall be difficult, I warn you, even for these two beauties, after all the rain we've had.'

'Let's try our best, Gregson. I've a message for you first, however, concerning the first trail you discovered. Have you your notebook?'

Holmes related our recent visit to Ballantine's Livery, and furnished him with enough detailed description to set the detective fairly hopping with anticipation.

'If you don't mind, gentlemen, I'd much rather be pursuing this other line of the investigation. Indeed, it is my duty. You may use Nip and Tuck here till your heart's content. Personally I believe it's useless. I'll send a man round to your flat this evening if convenient. They're no problem, I assure you. But mind, don't feed them the slightest morsel; they work best hungry and aren't worth a farthing with the taste of food in their mouths. Good day.'

He dashed off, brimming with excitement.

'Ah, Watson, we are free to use our canine friends here at our leisure. I had hoped our news would send him off. A nice fellow Gregson, and competent, but the police are more often than not a hindrance to me. They are far better serving as messenger boys and lookouts. I wish them every success in tracking down the wagon. Now then, you take Nip – or is it Tuck? – oh, well, we'll handle one apiece. Have no fear, man, for despite their size, they're as placid as sheep, as you can see.'

I took one of the sad-faced creatures and petted its domed head. It responded immediately by nuzzling and licking my hand, and whining softly.

'Quite right, Holmes, he's as gentle as a lamb. How then, do they attack criminals?'

'Ha! You are as ignorant as most of the public on that score, I'm afraid. Let us walk these two crime-fighters about a bit and see if we can't find another scent. In the meantime, I'll tell you something about them.'

We cast the scent again, from the scrap of bedclothes that Gregson had provided us. The dogs whined eagerly and began trailing, nose to the ground, almost pulling me off my feet.

'The breed's ancestor, the St Hubert's Hound, originated in the Abbeys of France, a descendant of the hunting dogs used since the time of Charlemagne. The name we English have bestowed, *blood*hound, refers not to the animal's lust for blood, nor its penchant for following blood spoor, but rather – whoa! whoa I say!'

Holmes and I spent the next several minutes attempting to persuade the dogs to pursue a course other than the one they intended.

'This is the trail Gregson found. If we find nothing else, we'll come back – where was I – oh yes, well, the name *blood*hound is used in the sense that the phrase blood horse, or blooded horse is used, that is, to indicate strict bloodlines and long lineage – for the strain has always been much prized...'

'Most interesting,' I answered, fighting the leash.

'We have here a beast with the keenest nose in the entire animal kingdom, and the only animal, the *only* animal save man, Watson, whose testimony is considered admissible evidence in a court of law!'

'You don't say!'

'Quite so, and – hullo, what's up?'

The dogs stopped their forward motion and were confusedly turning round in tight circles, whining shrilly and flagging their tails.

'Ah! What have we here, fellows? Eh? What's up? Have you found something, eh?'

After observing this behaviour for a few minutes I asked Holmes if it meant they had found a scent.

'Found and lost it, Watson,' said he. 'Do you observe anything remarkable about this portion of the quay? How does it differ from other parts of the area?'

'Not in many respects,' I answered, looking about. 'It does seem though, that there is a gradual sloping to the water's edge here, instead of a sheer drop of several feet.'

'Yes! Yes, Watson, go on – anything else?'

'No. I confess I cannot discover another distinguishing characteristic.'

'Oh really? I can see something from here that is most remarkable. Do you see that smudge of greenish-brown substance yonder? There is something we should both be interested in.'

I spotted the smudge some ten paces away, and went over to look closely.

'Axle grease!' I exclaimed. 'But what of it? Surely there are quite a few dray carts running up and down this quay –'

'Yes, running up and down this quay no doubt. But *across* it?'

'I'm afraid that's quite impossible,' I laughed. 'You can see for yourself there's the water on one side, and the iron fence on the other.'

As anyone familiar with the London Docks well knows, they are surrounded by high iron fences. The only gates are placed adjacent to the customs house. Thus, any comings and goings of either goods or persons may be strictly regulated by the officials.

'What you say is true. But notice the smudge itself. It was caused certainly by excess grease dripping off the front axle of some vehicle, then the rear wheel of the same vehicle running over the patch of grease and causing it to smudge.'

'That appears to be the case,' I assented.

'But we can both see that the smudge was elongated in such a way as to show definitely that the vehicle was bound in a direction *perpendicular* to the general flow of traffic.'

'By George, Holmes, you are correct! That means the cart has been dumped into the river – we should have it dragged for at once!'

'Not so fast, Watson. We should examine all the possibilities.'

'Yet you yourself have often stated that when the other possibilities are exhausted whatever remains, however improbable, must be the truth. I see no way in which a wheeled vehicle could clear the fence over there, unless it sprouted wings.'

'Let us make certain,' he cautioned, and left me with the hounds whilst he approached the fence twenty yards away. He inspected it carefully for a moment. Then, with a mischievous glance in my direction, he fetched it a powerful kick. To my utter amazement, an entire section of the wrought iron, perhaps eight feet square, fell away and crashed to the pavement with a tremendous clanging. For one of those extremely rare moments during my long association with him,

Sherlock Holmes lost himself in laughter. Chagrined, I looked away and pretended to busy myself with the dogs. They, however, gave me that look of cold aloofness which told me I was a fool.

'The railings were filed through – that is obvious,' remarked Holmes when I joined him at the fence. 'This could be done in silence. Then the section was temporarily lifted away to allow a vehicle to enter, take on or leave its cargo, then leave by the same gap in the fence. The section was, as we have seen, then replaced. To passers-by it was unnoticeable. A fairly remarkable feat.'

'Even more remarkable when one considers it's impossible,' I said. 'To file through this fence must have taken well over an hour. Why weren't they discovered in this time?'

'A good point. But think a minute. This occurred the night before last. That night, you and I were not more than a mile from this very spot –'

'Ah yes, the *fire*! Certainly it was an excellent cover for them. They could have put on a circus at the quayside and no one would have noticed –'

'Right you are, Watson.'

'No doubt the vehicle was the wagon that Ripley purchased from Ballantine's.'

'We can determine that easily enough in two ways. One, by comparing wheel tracks and axle length with the other remaining wagon that the smithy showed us. Secondly, we can take a bit of the smudged axle grease and compare it with the grease that is used at Ballantine's. The two checks should give us a definite answer, which I am confident will be the same one you offered. This spot was selected probably because of the feature you noticed: the wagon could be backed down to the water's edge. Here, let us try something.'

He took one of the hounds from me and led the animal down to where the first trail had ended. The dog again wheeled in tight circles, whining.

'Now Watson, bring your dog over here too. Now, lead him down to the water's edge, so.'

We took the dogs to the very edge of the embankment. The next instant I was nearly knocked flat by the tremendous agitation of my leashed animal. As I whirled madly round like a top, spun by the leash as a boy pulls the top's string, I saw that Holmes, not as heavy as I, was having even more difficulty remaining upright. Finally, after much tugging and shouting, we managed to subdue the dogs somewhat. Still, they howled and gnashed their fangs; their eyes rolled upwards in their deep sockets, revealing the crescent of white underneath. They appeared both angry and terribly frightened, and pressed close to us, great ridges of fur rising along their backs.

Surprisingly, the dogs seemed eager to leave the spot, even pulling us swiftly behind them. However, the ridge of hackles along their backs remained, and also the deep growling in their chests.

'Seldom have I seen dogs so agitated,' remarked Holmes a few minutes later. 'Well, this seems to prove one thing, Watson: whatever the giant rat of Sumatra is, it is most certainly *not* a "puppet contrivance" as you once suspected. No indeed, my friend, it is a living, breathing beast, and one so fierce that its two-day-old scent is enough to send these two brave hounds into a frenzy!'

But he needn't have reminded me – I was aware of the beast's authenticity when I saw the gashes upon the Captain's throat.

'There remains only one more avenue of investigation with our canine friends, Watson. Let us see if we can't pick up another one of Ripley's trails, even though the police failed to do so.'

We cast the scent time and time again, but without success. Finally, Holmes suggested that we go home to our lodgings and await the man who would return the dogs to Scotland Yard. We walked at a slow pace down the quay, past knots of onlookers staring wonderingly at the dark hull of the *Matilda Briggs*, past the customs house, and out through the tall iron gates. Holmes, in a pensive mood, declared he'd rather walk a mile or so than board a cab directly. So the four of us ambled on, the two *Homo sapiens* apparently being led onward by two gigantic specimens of *Canis familiaris*, the latter proceeding at a leisurely, sniffing pace.

Not far from the customs-house gates, we received a considerable surprise, for the dogs once again showed eagerness, flagging their tails and whining, and tugging at the leads.

'What have we here, my dear fellow? Could it be that Nip and Tuck have found something?'

It soon became apparent that they had indeed. They proceeded at first slowly, as if uncertain of a scent. However, after making steady progress for several hundred yards, they broke into a slow trot, and Holmes and I had difficulty keeping pace.

'We're off for the races it appears,' said Holmes, gripping the leash with both hands. 'Let's see where it ends.'

'This neighbourhood looks oddly familiar,' I remarked.

Holmes nodded, and I noted that his face had become grim.

It was over before we even half-suspected it: the dogs crossed an alleyway, whirled about in a small dooryard, and crossed the street in a mad rush. We found ourselves standing under the swinging wooden sign, and staring with amazement at the huge brass pedestal topped with two iron spheres and the hooded compass. To our astonishment, we were back at the Binnacle.

'Well, well,' mused my companion, and it seemed to me almost an attempt at levity. However, his countenance certainly was anything but light. In fact, it was one of those rare moments when Sherlock Holmes appeared lost. He stared keenly at the doorway to the public house for some time, then glanced carefully all round us. As the seconds ticked by, it became more and more apparent to me that he had been taken completely off guard. Knowing the rarity of such an occurrence, I became uneasy. I felt it necessary to break the silence.

'You were expecting the trail to lead elsewhere, were you not?' I asked.

'I must confess that I certainly was not expecting it to end here,' he replied, with a flicker of amusement. 'Surely you sense the irony, the brashness, eh, Watson? Very few criminals would have the gall of this Ripley... very few – wouldn't you agree?'

Some fifteen minutes later we were packed into a four-wheeler bound for Baker Street. Our friends Nip and Tuck (for which, to our annoyance, we were obliged to pay half-fare) were strewn between our feet. Holmes, still not fully recovered from the surprise of our last discovery, gazed out the carriage window.

'The cheek, Watson, the absolute *cheek*!'

'I don't quite follow you, Holmes.'

'You don't follow me, but Ripley *has*,' he snorted. 'Don't you see? He followed the three of us to the Binnacle yesterday. It is obvious from the trail he left. Did you note how the dogs wheeled and paused in the narrow doorway across the street from the pub? No doubt that is where he ducked in to wait until we entered. So our missionary friend is not jouncing over the countryside escaping in a wagon after all, but here in London, dogging us... which raises certain other questions, which you've probably asked yourself.'

'I have not been raising questions with myself, other than the most obvious one, which is where did Ripley go after he left the Binnacle?'

'Into a cab, I'm almost certain. As you saw by the behaviour of the dogs, he left no trail away from the pub. Therefore, he observed us leaving the docks, followed us to the Binnacle, then departed by cab after our luncheon was completed. But what is important is *why* he followed us, not when or how. Are you familiar with Joshua Hathaway's painting "Stag at Bay"? No? The painting depicts the wounded stag making a stand against a yew hedge. The dogs are closing for the kill, yet half their number lie dead at the stag's feet. I ask you, Watson, are we the hunters or the hunted? One thing is sure: *the stag is not running*. Furthermore, there's the incredible arrogance of Ripley... the eagerness to battle wits with me... certainly that is an unmistakable hallmark –'

He seemed to drift off into thought, and said nothing more until we were deposited inside our rooms. Mrs Hudson brought up some knuckle bones, and the two giant hounds stretched in front of the fireplace, cracking the bones between their jaws whilst Holmes and I shared a pot of tea.

'Now let us reconsider the events *in toto* in the light of all we now know. The tale, incredible and implausible as it seems, does have patterns and a chronology that make sense, does it not? It is, quite simply stated, the smuggling of some sort of monster into London aboard a merchant vessel. Most of our observations flow *with* the current of this strange story – agreed?'

I nodded.

'Yet, there are three events which stand out as being grotesque – that appear, to continue my analogy, to be going *upstream* instead of down, do you agree?'

'There have been many strange occurrences in the past two days, but I'm not sure I can identify the errant ones,' I replied.

'Then let me backtrack a little. The tale of John Sampson, while strange, has a certain logic to it. Likewise, the killing of Captain McGuinness, while horrific, is in one sense understandable.'

'You mean because of the possibility that he wished to betray the pact, or wanted to escape?'

'Exactly. These can be considered downstream events in that

they arise out of the basic plot, plan, or whatever, of Ripley and his confederates. But what of the fact that we were followed? Ah, that seems definitely in the *upstream* category, does it not? Yes, there is a counter-current running, and we must fathom it, or —'

'Or what?'

'Or we could be in a great deal of danger. I said from the outset that it was a dark and vile circle we were confronting. I say it again with even deeper respect. Now then, what of the other two upstream events? Another, I think, is the killing of Jenard. Why was Jenard killed and not any of the other crew — Sampson, for instance? If one of the crew was to be sacrificed for warning's sake, why pick a man as hale as Jenard, why not a little snip of a fellow like Winkler? And why not perform the deed on some dingy dockside, rather than Baker Street?'

'You said before that those who killed Jenard knew of you.'

'Did I? Why yes, I recall it. Well, we seem almost to come full circle. Who sent Jenard in our direction, and why was he killed? What did he know that no one else does?'

There was a long pause.

'What is the third event?' I asked.

'The third event is the writing in candle smoke above Jenard's bunk. It is not only mysterious in its meaning, but by its very presence. What does its author wish to gain by it? Does he wish to throw us off the track, or on to —'

Here he paused, and soon the hint of a grin formed on his lips. Slowly, he reached upward and back with his left hand. I saw the grimy clay pipe in his hands as he filled it. Having seen this ritual countless times before, I realized he was no longer in our quarters, but perhaps slinking around the East End like a wharf cat. Since further conversation was useless, I spent the remainder of the evening with Tennyson.

Departure

Except for the release of John Sampson from the Old Bailey, the next few days passed uneventfully. I busied myself with my practice and returned to Baker Street only to sleep, and then at odd hours. I seldom saw Holmes, and when I enquired into the progress of the case, received only a dismal grunt in reply. Assuming from these responses that all was not going well, I avoided him still further. Holmes could be distant and short-tempered when events frustrated him.

I noticed, however, that he was careful to bolt the door to our flat securely each night, and advised me to exercise caution whenever I left.

'Stick to the main thoroughfare whenever possible,' said he, 'and carry your pistol when you'll be out after dark.'

I followed the advice, although with reluctance, for it dented my pride. But the recollection of the two mangled corpses was sufficient to keep me on the lookout.

On the fifth day my duties relented. My final appointment failed to arrive, and I found myself at Baker Street in the early afternoon. I removed my coat and hung it on the tree. Holmes was standing in the bow window watching the leaves drift earthward in slow spirals. It was a bright, crisp autumn day and he seemed to be taking advantage of the clarity to scan the street in both directions. Behind him on the divan was the usual jackdaw's nest of papers including, from what I could gather from a quick glance, replies from various foreign offices of British Railways.

'Ah Watson! I see your last appointment was cancelled. I take it, then, that you are home for the day?'

'Holmes! How did you —'

'I'll tell you,' he said mischievously, 'only if you promise to accompany me to Bayswater Road, to the residence of Lord and Lady Allistair.'

'Certainly. I shall be glad to.'

'Fine. Then let's set off. Shall we walk?'

'Now how did you guess that my last appointment had been cancelled?' I asked as we walked briskly across Portman Square.

'I didn't guess it. I inferred it. You are regular, almost Teutonic in your habits, Watson, especially your professional habits. I dare say that's why we get along so well, for I, as you well know, am the opposite. In any event, your professional life is well-regulated and organized to the core —'

'Yes, but my days differ widely. Sometimes I see twenty patients, sometimes four.'

'Quite so. But always, Watson, *always*, you carefully write out your forthcoming appointments the night before in your pocket secretary. You sit in your chair with your right foot propped up on the coal scuttle —'

'Yes, that's true. I like to be organized for the next day.'

'And always, you depart each morning with your secretary in your right breast pocket — your fountain pen placed inside it.'

'How observant of you. Yes, I stick my pen inside to mark the place.'

'You *return*, however, with your secretary in your left pocket, *sans plume.*'

'I suppose I do. After my last patient, I make final notes in my secretary, tear out the pages, and file them.'

'But today, in addition to arriving home early, your pocket secretary and pen are in their "pre-work" positions, as I observed when you took off your coat. Ergo: your last appointment was cancelled. Now, see that forest of chimney stacks yonder? That, my dear fellow, is the house of the Allistairs. And two finer people you shall never meet. Come!'

Holmes' description was apt: the Allistair house at 13 Bayswater Road was indeed a forest of chimney stacks, and a sea of gables and cornices as well. The handsome red brick exterior was set off splendidly by an immaculate lawn and well-trimmed shrubbery. There was enough ivy about the house to provide a venerable feeling without seeming cluttered. I was impressed with its size as well as its beauty. The kidnappers were evidently well aware of the Allistair fortune.

'So you have remained in communication with the Allistairs. Have there been any developments?'

'Yes, as a matter of fact, and just about the time I expected, too. I must tell you at the outset, Watson: this won't be a pleasant call. In one sense, tremendous weight has been lifted from the Allistairs. In another sense, there is surely more pain to follow. I visited briefly with them this morning, and promised I'd return this evening with you. You can be of great assistance to all of us. Read this.'

He handed me a wire which read:

COME IMMEDIATELY — TERMS HAVE BEEN OFFERED.

'This is the first communication from the abductors to Lord and Lady Allistair?'

'Yes. I suppose one could take it as a cause for celebration, but I must tell you privately, Watson, I fear for the girl. But let us go up, and for God's sake, be of good cheer.'

We were shown through the front door by the butler, who, from his tense manner and sombre expression, evidently shared his master's distress.

Lord and Lady Allistair were seated on either side of a gigantic fireplace of carved stone. The high Georgian windows poured sunshine into the room, in which was displayed Her Ladyship's exceptional collection of rare china and porcelain. The sunlight on these objects lent a gleaming, cheerful atmosphere to the setting, but one glance at the couple was sufficient to convey the sense of anxiety that had overcome them.

Lord Allistair's appearance reflected his reputation. Tall, slender, around sixty years of age, he stood to receive us immaculately groomed and dressed despite the obvious emotional upheaval he was experiencing. His keen features were handsomely set off by a trim grey moustache and close-cropped hair. Her Ladyship remained seated, and one could only have admiration for her composure and cordiality at so trying an occasion. Only a few moments in their presence convinced me of their noble character and strong spirit.

A brief recollection of Lord Allistair's stunning career in government which, as the reader no doubt knows, was marked by compassion for the unfortunate, unrelenting pursuit of the corrupt, and zeal for progressive reform in all areas, only served to amplify my initial impressions of the man. The endowments, charities, and public works of his wife also came vividly to mind. As I took in the surroundings of the mansion, the thought struck me more than once that here indeed was a family of wealth and position that deserved every bit of it.

I was introduced as a trusted *confidant*, and was welcomed with a genuine warmth. Holmes and I seated ourselves on a luxurious sofa, which in turn was placed on an immense Persian carpet. The sunlight brought out the brilliant cobalt blue and deep burgundy red of its design and I couldn't help thinking that all in all, the room's size and appointments made our meagre Baker Street lodgings seem drab indeed.

'Gentlemen,' began Lord Allistair as he leaned tensely forward over the coffee table, 'as you know, this is the first communication we have received regarding our daughter's whereabouts or...' he faltered slightly, 'her well being.'

He handed Holmes a sheet of ordinary paper. On it were two messages. The first, as is common with messages in which anonymity is essential, was constructed by the pasting of words and letters upon the sheet. The other message, however, was written in delicate long-hand in ink.

'Lady Allistair and I are certain that the bottom message was written by our daughter. It is her hand, sure enough, although it shows obvious strain and nervousness. Since the letter was postmarked yesterday morning, we know that she is alive, at least,' said Lord Allistair.

'While we certainly share your optimism, sir,' remarked Holmes, 'we must not preclude the possibility, however unpleasant, that the handwriting was done some time ago, and merely posted yesterday.'

This possibility smote the couple like a hammer blow, bringing an onslaught of sobbing from Lady Allistair. Annoyed at Holmes' callous approach, I did my best to comfort them.

'I'm sorry,' he said, 'but it is a possibility that we must face, however remote. Here, Watson, what do you make of it?'

He handed me the note. The first message was short, clear and ominous: '£100,000 to be delivered in small bank notes from Strathcombe for return of your daughter. Harm shall befall her if you summon help or fail. Further instructions await you there.'

'Strathcombe is the country seat of Lord and Lady Allistair,' Holmes informed me. 'Evidently, the criminals feel safer in their plan by operating outside the city. The estate is in Shropshire, to the south and west of Shrewsbury, hard by the Welsh border. It is surrounded by nothing save craggy hills and great expanses of the Clun Forest. It is these rugged and desolate surroundings, perhaps, more than anything else, that have led the kidnappers to choose the place.'

'Strathcombe was originally built as a hunting lodge, and is still used for that purpose,' continued Lord Allistair. 'It is remarkable for containing the only wild boar in the British Isles. In the seventies, a few choice specimens were imported from the Black Forest by Prince Albert. Since then they've bred and flourished, although still confined to the single wooded valley in which Strathcombe lies. But we don't frequent the place much, since we prefer the city. It is, as Mr Holmes has stated, quite isolated, the nearest village being almost five miles distant.'

I nodded and read the second message which was written by the young lady. It was simple and heartrending: 'Dearest Mother and Father, for the love of God, help me! I am unharmed physically, but can maintain my sanity scarcely another fortnight. Please do as you are instructed if you wish to see me again. Your loving daughter, Alice.'

'The monsters!'

'Quite so. Knowing how you would react to this horror, Watson, and also knowing your sense of duty and your courage, I have brought you with me this afternoon in the hope, nay in the expectation, that you would render assistance.'

'Of course I shall, Holmes, and I appreciate your trust and confidence. Lord Allistair, rest assured that I will wholeheartedly give any service that I can, small as it may be.'

'We thank you, sir,' said Lady Allistair. 'Mr Holmes has spoken most highly of you, and we can see he is a good judge of character.'

Flushing slightly, I waved off these compliments as best I could and awaited further instructions from my companion.

'Your practice appears to be flourishing of late, Watson – is it possible for you to leave London for a few days?'

I nodded.

'Splendid. Then you can be of great service to this distinguished couple by accompanying them to Strathcombe tomorrow morning. Your presence will be beneficial in two ways. First, you will, by your engaging personality and indomitable spirit, be a source of companionship and comfort. Secondly, and more important, you will serve as a chronicler of events to me and as personal bodyguard to His Lordship and Ladyship as well.'

'Then you will not go?' I asked.

'I'm afraid not. As you know, there is another business afoot in London that requires my immediate energies; hence the need for your services. However, I shall be joining you all as soon as possible, perhaps in a few days, and certainly no later than a week. Is this agreeable to all? Excellent. Now, Watson, we shall return home where I will go over in detail with you your duties as intelligence gatherer and protector.'

We rose from the sofa and made our way back to the hall. Holmes paused, however, at the antique French secretary which stood near the doorway. He glanced keenly at a pair of framed portraits that stood upon it. Each was mounted in an oval cardboard. One was the face of a beautiful young lady; the other showed a young man standing in full military dress.

'This is your daughter, I presume,' said Holmes.

The couple replied in the affirmative in voices scarcely audible.

'And this young man is your son? Yes, I see he is. As is so often the case with sons, he looks like his mother...'

'Yes, that's young Peter,' said Her Ladyship smiling. 'This is his third year at Sandhurst —'

'Ah, a military man, eh? So he's decided not to enter politics. I seem to remember reading about your son in the newspapers last year... didn't he go to Eton?'

'Harrow actually.'

'Of course, I remember now, and a preparatory school, in the North?'

'That's correct, the Malton School in Yorkshire – you've a good memory, Mr Holmes.'

'But mainly for unimportant things, it seems. Well, I hope to meet your son one day, and I'm confident we'll be seeing your daughter before long. Good day, Lady Allistair, Lord Allistair. I shall see you all off at the train tomorrow. Adieu.'

We walked back to our quarters. I noticed a keen smile on Holmes' face.

'Another piece of the puzzle seems to have fallen into place, Watson. It grows clearer by the moment.'

If this were the case, it was indeed news to me. But, immersed as I was in my new role, I swept the 'puzzles' from my brain. I had enough to prepare myself for, and not much time.

'Let's get down to the maps and instructions,' I said, and quickened my pace.

The remainder of the evening and a good part of the night was spent in our chambers, where Holmes, with a survey map of the country around Strathcombe spread between us, explained precisely what I should beware of, and where I was to keep close lookout. He had also obtained from Lord Allistair a large-scale map of Strathcombe itself, which showed the floor-plan of the house, and the surrounding gardens, grounds and outbuildings as well.

'As you can see, the house is not large, being of some fourteen rooms. It was, as we've been told, built as a shooting lodge rather than as a mansion. It dates from the time of Henry VII, although somewhat altered in later centuries, and is in remarkably good repair considering its age and infrequency of use. Perhaps the good condition of the house is due in part to its smallish size. In contrast to the house, though, the grounds are considerable, encompassing some 900 acres of meadow, woods and marsh. Furthermore, because of its history as a shooting lodge, the grounds are riddled with outbuildings. There is a stable house with stalls and loose boxes, a kennel with runs and huts, a gamekeeper's cottage, and the ruins of a mews, long since abandoned. The reason I pay close attention to all of this, Watson, is because I fear the kidnappers have chosen their site well. It is rugged, inaccessible, unpopulated, and possesses myriad hiding places and vantage points. It is no fool's errand you have volunteered for, my good fellow. The way is fraught with uncertainty and danger. You must be armed at all times and take no chances. Furthermore, you should communicate with me by telegraph daily. Your failure to do so will cause me to call out the militia, do you understand?'

'Perfectly. By the bye, considering your feelings on the "other problem" here in London, I might give you the same advice.'

'It would be well-taken, I assure you. Now the required amount of cash will be conveyed to Strathcombe in a strongbox which you will guard. In the event that the "further instructions" come fast upon your arrival, it would be best not to try and contact me, as it would arouse suspicion. You remember from the note that Lord Allistair was *not* to seek help.'

'Certainly. How, then, will my presence be explained?'

'Quite simple: you are a distant cousin of Lady Allistair's, and are joining them for a stay in the country. I doubt the criminals will see a connection, but if they do, you had best be prepared for the worst. Also, there is something else you should know: none of the household staff at Strathcombe knows the *real* purpose of the Allistair's country visit. For safety's sake, this is to be kept secret as long as possible.'

'I understand.'

'Furthermore, considering the emotional state of Lord and Lady Allistair, I need hardly mention that the dreadful business surrounding the *Matilda Briggs* –'

'You needn't fret about that – the tale of the giant rat of Sumatra shall stay locked in my bosom.'

'Excellent.'

I rose early the following morning and packed my grip. Extra items included a Webley-Smith revolver and box of cartridges, field glasses, and Holmes' split-bamboo fly rod, which he was gracious enough to loan me.

'I doubt if you'll have time to put it to use, but it makes your appearance more legitimate,' he commented over the breakfast muffins, 'and pray, don't forget the maps – you'll want to familiarize yourself with the surroundings as soon as possible. We'd best be off; the train to Shrewsbury departs within the hour.'

Paddington Station was crowded; we trundled about for what seemed an age before we caught sight of the Allistairs boarding the second to last railway carriage.

'If they've followed my instructions, they have booked an entire compartment. This will ensure comfort, safety, and privacy. However, you should carry your pistol on your person, not in your luggage.'

I did as he bade and clambered aboard. Finding the compartment, I entered and was warmly received by my recent acquaintances. They appeared in better spirits. Whether it was the freshness of the morning, or perhaps the anticipation of the dreadful trial coming to a close, I cannot say, but they appeared almost cheerful, although the anxiety showed through occasionally. I pushed the carriage window down to bid Holmes goodbye.

'The very best of luck to all of you, including your daughter,' cried Holmes as the train began to roll, 'and mind, Watson, keep in touch daily. I'll be joining you when I'm able.'

Then, it seemed to me very suddenly, he turned and plunged into the thickest part of the crowd and disappeared like a stone in water.

Almost immediately, I was aware of another man following him in to the crowd. The glimpse lasted but an instant, due to our quickening speed, but he appeared intent, even grim, in his mission.

'Who might that be?' enquired Lord Allistair.

'I've no idea, but I don't like his manner I'm bound to say,' I replied. 'My friend has emphasized caution time and again – I only hope he heeds his own advice.'

With this unexpected turn of events, the journey, of more than two hours, passed more slowly than it might have. My mind could not help dwelling upon the possibility that Holmes' life was imperilled. Accordingly, at the next stop. I disembarked and sent the first of my wires, albeit prematurely. It read, 'Beware, you were followed this morning at Paddington.'

Feeling slightly relieved, I passed the remainder of the trip in pleasant conversation with Lord Allistair and his lovely wife. The rocking of the carriage, and the soporific rumbling and clacking of the wheels soon caused Lady Allistair to doze, albeit fitfully, and Lord Allistair and I talked of Holmes' last exploits, and the assurance we both had that if anyone could set things right it was Sherlock Holmes. One thing he showed me, however, that returned some feelings of apprehension was a compact leather pouch. Upon opening it, I saw a sight which almost took my breath away: £100,000 in small and medium banknotes.

I drew the compartment curtains and placed my loaded pistol on the seat beside me.

The remainder of the journey passed uneventfully, his Lordship reminiscing about his youth in the Cornish countryside, and his younger years in Parliament; and I felt fortunate in having the opportunity to have become intimate with so illustrious a man. The country rolled by, and the meadows and pastures gradually gave way to dense forests and craggy hills. One saw fewer farms and villages, and less of civilization in general.

'We are entering the valley of the Severn,' explained Lord Allistair. 'To the south, it is a sportsman's paradise. Clear lakes and deep woods abound there; the only open areas are rock-strewn meadows, and occasional clearings for farms and houses.'

'The woods are very dense, are they not?'

'Ah, I can see you've never been to this part of England before, Doctor Watson. These are the finest forests in the land. They are primeval, and have been for centuries some of the favourite hunting grounds of English kings. They are mostly oak and beech. Some of the older trees, dating from the Middle Ages, are gigantic.'

I was amazed to see trees with trunks the size of cottages, and limbs the size of trees. The woods had an eerie, fantastical quality; their size and grandeur defied belief – one expected them to be inhabited by goblins, witches and monsters.

Some minutes later, as the train eased to a stop, the faint clangour of the bell could be heard over the hissing of steam and squeaking of brakes.

We gathered our things (most carefully, of course, the satchel containing the fortune in ransom money) and quit the compartment. I took the lead. I carried my grip and fly-pole with my left hand, my right hand casually thrust in my pocket clutching my revolver. While I didn't wish to cause the Allistairs any undue alarm, I knew that if the kidnappers wished to make an early escape with the money, the railway station, or nearby, was the logical place to lie in wait. However, the corridor was deserted, and we alighted on the platform without incident. Also, to my pleasant surprise, the only other disembarking passengers consisted of an elderly couple. Evidently then, we weren't followed from London.

We were promptly met by Brundage, the head of the household staff at Strathcombe. He was a middle-aged bald man with greyed temples and a dreamy, wistful expression. His meeting with the Allistairs was charged with emotion: there wasn't a dry eye amongst the three of them. I took this to be another good sign – the head servant was an old and trusted employee, and one with great attachment to the family. As he packed our luggage expertly in the landau, I glanced keenly about. The station platform was deserted save for several gossiping bumpkins whom I took to be farm labourers, and a lounging gypsy.

All in all, I was much heartened as we boarded the open coach and set off for Strathcombe, some eleven miles distant.

'We shall lunch at the White Hart in Rutlidge,' called Lord Allistair to his servant as we set off.

Shrewsbury is a small but prosperous city, having a large business in tanneries, and is an outlet for the various minerals and timber taken from the countryside. We skirted a handsome park and rumbled through several narrow streets, each lined by the black-and-white timbered houses. Leaving the city, we caught a glimpse of the old abbey and castle, built in the eleventh century as a Saxon stronghold. Soon afterward, however, all traces of civilization were left behind, and the road cut its way through more of the towering forests I had seen from the railway carriage.

The only break in this rugged and wild scenery was the hamlet of Rutlidge, which consisted only of a score or so of buildings, one of which was the charming country inn called the White Hart.

We had an excellent and hearty lunch of cold ham, creamed potatoes, custard pie, and cider. Neither the innkeeper nor any of the guests, of whom there were several in the dining room, showed the slightest interest in us. Apparently, they did not even recognize the famous couple.

'We aren't well known hereabouts, except by reputation,' explained Lady Allistair. 'I doubt if there are a score of people round the countryside who could know us on sight. As we've told you before, we do not spend much time here, and when we do we keep pretty much to ourselves.'

How ironic, thought I, that these kind, simple country folk go about their tasks blissfully unaware not only of the presence of one of England's foremost political figures, but of the ominous exchange that would possibly take place within a matter of days.

'Get out!' I heard the innkeeper cry. He entered the dining room with a look of loathing on his coarse features. Looking beyond him, I saw a figure reluctantly slink down the dark hallway of the public house. As he swung open the door to leave, I saw it was a gypsy, whose earrings, slouch hat, and swarthy features were unmistakable. Furthermore, I noticed it was the same fellow who had been idling about on the railway platform. He ambled dejectedly out into the autumn sunshine.

'Sorry to trouble you,' pursued the innkeeper as he passed our table, 'but I fear I've lost all patience with that lout. He's been loitering about the place for two days.'

'And you have never seen him before then?' I asked.

'Not that I can recall, sir, no. But they come and go, living off thievery, and poaching. With their bad habits and ill manners, it's no surprise they're forced to keep moving. Oh, they're thick around these parts. They like the woods, for it enables them to hide from the law. There's plenty of game and fish, too, for them to live off of. Plenty of gypsy camps hereabouts, but I don't recall that shirker before, no, sir.'

The early afternoon sun was warm for an autumn day, and the four of us proceeded at a leisurely pace. The horse, who knew the way, kept at a slow trot, and Brundage soon forgot whip and rein. The autumn colours were just beginning to turn their rich reds and golds, and the aroma of damp leaves and fallen fruit was thick on the wind. The famous couple held hands together in the rear seat. It was obvious they were still deeply in love, and enjoyed showing affection to one another. To think that somewhere in the surrounding wilderness there crept villains who would stoop to an act so vile as to kidnap their daughter filled me with rage and revulsion.

Soon we came out of the beech forest and ascended a long, gentle rise, the summit of which provided an excellent view of the entire countryside. Here there were few trees, owing to the great abundance of boulders and cliffs. As I looked back down towards the forest, I was aware of a slight movement along the side of the road. Without comment, I took the field glasses from their leather case and raised them to my eyes.

It was a man on horseback, perhaps a mile behind us. Though still in the woods, I could see his outline as he passed through the myriad shafts of sunlight that pierced the gloom of the heavy wood. For a brief second, he was entirely illuminated by the sloping rays of the sunlight. I could see that it was the gypsy. The third appearance of this character, travelling apparently aimlessly, yet in our direction, made me uneasy. Had Holmes observed him thus, I am sure he would have said that there was an ominous deliberation about the man – that although possibly only a coincidence, a coincidence was unlikely. The gypsy was following us. I was about to tell Brundage to reverse and confront the lout, whereupon I could threaten him with my revolver. However, I recalled the portion of the ransom note which warned of any involvement with the police or other parties. One glance at the Allistairs, so brimming with hope and confidence in me, and I realized this was a foolish course, however much I yearned for action. A few minutes later, we topped another rise. Again, I looked back. Even with the aid of the glasses, I was unable to see anyone upon the road. The man had vanished into the forest. Somewhat relieved, I returned the glasses to their case and, not mentioning the incident, sat out the remainder of the ride in silence.

Unlike most country houses with which I have been acquainted,

Strathcombe was not set off in full view of passers-by. It had neither an open approach to the grounds, nor a high fence with elaborate gates. It was, rather, set halfway into a copse of tall trees that all but obscured the house and buildings. One did not approach it, but stumbled across it gradually, as if by accident. The gravel path turned, and we passed several of the outbuildings before the house itself came into full view.

With an expertise that had grown from long practice, Brundage swung the open carriage round and we alighted upon the stone steps that rose gradually to the open terrace in front. Ascending the steps, the three of us paused on the bricked terrace to admire the view. The terrace, enclosed by an ancient lichen-blotched stone balustrade, looked out over a broad valley through which meandered a small trout stream. Clumps of willows abutted the stream, and the meadows on each side were bordered by woods. Save for the small outhouses, there was not another sign of civilization to be seen – not so much as a farmer's cottage nor a church steeple. The dying sun cast a reddish glow in the West, and the setting seemed already to work a soothing spell upon the couple. Accustomed as I was to city noises, it was a pleasant change indeed to hear the myriad bird sounds – the mewing and twittering of the swallows as they crisscrossed the dusk on crescent wings, the trill of the larks and blackbirds.

Having been shown to my quarters, which consisted of a bedroom, dressing room and parlour, I unpacked my belongings and dressed for dinner.

After changing my clothes, I placed the map of the estate that Holmes had given me on the bed, and, by looking out of the double window, proceeded to orientate myself.

The house consisted of four large rooms downstairs surrounding a great hall. Upstairs were ten smaller rooms, at one time no doubt serving as individual bedrooms to accommodate guests. Now, however, these rooms were split into three suites, one of which I now occupied.

My suite was in the left wing, in front, and commanded a splendid view of the main approach to the house. In the dimming light, I could barely make out the grey tower of the ancient lime kiln.

A motion caught my eye near the lime kiln. It was a man on horseback. Could it be the gypsy? Would he have the effrontery to follow us on to the very grounds of Strathcombe? I raised the field glasses to my eyes for a better view. The man was certainly not a gypsy: he had blond hair. I glimpsed him only for a moment, however, because he wheeled his horse quickly about, dashed over the meadow, and cleared the stone wall in a prodigious leap. Whoever he is, I thought, he can surely handle a horse. Who was this man? I must remember to mention him to Lord Allistair.

Continuing to examine the grounds from my vantage point, I took in the meadows and deep woods beyond with a sweeping gaze. Holmes was correct; the kidnappers had indeed chosen their site with cunning. Hidden in the deep woods or on the rugged hillsides, they were secluded and safe. To search them out would require a score of men and horses, and hounds as well. Obviously, this course of action would spell disaster for Lady Allistair. Clearly, the criminals could remain safe as long as they wished. On the other hand, the close-lying woods and broken stone walls would allow them to skulk about close to the house itself without being detected. This would enable them to come and go as they pleased, to leave notes of instruction and, ultimately, to obtain the ransom. It is an old soldier's saying that 'the unseen enemy is the most feared'. I have always believed this, and standing at my window in the twilight in that desolate place I was profoundly convinced of the saying's veracity. To add further to my feelings of uneasiness was the evidence of high intelligence and assiduous planning behind the kidnapping plot. Already I longed for Holmes' presence and support. However, determined to fulfil my role as Holmes had described it, I assumed a cheerful, almost jaunty air and descended the staircase to meet Lord and Lady Allistair in the great hall.

Strathcombe's history as a shooting lodge is never so vividly pressed into the mind of a visitor as when he ambles about, glass in hand, under the innumerable mounted heads that stare balefully down from the high dark walls of the great hall.

'The vicinity is most famous for boar,' observed Lord Allistair as he refilled my glass. 'But there are fine stags hereabouts as well. We used to keep a pack of hounds to hunt them, but not in recent years.'

My attention was directed to a massive head over the great hall fireplace. It was as large as the head of a colt, and was set off by curving ivory tusks as long as a man's fingers.

'That boar was brought down three years ago by Count Le Moyne during an official visit to this country. As a goodwill gesture, he left the head for our hall.'

'It's immense. Surely there are not creatures like this roaming the woods?' I asked.

'To be sure, Doctor Watson. They may weigh as much as four hundredweight. It's fortunate that Le Moyne is a crack shot, for it took two rounds at close range with a Holland and Holland double rifle to stop that brute. He wouldn't be alive today, I can assure you, if he'd missed with either barrel.'

I gazed in awe at the head, frozen in a horrid snarl. Truly this was a wild stretch of country that lay roundabout us, and the realization made me feel further for the safety of Alice Allistair.

'If I may interrupt, sir,' said Brundage, 'Ian Farthway, the gamekeeper, tells me that there is another boar newly arrived in the river bottom. From the prints it leaves, it promises to be even larger than our present specimen.'

'You don't say so!' replied Lord Allistair. 'Then it must be huge.

God forbid it has a temper to match its size. Perhaps our friend, Doctor Watson, would like to go after it.'

'No, thank you,' I protested. 'Having once been shot myself, I am loath to take up firearms, except in defence.'

'Well then, since I share the doctor's distaste for blood sports, we shall leave our wild pig to roam and root about the bottomland as he pleases.'

'He shall never be hard to locate, your Lordship,' continued Brundage, 'as Farthway claims he leaves a curious print…'

'Eh, curious print? What do you mean, Brundage? Explain yourself.'

'Apparently, sir, this boar leaves a three-toed print instead of a cloven one. It's some sort of deformity, no doubt.'

'On one foot, or all four?' I enquired.

'I don't know, sir.'

'Well, it's a curious thing. And now, doctor, I believe Meg has announced the evening meal.'

'Tell me about this man Farthway,' I asked as we made our way upstairs, claret in hand.

'Our gamekeeper – knows the countryside like the palm of his hand.'

'Is he a blond fellow – good horseman?'

'The very same – but have you met him?'

I then explained my brief glimpse of Farthway, and we entered the dining room.

Our dinner was pleasant, and only slightly subdued considering the enormous tension that the noble couple was striving to conceal. The partridges were excellent, served with a delectable orange sauce and accompanied by a choice bottle of burgundy. When the meal was over, Lady Allistair excused herself and repaired to her room. From the look on her face when she went upstairs, I foresaw a bout of crying. Saddened as I was by this, as a medical man I was aware of the purgative effect of tears, and felt it would help her sleep. After her departure, His Lordship and I seated ourselves before the dying fire. With his wife out of earshot, Lord Allistair's conversation assumed a harder tone, a tone that was, I felt, grounded in sober realism. Hearing him speak thus, I was aware of another side of this benovolent human being: one that showed his iron will and keen determination against long odds.

'God knows where they've hidden her,' he said in a low tone, 'but I think it best not to foray out after them –'

'No, by all means we must wait, if even for a short time...'

'Quite. We should attempt a peaceful, if expensive solution to this. The money is nothing; were it my life savings I of course wouldn't care. But if my daughter has been in any way harmed –'

He gripped the arms of his chair until his knuckles grew white.

'Steady, Lord Allistair, I have every confidence that she will be returned unharmed.'

'Ah, were it so! I, however, have no illusions as to her grave danger. The one thing, in fact, that saves me from breaking down utterly is the numbness brought on by a too-lengthy wait.'

I nodded in sympathy.

'But Doctor, there's another element working here. I can't help but feel that in addition to wanting money, the kidnappers seek a personal revenge against me – or my wife.'

'How so?'

'Why was there no word about Alice for over two months? *Why*, when a short telegram – that could have been sent with discretion and safety – would have done so much to alleviate our suffering?'

'Ah. I see your point. And yet they chose not to send any message whatever until now – and so have kept you in misery these ten weeks.'

'Who could have such a hatred of me? I have enemies as anyone in public life is bound to. Yet I consider them political opponents – not personal ones.'

'And you can think of no one in your past who would deliberately seek to hurt you?'

He knitted his brows in thought.

'No,' he said at last.

And I wasn't in the least surprised. If I could think of any great man who had risen to power without making enemies, it would be Lord Peter Allistair. As I looked at the man who sat within a few feet of me, I was aware of how old he suddenly appeared. The renewed hope then, the warm optimism of our outward journey was a sham, perhaps a temporary show for my benefit. Clearly, these two people, noble in every sense of the word, were close to being permanently shattered by this experience. As I said goodnight to Lord Allistair, I renewed my resolve to do anything in my power to secure the safe return of Alice Allistair.

I was enervated by the journey and the nervous strain. But though I longed for bed, I sat down at his Lordship's study desk and penned the following wire to Holmes:

> HOLMES: REPORTING DAILY AS INSTRUCTED,
> ARRIVED STRATHCOMBE SAFE. STAFF APPEARS LOYAL
> BUT SURROUNDINGS FORBIDDING. NO INCIDENT
> EXCEPT FOLLOWED BY GYPSY. LETTER FOLLOWS
> — HOPE YOU COME SOONEST. WATSON.

I sealed this message with instructions to Brundage that it be sent in the early morning to Baker Street. And then, with a weary body and heavy heart, I ascended the carved oak staircase to bed.

Seven

SOUNDINGS

Perhaps it was the sunshine that flooded my bedchamber, or was it the warblers and finches outside the window that so improved my frame of mind next morning?

Another reason, particularly apparent to me as a physician, is that the human soul is adaptable and resilient; we can go only so long in an anxious, depressed state before a voice from deep within us cries 'enough!' and we summon up from the depths of our spirit a strength and optimism we had not realized were there.

I dressed and joined my hosts for a hearty breakfast of scrambled eggs and fried trout, with plenty of toast and honey.

Afterwards, at my suggestion, Lord Allistair took me on a tour of the grounds. The morning was lovely, filled with the brisk air of autumn. I donned a shooting jacket and, following Holmes' strict instructions, carried one of Lord Allistair's seldom-used shotguns, a magnificent Purdey twelve-bore, at my side. I had made the suggestion of the tour deliberately, of course, because Holmes considered it imperative that I familiarize myself with the grounds and terrain, paying particular attention to any sites of possible concealment, or hidden approaches to the house.

'I'll show you the kennels first,' said Lord Allistair, 'since they're in the best repair, having been used until quite recently.'

We strolled over the lawn to a low stone building with a slate roof almost entirely intact. Looking inside, I could see two low hallways and about a dozen runs. The building was slightly over a hundred yards from the house.

'The stables are still in use, of course,' Lord Allistair continued. 'I'll show you those when we meet Wiscomb.'

'He is your stable-boy?'

'Stable-boy and gardener both. He's been with us quite some time, even longer than the Brundages – a bit infirm nowadays –'

'Do you consider him reliable?' I cut in.

'Oh, entirely.'

'I don't wish to pry,' I continued, 'but it would be most helpful if you could briefly relate the histories of your household staff.'

'Ah, I feel the presence of our mutual friend, do I not?'

I admitted frankly that Holmes had given me certain instructions.

'Then of course I'll do exactly what you wish. On our way round the place, I'll tell you everything I can.'

So as we strolled across the grounds, our shadows playing across great stretches of lawn in the early sunlight, I was given a brief thumbnail sketch of each of the servants.

The Brundages had been with the family for more than twenty years, and distinguished themselves by superior service and loyalty. Clearly, we could exclude them as far as any sort of foul play was concerned. There were two maids: Julia and Betsy, Julia being Lady Allistair's private maid and Betsy serving guests and visiting relatives. Neither had served the household for long, but both seemed of good character.

Betsy, however, was apparently in the midst of a lover's quarrel, and appeared upset.

'Is he a local fellow?' I asked

'Who?'

'Betsy's beau. Is he from hereabouts?'

'Nobody knows, for we've never seen him. She goes off to town to meet him, and she never speaks at all of him, according to Julia. Now here are the mews, Doctor. As you can see, they are fairly tumbledown.'

The building, almost roofless, contained two rooms (I supposed for different sized birds), but the walls were largely missing. For a place of concealment, the building was useless except at night.

The lime kiln, located out towards the front stone parapet, was singular. Being twenty feet across, the hollow cylinder rose almost the same distance, and was approached by walking up the earthen wagon ramp that sloped up one side. An iron door was placed at the base, through which the rendered lime was removed. It had not been used for generations. We looked briefly at the trout pond and garden, and returned towards the stables.

'That leaves only Farthway, the gamekeeper,' continued Lord Allistair. 'We know less about him than the others since he's quite new, having been brought into our service less than a year ago. He's a superb gamekeeper. I sometimes think he's not entirely happy here though. He's a fast-paced young man, having served in the Black Watch. I can't help wondering if he doesn't get bored in his present job.'

'You say he was in the Black Watch?'

'Yes indeed, and an officer to boot.'

'You don't say! But doesn't that still require money?'

'Certainly. I think that's why he left. Of course it's pure conjecture on my part. It would never do to ask —'

'No, of course. So his family suffered a decline?'

'So it would seem. I believe the Farthways were once one of the most respected Scottish families. Well – for whatever reason, Farthway quit the service and joined us as gamekeeper.'

'That seems odd, and surely a fall in station, wouldn't you think?'

'Certainly. But of all the applicants, he was the most insistent, and qualified, as you'll see. But as for his reasons – well, as I've said, we know very little about the man.'

'I should like to make the acquaintance of this Mr Farthway,' I said.

'No doubt you shall in the near future. And now, here we are. Hello, Wiscomb, I see you've saddled our horses.'

We were met in the stable yard by the elderly and somewhat uncouth Wiscomb. Upon taking note of his trembling extremities, and the colour of his nose, I assumed him to be a part-time drunkard, and thus Lord Allistair's statement that he was 'a bit infirm' made sense. He seemed dutiful and obliging enough as he guided us into our saddles, yet what inner torment racked him so that he sought solace in the bottle?

'Tell her Ladyship we shall return for luncheon,' was all Lord Allistair said as he adroitly wheeled his horse about and plunged across the sparkling lawn.

I followed him as best I could, and after a brisk trot, we'd cleared the near fences and started off across the meadow. This portion of the grounds was well-kept grass, but in less than two hundred yards the meadow gave way to a deep and towering forest of ancient oaks and gigantic beeches, the latter towering over a hundred feet. We pursued our way directly into this natural labyrinth, following ancient narrow paths that criss-crossed infinitely into the deep recesses of the wilderness. The old trees formed a canopy above us, and, the ground being free of undergrowth, one could see between the massive trunks for quite a distance in any direction. Lord Allistair informed me that during Strathcombe's time as a hunting lodge it was the custom for mounted hunting parties to pursue game through the woods at full chase.

'And we've never been the only ones to take game from this country, Doctor Watson,' added Lord Allistair as he cantered by my side in the gloom. 'I must admit to being somewhat lax about the poaching. You see, these woods have long been the temporary home for woodcutters, poachers, gypsies and, I'm afraid, occasional felons of every description who've grown used to taking game from the vicinity. They take it both by gun and snare, and without regard to season.'

He reined in, and pointed down.

'Evidence of their comings and goings can be seen here, and even more clearly in the dried mud of the river bank...'

The loam of the forest floor was heavily marked with recent prints, both of horse and man. Lord Allistair, in a discursive mood, continued:

'Strathcombe, as the name implies, is a broad river valley cut through deep forests and steep hills. Although there are remnants of stone walls bordering the park and gardens, there are no formal boundary arrangements; people and animals are free to come and go as they please.'

Needless to say, this last confession worried me a great deal. As *confidant* and guardian to this couple, how could I possibly oversee their safety with countless transients and ruffians trespassing their borders?

'As you can see, Doctor, the terrain is decidedly to their advantage. The maps Mr Holmes and I pored over last week are unfortunately correct: there are numerous dips and rises, copses and stone walls within close reach of the house. Even a child, if he wished, could approach the house in secrecy – especially after twilight. Now the reason for this jaunt is for me to show you two places of considerable interest: the Keep and Henry's Hollow.'

'They are nearby?'

'Oh yes – the Keep is three-quarters of a mile to the east.' After twenty or so yards, we came to a slight break in the forest. Lord Allistair turned in his saddle and raised his arm. 'There it is.' He pointed to a towering crag of rock that rose skyward with steep sides. It did in fact resemble an ancient castle keep, at least in profile.

'From its summit one can get a bird's eye view of the entire estate and the country around. Years ago it was our custom to post a gamekeeper there to watch the hunt and spot stags. He would then, by means of waving flags mounted on long poles, signal the hunt as to where the game was to be had.'

'How is it approached?' I asked.

'There is a precarious footpath that winds round it to the top. The summit is bare save for a few clumps of bracken and several wizened pines that sprout from crevices in the rock. Just below the summit is a flat outcropping of rock under which is a small cave, large enough for several men to sleep in, sheltered from the elements. There, can you see it?'

Up near the craggy peak I could barely see a ledge of rock and a dark depression underneath. It must have been hundreds of feet above the woods. Considering the present circumstances, I definitely did not like the look of it.

'And the other place?'

'We are headed for it now.' Lord Allistair pointed with his riding crop straight ahead. 'Henry's Hollow lies less than two miles down this path.'

'What sort of place is it?' I asked.

'A very interesting one, I can assure you. If the legend is true, it is an historical site. But whether the tale that surrounds the place is truth or fiction, Henry's Hollow is an eerie place, as I'm sure you'll agree. It is the one thing about coming to Strathcombe that the new visitor remembers most.'

We trotted on along the faint path that was marked with tracks of other horses, and deer as well. Twice Lord Allistair paused and pointed to other cloven tracks that were massive, and sunk deep into the hardpacked loam.

'Wild boar,' said he. 'But not the monster one that Brundage mentioned.'

The horses, catching the scent of the wild pig, shied slightly and needed no urging from us to continue our jaunt at a rapid pace. So we rode on through the forest. The horses' feet rustled the fallen leaves, woodpeckers hammered against the huge trunks, and jays flew shrieking overhead.

'Ah, jays and crows are the watchman of the forest. None can enter without the announcements you hear.'

I was amazed at the distance the crying of the birds carried, reverberating through the moss-covered trees for hundreds of yards. The gloomy forest seemed to stretch away infinitely.

'Do you see it?' His Lordship asked a few minutes later.

'I don't see anything out of the ordinary,' I confessed, peering into the dimness ahead. Shafts of sunlight pierced the gloom at random intervals, but even with this illumination I could see nothing remarkable.

'Let us draw a few feet closer,' he said.

Never shall I forget the eerie spell which came upon me when I finally realized that I had been staring at Henry's Hollow for the previous ten minutes. Even as I write these words, I can once again feel the tremor of excitement that comes when witnessing something unique and grand.

Not thirty yards ahead was a line of immense oak trees, each with a trunk as wide as a carriage. The distance between the trunks was only slightly greater than their diameters. Their massive lower branches, each as big as most trees, interlaced to form a barrier as stout as the strongest castle walls. It was then I realized that the line of trees was not straight, but circular. We dismounted and, leading our horses, approached the ring of giants.

Lord Allistair and his horse passed through first. I followed and joined him on the edge of a ridge, and gazed with wonder and amazement at the depression in the forest floor: an oblong-shaped hollow resembling an amphitheatre, some two hundred yards long and perhaps one hundred feet deep at its centre – the whole surrounded at the rim by the palisade of huge trees whose branches all interlocked in frozen majesty.

'So this is Henry's Hollow…'

'Quite so. You are probably supposing that it takes its name from this earthen hollow. However, there is another story of the name's origin, and it is linked with the general legend of Henry's Hollow which, by the way, historians now regard as true.

'This place is named after King Henry IV. It is said he camped here with his troops on the eve of the battle of Shrewsbury in 1403. As anyone can surmise, this spot is an ideal camping place, and, if need be, an effective defence works too. Now obviously these trees were planted long before even Henry's time, perhaps by druids or other forest folk who made this natural dell into a defensible, sheltered home.'

'It is remarkably well-hidden, too, especially considering its size.'

'Follow me down, Doctor,' said His Lordship, and we wended our way, horses in tow, down into the centre of the strange place. There were oaks in the hollow as well, and under their protective arms the troops of Henry IV must have slept in preparation for the great battle against the Welsh rebels almost five hundred years ago. In my mind's eye I could picture them squatting or lying about on rude beds of ferns and leaves, their helms and armour glinting in the firelight as they ate and sang to summon up courage for the ensuing fight.

We wandered about under the trees and stopped in a small clearing towards the very centre of the dell.

'Supposedly, King Henry constructed a crude forge on this very site by building a fire in the base of a hollow tree. Some still think this weird place took its name from the hollow tree rather than the depression in the earth. According to legend, Henry had the forge constructed to re-temper his sword. With it he vowed to kill Owen Glendower. But as we know, he failed in this, although he slew Harry Percy, called Hotspur, and displayed his body to the people of Shrewsbury as proof of the deed. The rebellion was crushed. Since then, Henry's Hollow has changed little, if at all. No one lives here permanently, but because of its isolation it has attracted vagrants, felons and ne'er-do-wells of all description for centuries.'

Upon hearing these words I scanned the rim of the hollow uneasily.

'Perhaps it is best if we return to Strathcombe,' I suggested, and unslung the shotgun from my shoulders.

'You are quite right, my friend. It's nearly noon, and I don't like to leave Lady Allistair for long these days.'

We led the horses up towards the rim. We were almost to the ring of oaks when Lord Allistair paused.

'I forgot to point out these caves in the sides of the hollow,' he said. 'They are all round the place, dug in amongst the roots.'

To my amazement, I saw numerous holes in the sloping bank of the dell. Drawing closer, one could see they were tunnels dug out between the roots of the large trees. The roots no doubt acted as joists and rafters, holding the soil together and thus preventing collapse. They seemed to wind into the earth for some distance, but as we were both anxious to return to the Lodge, I cut my inspection short.

We left the hollow and returned to the forest path. In less than half an hour we were at Strathcombe, but two things occurred which I must relate, although I did not mention them to Lord Allistair.

The first was the unmistakable odour of woodsmoke in Henry's Hollow. It was faint, and had the dank and musty smell that comes when a fire is doused with water. But it was evident nevertheless. Someone was living in Henry's Hollow. Somewhere, among the giant trees and dismal hillside caverns, was lurking a fugitive, or an enemy. Was this person, or persons, warned of our approach by the jays and crows?

The second thing was even more alarming, and was observed in the twinkling of an eye. Upon our return journey I chanced to look once again at the high walls of the Keep. The rock was bright grey as the sunlight struck it. I remember musing on what a charming place its summit must be – what a pleasant spot for a picnic lunch. The midday sun made the rocky ledge and the cave beneath even more noticeable. I was about to turn my head when I saw it: a pinpoint flash of light coming from the dark mouth of the cave. It lasted no more than half a second. I am sure His Lordship did not notice. I of course knew instantly what it was; my days as an artilleryman had taught me to recognize the flash of field glasses in the sun. Someone was watching us.

Eight

NEW HOPE, AND A PUZZLE

I decided to mention neither the odour of woodsmoke nor the reflection on the Keep to Lord Allistair. He was bearing up well under the tremendous strain, but I had a feeling he was near the breaking point; more bad news could severely tax him.

As we approached the house, we were struck by the silence and deserted appearance of Strathcombe.

'This is odd. Usually one sees some of the staff at work, especially on so pleasant a day.'

We drew closer and with each passing second, my apprehension grew. Before we'd even reached the stable yard, we were met by Wiscomb, who came hobbling at top speed from the house waving his arms wildly. He was followed almost immediately by Lady Allistair, who appeared as distraught as the manservant.

'Something's amiss!' whispered His Lordship under his breath.

'Peter – Peter!' cried the Lady as she ran towards us. As she approached, it became obvious that whatever had occurred, it was cause for happiness; her face was joyous.

We dismounted and Lord Allistair ran to his wife, caught her in his arms, and bent over close to hear what she had to say. After a few seconds, he turned round and shouted.

'Alice is safe! There's a note inside that proves it so!'

I followed the jubilant couple inside and watched as Lady Allistair plucked an envelope from the mantelpiece.

'Where did you find this?' he asked Lady Allistair.

'Meg found it this morning on the terrace balustrade directly after you and Doctor Watson left. It was weighted with a brick.'

'It's amazing, and shocking – the ease with which they placed it there,' he added and, his hands trembling with emotion, opened the envelope and extracted what appeared to be a sheet of newsprint.

'It's the front page of the *Manchester Guardian*,' he exclaimed, 'this morning's edition. Ah! See here, Doctor Watson, her note is penned directly on the margin, thank God!'

A brief message, in the same handwriting I had observed in the living room of the Allistairs in London, was penned on the right margin of the newsheet. It was obvious that the newspaper proved that early that morning Alice Allistair was alive and well. As can be imagined, this crude epistle had a marvellous effect on all of us – Lady Allistair in particular, who wept with joy.

The message read: 'My dearest Father and Mother, I am safe for now. I am assured of prompt release to you if the total ransom, in amount and form previously indicated, is paid upon request by those who hold me. Instructions will be forthcoming shortly, and must, upon pain of my death, be obeyed to the letter. I am unharmed and well, and joyous at the knowledge that I shall soon be with you both.'

The note was signed, as before, 'Your loving daughter, Alice.'

'They have kept their word so far!' cried Lord Allistair, beaming. 'Pray we can get through these next few difficult days – then our sufferings will be over. Come, let's have some sherry.'

Our spirits raised, we gathered in the conservatory, which was really an extension at the back of the central hall, with huge windows on three sides. It was, in contrast to the rest of Strathcombe, bright and cheery. We seated ourselves in front of these windows and awaited Brundage, who soon appeared with a silver tray laden with bottles and glasses. Lady Allistair again picked up the sheet of newsprint with her daughter's writing on it. Tenderly, almost lovingly considering the blessed news it had brought, she fondled the page of newsprint and read and re-read the message of hope written a few hours earlier. She held the paper as one would hold a book, and inclined her body forward slightly in a posture of deep concentration. The strong rays of early afternoon sun streamed down upon her from the tall windows behind.

'Well, this is indeed encouraging,' said His Lordship, draining his glass. I could see before me the weight of weeks of worry lifting visibly from the couple.

'Since it's this morning's paper,' I offered, 'instead of last evening's, your daughter and her captors must be hereabouts. I venture they're not more than ten miles distant. You see my friend Sherlock Holmes has taught me –'

I was struck by a most curious sight.

'Yes, Doctor, what were you saying?' asked Lord Allistair.

'I was saying…'

'I say, Doctor, are you all right?' Her Ladyship asked, putting down the paper.

'Fine, thank you,' I replied. 'But pray, don't put the paper down just yet. Please hold it as you were a moment ago.'

'Like this?' she asked.

'A little lower, please,' I instructed. 'Just above the tray –'

Her Ladyship did as instructed, and brought the paper down to within a few inches of the silver serving tray that sat upon the coffee table.

'Now this is most interesting,' I pursued. 'If you'll excuse me, I would like to remove the sherry bottles for a moment, and leave only the tray...'

The couple looked at me as if I'd lost my reason, but I proceeded to remove the bottles.

'Now see how the sunlight comes strongly down through these windows at this time of day,' I said, the excitement growing in me.

'One would expect so in a conservatory,' said Lord Allistair, not without a touch of irony.

'... and strikes the paper full force, as you see. Now Lord Allistair, look down at the tray.'

He followed my instructions, and a look of amazement grew upon his face.

'Good God – look at those tiny sparks!'

Reflecting off the shiny silver were many small pinpoints of light, resembling a miniature constellation. I took the sheet of newspaper from Her Ladyship and held it up to the light. The tan translucence of the newsprint was pierced by a score or so of tiny pinpoints of bright light.

'These tiny holes were made by a pin or a needle,' I said, 'and they appear to be arranged somewhat symmetrically. Also, they occur only in this one section of the page and nowhere else.'

'They seem to be arranged in rows,' continued Lord Allistair who was looking over my shoulder, 'and are placed sometimes singly and sometimes in pairs. Now that's a queer thing, Doctor. What do you make of it?'

'I can't make anything of it,' I replied, 'except their arrangement is certainly not random – they must have some meaning. Here – you'll notice that all these pinpricks are spaced within this single short article entitled "Foreign Investment". Let us first read through the article.'

The article, if it could be called such, was a mere 'filler' piece used to round out the column. It was a scant two sentences in length, and ran as follows:

'LONDON – The Home Office today announced a joint production agreement signed with Belgium. It involves the manufacture of internal combustion engines.'

'The article is unimportant surely,' said Her Ladyship after reading it. 'It's simply one of those snippets tacked on to a column for appearance's sake.'

'Perhaps, but if my long association with Sherlock Holmes has taught me anything, Lady Allistair, it is that things that appear trifling are often not. It is possible that these small pinpricks in the paper were deliberately placed there to convey something.'

I then briefly related the events, and the apparently nonsensical message surrounding the 'Gloria Scott' adventure. Upon hearing of the dire fate proclaimed by that message, Lady Allistair once again fell into a fit of depression and worry over her daughter's well being. Enraged at myself for having unwittingly shattered the calm that had so recently descended upon her, I tried to allay her fears by assuring her that the tiny holes in the paper were probably without meaning.

'You are not a good liar, Doctor,' said Lord Allistair. 'I agree that there is some meaning to these strange marks. However, we know Alice is well. Perhaps they bear further good news, or extra instructions. There's no reason to assume that they carry bad news.'

And so saying, he instructed his wife to retire to her room for a short nap while we adjourned to his small study. Soon a pot of coffee was brought in, and we sat smoking before the fire, attempting to decipher the meaning, if any, of the tiny pinholes in the paper.

'We miss your friend terribly at times like these,' said Lord Allistair.

'No doubt he is capable of arriving at answers to puzzles like this one?'

'If it is penetrable to the mind of man, it is child's play to Holmes,' I replied. 'But since he is not here, then we must proceed as best we can. Let me shut the door to ensure privacy, then we shall, with the paper on your gaming table, set ourselves to the problem.'

The short piece looked like this with the pinprick marks filled in with pen dots:

LONDON – The Home Office today announced a joint
production agreement signed with Belgium. It involves
the manufacture of internal combustion engines.

We stared at the words and markings for some time, each advancing his own hypotheses.

'The most obvious explanation is of course that the pinpricks point out the letters in the article either directly above or below them,' advanced Lord Allistair.

'Yes, I think we can both agree on that. But why are some marks above the letters and others below? Also, why are some pricks paired while others are alone?'

'Let's first spell out the letters that are indicated regardless of the position or number of marks,' he suggested.

We spelled out AJOTPRIASWHNSEATREBE.

'There's no meaning whatsoever in this hodgepodge – except that the word *seat* is spelled,' said I. 'I take it we can dismiss this message.'

'I have it!' he cried, jumping up from the table. 'The various pinprick positions and numbers indicate different words. See here: let us take the single dot on top first. Tracing the letters where this dot appears, we will have the first word, or *a* word at least, of the code.'

Following this scheme we arrived at the word ATRA.

'Is that a word you know of, Doctor – perhaps in Latin?'

'No. However, let's go on to the next set of markings which would logically be the single dot *underneath* the letters.'

Following thus, we arrived at the word WARE.

'Still no sense to it. And the next word?'

'P-I-S-S-E-T-B-E-,' I spelled aloud, and wrote PISSETBE next to the other words.

'I suppose it's useless,' said Lord Allistair. 'There must be another key to the puzzle. Or else, like as not, there's nothing to it.'

'Let us try the last group: the double dots underneath...'

To our utter amazement, the dots spelled JOHN.

'That's more than coincidence surely, Doctor. Now the question is – if this is indeed a word, why then aren't the others?'

We tried re-arranging the letters of the other 'words' in the event that they appeared out of order, but still could make no sense of them.

'All we know is the message is from John, or *to* John. But who is John?' I asked.

'No one in this household... unless –'

'Unless what?'

'Unless its you: John Watson.'

'But that's absurd!' I cried. 'Nobody in these parts has ever heard of me. Besides, what have I to do with the return of your daughter?'

'Nothing directly. But perhaps those who hold Alice aren't aware of this. Perhaps they see you as a threat to their plans.'

Upon thinking about this for a moment, I decided to reveal to Lord Allistair what I had seen earlier in the day.

'Someone was up on the Keep watching us you say?' he asked incredulously. 'But if that is the case they, whoever they may be, were aware of your presence even earlier, because the letter was awaiting us upon our return.'

'Quite so! I confess I'd forgotten it. Dash it! I wish Holmes were here.'

'But since he is not, we must continue with our search for the wisest course of action.'

'Lord Allistair, if I am in any way endangering the return of your daughter, I must leave at once —'

'Nonsense. If I were convinced of that, I would of course insist that you depart. It is extremely unlikely that this is the case. Furthermore, Mr Holmes' instructions were, as we can both recall, quite strict: you are to remain at my side until his arrival. So be it. In the interim, we shall continue our quest for this message within a message. The more I brood upon the matter, the more convinced I am that these tiny pinprickings are the work of my daughter.'

'Why do you say that?'

'First of all, because they are meant to be discovered upon close inspection but not noticed casually. As a matter of fact we were very fortunate to have noticed them at all — thanks only to your keen eyes and our silver serving tray. No, it was definitely done secretly and perhaps hurriedly — a message within a message. Who else could wish secretly to convey a second message but my daughter? Secondly, there is the mode in which the message has been executed: a needle or pin as you have suggested. Does a man carry these about? Not usually. Furthermore, note how precisely the pinpricks are placed: not one out of line and no tears in the paper. All the more difficult when we consider the fragile texture of newspaper, the small type, and the speed and secrecy with which the message was transcribed. Do you, a surgeon, think yourself capable of this?'

I replied that I wasn't sure; the precision was extraordinary.

'And you begin to sound like Sherlock Holmes,' I added.

'I'm surprising even myself,' he laughed. 'But I know that Alice is very good at needlepoint, and would therefore have the skill to do something like this, and in a hurry as well.'

'It's a pity we cannot decipher the message. I think the best thing to do is summon Holmes as quickly as possible. So I shall ride to town this afternoon and dispatch a wire to that effect. All indications point to events coming to a head imminently.'

He nodded his head slowly.

At this point, we were interrupted by a gentle knock from Brundage, who informed us that Betsy, the upstairs maid, wanted a word with us.

'Can't it wait, Brundage?'

'She is quite distressed, sir. It is partly at my recommendation that she has come, Your Lordship.'

'Very well, show her in.'

Betsy appeared, visibly trembling. Her eyes were tear-stained and her face was contorted, evidently from a recent and lengthy bout of crying. Upon seeing her condition, Lord Allistair rushed to her side, put his arm round her, and led her gently to his chair and sat her down, all the while speaking in soothing tones. I was much struck with his fatherly concern for her, and was once again reminded of his compassion and concern for his fellow men, no matter what their station. After a few moments of this kindness, the girl grew more composed.

'My Lord!' she entreated, breaking out into fresh sobs. 'God have mercy on me. I shall hang for what I've done!'

'What's this? There, girl, it cannot be that bad. Now tell me and the good doctor what it is you've done, or haven't done, that's got you so upset. There, there.'

But she grew uncontrollable once again, and it was only after several more moments and two sips of brandy that she was again able to continue.

'Is your distress in any way related to the finding of the letter on the balustrade this morning?' I asked.

She hesitated for an instant, then nodded quickly, her eyes brimming over with tears.

'Did you see who placed it there?'

'It was *I* who placed it there!'

Shocked at this admission, we both plied her with questions in rapid succession. Was she one of them? Where were they? Was Alice unharmed? But to all of these she was unable to answer, so distraught was her state. Finally, following Holmes' example in instances of this sort, I convinced her that whatever secrets she held from us, it was better to reveal them.

'Betsy, both His Lordship and I realize that you have come to us of your own volition. Whatever difficulty you are in – no matter how serious – it will not be made better by your silence. We are on your side and wish only to help. Now please, tell us everything about how you came to be involved in this.'

'Oh please, sir – you must believe me! I was never involved with them directly, I swear it! It was Charles –'

'Who is Charles?' asked Lord Allistair.

There was a pause, and the girl fell silent, looking shamefully at her hands, which were twitching in her lap.

'We were to be married,' she said quietly.

'Is this the young man you have been seeing in town?'

'Yes, My Lord. I'm in love with him, My Lord.'

'And he with you?'

'I was so sure of it until recently. Oh he's so winning in his manner, and generous. I only hope nothing ill's befallen him!'

'You must begin at the beginning, Betsy. When did you meet this man, and what connection has he to the abduction of my daughter?'

'I met Charles Compson three months ago at the Shrewsbury Fair. We were attracted to each other almost immediately, and it wasn't long before we were seeing a lot of each other. He works as a tanner in the village, and always dreams of being rich enough to buy his own tannery in Australia. He's always talked of somehow raising the capital, and the two of us would marry and set off to make our own way. Well, happy as I've been here, My Lord, the dream has had a certain appeal, if you can understand —'

Lord Allistair nodded.

'Things have been marvellous up until a few weeks ago. At that time, a change occurred in Charles that has perplexed and bothered me ever since.'

'What sort of change?'

'He seemed secretive, as if he were holding back. Three nights ago, he asked me to meet him in the village. We met at the public house there, and he confided that he'd got the opportunity to raise the money needed to fulfil our dream. Of course I was overjoyed, never dreaming for a moment it would end like this.'

She bit her lip and fought back a recurrence of her sobbing.

'He said that I must first promise not to tell anyone what it was that he would confide in me. I promised, and he revealed that he had been in contact with two gentlemen who knew the whereabouts of your daughter. He made it clear that they weren't the ones who had taken her but merely knew her whereabouts…'

Lord Allistair and I exchanged a momentary glance, half disgust and half pity, that a poor innocent country girl should be so cruelly deceived.

'Charles told me that all I had to do for my part was to keep a sharp eye out round the house to see who came and went. I was also to watch for any strangers or friends,' she continued, looking up in my direction.

'Charles said that when the time came for the release of Lady Allistair, these observations would make things go more smoothly. For his part in helping with the release, Charles was to be paid handsomely;

enough money for passage to Australia and several tanneries.

'Early this morning, before the break of dawn, I met him at the foot of the village road to report your arrival, Doctor. He handed me the letter, saying I was to place it on the stone balustrade and call attention to it. "It won't be long now, Betsy darling," he told me. "The young lady is safe and sound and, thanks to us, will be delivered up to her parents quick as a wink." So I did as I was told, and now...'

'And now what?'

'I fear harm may have come to him.'

'To Charles?'

'Yes, he was supposed to meet me at two, and he was not there. It's not like him to miss appointments, My Lord.'

'Where was this meeting to take place?'

'Where we usually meet: at the foot of the town road.'

'Now Betsy, we are going to try and help you. But first there are a number of important questions we are going to put to you. You must answer them completely and truthfully if you expect any mercy on our part concerning your involvement in this foul scheme – whether deliberate or accidental.'

She indicated that she would comply totally.

'First,' said Lord Allistair, 'to your knowledge, is my daughter unharmed?'

'From what I hear, she is.'

We both breathed a sign of relief.

'Have you any knowledge of the contents of the envelope handed to you this morning?'

'Yes, My Lord. It was a handwritten note from the young lady.'

'And anything else?'

'No, My Lord.'

Lord Allistair and I exchanged a quick glance. In all probability, neither Betsy, Charles, nor the kidnappers themselves knew anything about the second message done in pinpricks.

'Have you ever seen the "gentlemen", if such they can be called, that your friend Charles referred to?'

'No, My Lord, never.'

'Did he tell you anything about them — what they look like, where they are staying?'

'No — nothing. Except that they cannot be far away, since I know Charles goes often to speak with them, and returns to his lodgings in the town.'

'Is there anything else you can remember that may be of use to us? Anything you can do to help us is to your advantage as well as ours.'

'I am sorry,' she said at last, 'but I cannot think of anything. You both must believe me, gentlemen, I never thought I was engaging in anything that would in any way endanger Lady Alice. I am sure Charles feels the same way —'

'Does he?' asked Lord Allistair sternly.

'Oh, I am sure of it! And that is why we must find him. I'm so afraid...'

'You are convinced in your own mind that he is in trouble? How do you know he hasn't fled with the others?'

The poor girl lowered her eyes again, as if ashamed to admit that the possibility might in fact be true. Her face trembled slightly, and after some time she spoke.

'Because he loves me,' she said in a barely audible voice.

Lord Allistair placed his hand gently on her shoulder.

'I must tell you that you have behaved foolishly, Betsy. And there's a possibility you have been cruelly used as well. However, you have been a good servant to us both. We know you didn't enter into this pact with bad intentions. You must leave us while we decide upon the best course of action. Kindly wait in the kitchen. We will send for you shortly.'

The poor girl departed, and left the two of us to determine her fate. 'I'm afraid she has been taken advantage of,' he said. 'And her young man, this Compson, seems a bumpkin as well. No good can come of it.'

But Lord Allistair called her back a moment later, and she reappeared, still shaken.

'Betsy, so that we can find this friend of yours – eh, what's his name again?'

'Charles, My Lord. Charles Compson.'

'Yes. Can you give us a brief description of him?'

'Of course, My Lord. He's medium height, sandy hair, a big moustache.'

Lord Allistair paused.

'That description may fit many people hereabouts. Is there anything particular only to him?'

'No, My Lord, unless it's Clancy.'

'Who is Clancy?'

'His Kerry Blue terrier, My Lord. They're inseparable, are he and Clance. Go just about everywhere together – and have for years. Yes, My Lord: where you'll find Clancy, you'll find Charles not far off.'

She was again dismissed, and Lord Allistair and I were left to ponder this revelation.

'I can't help wondering,' I said slowly, 'to what extent her revelation of me will jeopardize the exchange.'

'Hardly, if at all. She doesn't know your real purpose here. I'll give Betsy's description of this Charles Compson to Farthway, the gamekeeper. He'll then keep a sharp lookout for him throughout these parts. If you're going to send a wire, Doctor, you'd best get started. Do you want a horse or carriage?'

I selected a horse and, placing my Webley in my coat pocket, started off on the nine-mile trip. Ian Farthway was to start an impromptu search for Betsy's man, and I was to keep my eyes peeled as well along the road. Lord Allistair and I had agreed that should Betsy find Charles of her own accord, she was to tell him that I had departed for London. In this way, it was thought, the kidnappers would feel less threatened and the exchange could be handled more smoothly.

Seldom have I been in gloomier spirits than when I wheeled at the outer stone fence and swung away towards town. The sun was gone behind a gathering cloud bank, and what had appeared bright and cheerful earlier now seemed gloomy and still. I made my way at a medium trot down the first long slope and entered the woods. There was no sound save the clip clop of the hooves upon the road, and in the stillness it seemed ear splitting. I recalled the gypsy who had followed us earlier, and the strange events of the morning. The letter from Alice Allistair was an optimistic sign, to be sure. And yet, of all the events of the past two days, it was the only cheering note. The smoke in Henry's Hollow, the watchman on the Keep, the puzzling message within a message, and the league between the maid and the abductors, all pointed to the utter encircling of Strathcombe by unseen forces, and their deep penetration into our defences. And the gypsy: was he simply a lout, or was he, too, in the employ of the criminals? So overwhelmed was I at the sudden and foreboding turn of things that I was convinced it was time to summon Holmes. For if any man could devise a productive strategy against these ruffians, it was clearly he.

The forest closed around me, and it seemed to grow darker by the minute. I spurred the horse onward, keeping my eyes about me. The visibility was poor, and the great trees of the forest loomed out as if to devour me. I was thankful I'd brought the Webley, and hurried on towards Rutlidge, four and a half miles away.

I arrived there in less than forty-five minutes, dashed straight to the telegraph office, and sent the following wire:

EVENTS MOVING SWIFTLY — REQUEST YOU COME AT ONCE.
SPIES IN THE HOUSE AND THE ENEMY EVERYWHERE.
WILL WAIT FOR ANSWER. WATSON.

I had thought it best to wait for a reply so as to have some news to tell the Allistairs upon my return to Strathcombe. I was obliged to wait for well over an hour for his answer — much longer than I anticipated. This struck me as curious, since Holmes had promised to remain within a few minutes' walk of the nearest telegraph office. Finally it arrived and read as follows:

SHALL ARRIVE ON TOMORROW'S TRAIN 1:30 P.M.
SEND CARRIAGE. HOLMES.

Thank God, Holmes was on his way! But what else could transpire within the intervening time? I shuddered to think. As I opened the door to leave the office, a thought struck me.

'I say,' I asked the key operator, 'have you seen a gypsy hereabouts in the past day or so?'

'I certainly have. There was a vagabond in this very office late last night, enquiring about a wire.'

'What did he look like?'

'Tall lean chap with a hook nose and a scarf tied round his head.'

That didn't sound like the gypsy I'd seen, but I did not rule out the possibility that the two could be in league. In fact, this was most probably the case.

'What sort of wire was he enquiring about?'

'He wished to know if there had been any messages to Strathcombe, the Allistair estate.'

A tremor passed over me at his words.

'And what did you reply?'

'That it was none of his affair, and to leave the premises.'

'That's a good man!' I said, tossing him a half-crown. 'Goodnight!'

Needless to say the appearance of the second gypsy made a dismal situation seem yet darker, more ominous. There was obviously a band of them, and they appeared to be well organized. The thought crossed my mind that careful planning and close communication weren't marks of these wandering, lazy, hot-blooded folk. Yet this group appeared to be an exception. I swung into the saddle resolved to keep silent about this development – at least until Holmes' arrival.

It was past nightfall when I struck the forest road. It looked still more dismal and ominous, and I passed through it at a brisk trot. My horse, for some reason, displayed a nervousness that was unnatural for a seasoned hunter. I sympathized with her, because some sixth sense inside me said all was not well, and I had best reach Strathcombe soon. Accordingly, I took her to a canter, and then to a gallop.

It was with a deep sense of relief that I topped the final rise and saw the few twinkling lights of Strathcombe ahead. I looked behind me. There was no sign of anyone. I hadn't been followed and help was on the way. Evidently, Alice Allistair was safe and unharmed. Surely, then, things weren't all that bad. Hopefully, within two days the trial would be over, and Holmes and I would be free to take two days of fishing at Strathcombe and then return to London, perhaps to continue our hunt for the giant rat of Sumatra. In lighter heart, I proceeded past the outer stone fence.

I was abreast of the lime kiln when I heard the howling of the dog.

Nine

CONFLUENCE

A chill shot through me at the sound. In the deep recesses of my mind I could feel a dark blanket of dread drawing ever closer.

My horse shied and whinnied at the eerie sound, and raced eagerly to the stables. It seemed to have suddenly grown much colder, and I longed for the parlour fire.

'Who goes?' cried a shrill voice as I approached the stables.

'It is I, Doctor Watson.'

'My apologies, Doctor,' said Wiscomb, as he made his way feebly from the stable door. 'I am unused to riders arriving at this hour.'

He appeared slightly the worse for drink, and his hands trembled as he took the reins. 'It's got right chilly, eh Doctor? And there's something else, too, about tonight. I've the feeling something's up. Can't put my finger square on it, but there's something in the air, someth –'

'There, you hear it!' said I. 'It sounds closer now.'

'Ah, the dog. He's been at it all night. Chase 'im off four times already I have –'

'What does he look like?'

'Oh, smallish, wire-haired. There! He's comin' back. I'll give 'im what for –'

'Hold on!' I cried. 'I'll go outside and see to him on my way to the house – no need to bother.'

He relented, put down the crop he'd picked up (I assumed to teach the dog a lesson) and ambled off to finish dressing down the horse.

It had indeed grown chilly outside; as I left the stable building I could see my breath, and the wind had quickened as well. I was halfway to the house when the howling commenced once more. Looking to the head of the drive, I observed a small dog hurrying to me. Forty feet away, it paused, whining. I knelt down and stretched out my hand.

'Clancy!' I called, and instantly the dog sprang forward with a joyous yelp. Upon reaching me, however, and sniffing my person, he again backed off, looked slightly confused, and resumed whining. He then paced to and fro, occasionally proceeding in the direction of the drive then hesitating, with a backward glance in my direction, and returning. It was plain the animal had lost his master. Considering Betsy's earlier concern, I didn't like the look of things.

I entered the hall to the sound of sobbing. Julia the maid met me in the main hallway.

'Good evening, Doctor Watson. Lord and Lady Allistair are waiting for you in the library. We are so glad you have returned, sir –'

'Julia, may I enquire who is crying?'

'It's Betsy, sir, afraid for her man.'

'He has not turned up yet?' I asked.

'No, sir.'

I entered the library to find Lord and Lady Allistair in a semi-darkened room, pacing nervously to and fro. They greeted me with visible relief. The relief turned into delight when I told them that

Holmes would arrive the following day.

'Shall we meet him at the train?'

'Brundage can do that – he requested a carriage. He seldom – hullo, who's this?'

I was surprised to see a shadowy figure emerge from the doorway and approach us. As he neared the fireplace, which was the primary light source, I could see that he was the tall, blond man I saw on horseback the first night at Strathcombe.

'Ah, I remember now, you have not met. Farthway, this is Doctor Watson, second cousin to my wife.'

'How do you do, sir,' said Farthway coolly. He had the air of dash and daring about him. At first glance, he seemed frank and open enough, yet there was a coolness, a hesitation, that set my guard up slightly.

'What is it, Farthway?' paused Lord Allistair.

'Your Lordship, I understand from several of the staff that you and the Doctor rode deep into the forest this morning.'

'That is correct, but I cannot see how this concerns you, Farthway.'

'I beg your pardon, Your Lordship, but I feel it concerns me in a personal way, since the woods are dangerous now.'

'How do you mean?' I demanded.

'There are a good number of vagabonds about, sir,' he replied, still looking at Lord Allistair. 'And there is the big boar in residence along the river bottom.'

'And no doubt you have also some knowledge of the letter delivered to us this afternoon?'

Farthway nodded. Lord Allistair hesitated a moment, as if undecided whether to reprimand or praise his gamekeeper.

'Very well, Farthway. Thank you for your concern. But I must remind you that it is my decision entirely to enter the woods or avoid them. As a matter of fact, we shall no doubt be going there again tomorrow, and would like you to act as guide.'

'Very good, sir. Will you shoot?'

'No,' answered Lord Allistair, after an inquisitive glance in my direction. 'You may go.'

But as he turned to depart, I called him back.

'Mr Farthway, from what I have seen and heard of you, you handle a horse very well, and a gun, too, I understand.'

'Thank you. I endeavour to give satisfaction to my employer and his guests.'

'Are you engaged tonight?' I asked.

'*Tonight*, sir?'

'Yes. Could you find your way about in this countryside in the dark?'

Farthway hesitated, his keen features working in the firelight as he attempted to look beyond my simple, and no doubt perplexing, request.

'I'd venture to say,' he answered at last, 'that I could find my way about blindfolded − anywhere you'd care to go but −'

'But what?'

'I don't think it would be advisable to venture out tonight, sir,' he said nervously.

'Why not?'

He shifted, and his eyes refused to meet mine directly. 'I just don't think it advisable,' he said.

'Could it be, Farthway,' I taunted, 'that you fear for your safety?' and saw his eyes flash with anger.

'I might remind you, Doctor Watson, that I have spent a good many of my years defending the Empire all over the globe, often in the face of hostile fire. You have, in all probability, spent your time quite differently. It is for your safety I fear, not my own. But if you are determined, I shall have the horses ready in twenty minutes.'

With this, he turned like a Prussian on his heel and departed.

Meantime, Lord and Lady Allistair had been standing by, apparently thunderstruck at my request.

'You are not serious, I hope. I take it your request was a form of humiliation for him – and well deserved, too, I might add,' said Lady Allistair to me.

'Quite an outburst for a gamekeeper. I may have to sack the man, good as he is.'

'No doubt he is regretting his shortness with me already,' said I, 'yet I was, and am, entirely serious about venturing out tonight. From all accounts, the one man to accompany me is Ian Farthway.'

I then briefly explained the episode of the lost dog to them. Although they showed some concern for Betsy, it was obvious that, in the light of recent revelations, their concern and affection for her was not infinite. Moreover, their concern for me was paramount. At some length, however, I managed to persuade them both that Betsy's difficulties were in some way connected with their own.

'So we really must go and look about the place,' I said, 'and though I challenged Farthway, I achieved my end, for it is imperative to have his services this evening, even if it was necessary to taunt him into it.'

'Then if go you must, for God's sake be careful. I'll have flasks of coffee and brandy brought up for you both. Remember your pistol, sir, and do as Farthway says.'

'Thank you, Lord Allistair.'

It was a sullen Farthway who met me, horses in hand, at the foot of the terrace steps. I presented him with his flask and he grunted a reply. As we mounted, I noticed he had the familiar fowling piece slung over his shoulders, yet somehow it looked heavier.

'Holland and Holland double rifle,' he replied shortly when I asked him about it. 'Not a fowling piece. This can stop an elephant. Now Doctor, would you mind telling me why you've proposed this nocturnal jaunt?'

'Here comes the answer, I think,' I replied.

At that exact moment, Clancy, the terrier, came round the drive whining and wheeling in tight circles. I simply told Farthway that the dog's master was missing, and perhaps the animal could lead us to him. It seemed as if some of the daring and excitement of his earlier career was returning to the ex-soldier. With a keenness that bordered on enthusiasm, he started down the drive at a brisk trot. The small dog led the way, alternately yelping and dashing ahead into the darkness, then, less sure of himself, returning in our direction in the same whining, turning fashion as before.

'It seems to me I've seen this dog before,' said Farthway after a quarter hour's ride. 'Is his master a loutish fellow, leather apron, walrus moustache?'

'That sounds like him, a tanner's apprentice named Charles Compson. Was he often about?'

'I've seen him on the main road here a dozen times during the past few weeks. A simple fellow – always the little terrier was at his heels. The man has not been seen?'

I retold Betsy's story, but only mentioning their love affair and eventual plans to emigrate to Australia. I mentioned nothing of Compson's supposed involvement with the abductors. We hurried on down the road in the darkness. In my haste, I'd forgotten a lantern, and quietly cursed myself. However, I realized too that a lantern enables one only to see immediate objects; it is useless for seeing distances at night. Perhaps it was just as well I'd not brought one. We were headed not towards Rutlidge but rather in the opposite direction – towards the Welsh border. The dog was alternately running and trotting now, and his howling increased in intensity. That sound, with the hollow clatter of our horses' hooves along the cold road, sent chills through my body. The night, having grown even more overcast, was dark as pitch. Nothing was visible save occasional glimpses of the small dog as it flitted gingerly between the horses.

'I must say,' he offered at length, 'that I was a bit short with you, Doctor. I apologize.'

'You needn't worry yourself over me, Farthway. But your remarks to Lord Allistair could have more serious consequences.'

'Ah, but what does *he* know of the dangers that lurk about here? He and the Lady come here twice a year at the very most. It would not surprise me in the slightest if he were to get lost in his own woods some day –'

'You speak in a tone of contempt for him,' I returned. 'For a man of his stature, that is surprising. And for a gamekeeper and employee your tone is offensive.'

'I did not wish to give that impression. Quite the opposite is true. I came into Lord Allistair's service more out of admiration than for any challenge and excitement this job would offer me which, as you can see, isn't much.'

'Until recently.'

'Aye. And therein, Doctor, lies my concern. The woods are always full of thieves and brigands, but now they are more dangerous than usual. I reacted tonight out of concern, not insolence.'

'Tell me, don't you ever fear for your own safety in the woods if they are as dangerous as you say?'

'No, sir. There's no one that knows this country as I do. I can lose anyone in these woods, sir, quick as a wink. I know every dell and copse in the Clun Forest, from Henry's Hollow and the Keep clear over to the Clee Hills and the Wrekin.'

'You were born here?'

'I was born in Glasgow, but moved to Ludlow as a boy – so it was here I spent my youth. I dare say that there's none know this country better than Ian Farthway.'

'I understand that until recently you were with the Black Watch.'

'Indeed I was.'

We continued for some minutes in silence.

'Why don't you ask me why I left the regiment, Doctor?' he asked.

'Well I...'

'Come now, you're probably dying to know. The truth is, I was forced to retire from the service for the same reason I moved to Ludlow as a young man: lack of funds.'

I said nothing.

'You see, my family, for all its veneer of respectability and wealth, has had more than its share of drunkards – the worst of which was my late father. In his short lifetime, he managed to squander our family's remaining fortune and ruin our name in Scotland. So I headed south and took a working man's job, saving all the money I could. My stint with the Black Watch was enjoyable, and I was a good soldier, but the money ran out, so here I am. I tell you this because I harbour in my soul some resentment for those who've never done an honest day's work.'

'Are you referring to me?' I bristled.

'No. Neither you nor His Lordship. But I suppose my temper gets up when I see Strathcombe, and think of the life I might have had if my forebears had been more prudent. Well, I've said enough.'

And so we rode on, following the lively gait of the little terrier. But I could not help wondering about this young man. Even considering his financial situation, why was he content at being a common gamekeeper when his record and personal bearing suggested he was capable of greater things? Why was he distant and aloof, even with his employer? And finally, where did this young man go to on his fine stallion? Where did he spend his time between sunrise and sunset? More particularly, where was he bound the evening I arrived, when I saw him clear the stone fence in a magnificent leap? These questions specifically, and his mysterious manner in general, concerned me. But clearly, there was urgent need of his talents that night, so I decided to put aside my suspicions for the time being.

After perhaps twenty minutes, the dog grew noticeably more nervous. Suddenly he stopped altogether and, nose to the ground, made his way to the edge of the road. There, he slowly lifted his head and peered into the tall forest that began less than twenty yards away. A low growl began in his throat. It rose higher, louder, then ended in a terrified shriek as the dog bounded back in our direction and cringed between us.

We tried to urge the horses forward in the direction in which the dog had gazed but they too, as if taking a cue from the smaller animal, refused to proceed further. Even Farthway, with his tremendous skill as a horseman, couldn't budge his mount. They snorted and whinnied, then reared, but no amount of spurring or oaths would move them.

'We'd best dismount, Doctor,' said he, 'and approach on foot.'

But no sooner had we left our saddles than the horses turned tail and broke for Strathcombe at full gallop.

Farthway, sensing that this turn of events cast some doubt on his abilities as gamekeeper and horseman, let out a string of oaths that was remarkable indeed.

'Well, there's no retrieving them now. We may as well go and have a look – we'll be walking back anyway,' I said.

Farthway unslung the rifle and I drew out my Webley and cocked the hammer.

The terrier had stayed with us, as one would expect of a dog, particularly of the terrier breed. It was frightened, however, and seemed even to regret that it had led us to the dreary place. We left the road and walked slowly through knee-high bracken until we were at the forest's edge. The dog, barely leading us, would never venture more than a yard or so ahead without looking round to see for certain that we were close behind. It was quiet now, as if afraid of disturbing some sleeping monster. The only sound it made was a barely audible deep growl that always changed to a shaken whine. I placed my hand on its neck, and could feel, through its wiry fur, the little pulse pounding wildly.

'Have you a light?' I asked, after gazing at the ominous wall of trees. 'No? I have only a pocketful of matches for my pipe. We should feel our way forward in the darkness then, and save our light for the end of our mission – if there is one.'

As we strode cautiously into that looming black mass of the forest, I was overcome by one of those peculiarities of life known as *déjà vu*. Where and when had this occurred before in my life? In a few moments I remembered, and grew all the more wondrous at how strange a thing the mind is, for the instance in my youth that had brought on the *déjà vu* occurred when I was only seven, and though I could not have thought of it more than a dozen times in my thirty or so intervening years, yet there was the incident called up from the murky deep, and recalled clear as a bell. Soon after my seventh birthday, my mother took me on a journey to France, and we boarded the night ferry at Dover. I remembered clambering up the gangplank, hands clutching at my mother's dress, towards an enormous black shape that was the ship. Since the gangplank seemed to terminate in the very centre of the ominous mass, it was terrifying indeed. I had the dread feeling that we were about to be swallowed up by the huge dark thing, and never were to see the light of day again.

But as I was terrified as a boy, I must admit that approaching the looming mass of the forest that night in the wilds of Shropshire (even considering my age, my companion, and the fact that we were armed and capable men), the same feeling of dread crept upon me. For just as a small boy has his fears, he also has his mother, in whom he may invest boundless quantities of wisdom and courage. And so when he becomes a man, while he is the more capable and strong, yet he no longer has the all-protecting figure to watch over him and he realizes that he is entirely on his own. So it seemed to me to be a bob for a shilling: we never can shake off the anxiety that dogs our heels from the cradle to the grave, and is always ready at a moment's notice to clutch its icy fingers round our hearts.

We had slowed to a snail's pace, owing to the blackness and the tangle of trees and branches. We could feel the terrier slinking between our legs and hear its frenzied panting, for so terrified was the animal now that no other sound emerged from it.

'You see,' said Farthway in a low voice. He raised his arm and pointed ahead into the darkness. 'There's a clearing yonder – can you see the gleam of pale stone?'

I confessed I could see a patch of faint grey, but nothing else. As we drew nearer, however, I could see it was a clearing made by outcropping stone, on which no trees could grow. Drawing still nearer, I could see that the outcropping, as is common with formations of the sort, projected from the earth at an angle, and had almost the appearance of a miniature Gibraltar. After several minutes we came into the clearing but, even though it was an area devoid of trees, the darkness was complete. We walked twice around the rock, which was about sixty feet long, without noticing anything amiss. At its highest, the projecting rock rose in a wall almost perpendicular – a miniature cliff ten or twelve feet high.

'Clancy!' I called softly, for it was he, and only he, who could show us the way.

But the dog had vanished.

'When did you last see him?' asked Farthway.

'I remember him at my side just as we saw the clearing,' I replied, 'and can't remember seeing him since.'

Then there came to our ears a low crying sound. We were almost positive it came from the dog – but from which direction?

'It seems to come from nowhere,' said Farthway.

'And yet from everywhere…'

'It seems nearby…'

'But far away as well.'

Again we cocked our ears. Again, the sound came. It was not more than ten feet away.

'Doctor – above you!' said Farthway in a hoarse whisper.

We had been standing under the cliff end of the rock. I looked upward and in the darkness could see the faint moving silhouette of the small dog's head as he peered down at us, whining.

'There, Clancy – how did you get up there?'

'He must have walked up from the other end of the rock – but why would he venture up there?'

I took a match from my pocket and struck it. Its first flash momentarily blinded me, but once the flame had steadied, I held it up as far as I could reach. Clancy's alert face came into view.

'Good God!' cried Farthway in horror.

Just as he shrieked, I uttered a cry of terror as well. We both saw it.

At the dog's feet, projecting over the edge of the rock and placed as though delicately shading the flame which I held aloft, was a human hand.

We stood for some seconds transfixed by the mute horror of it. The terrier, as if bidding us to ascend the rock, began barking. We stared in disbelief at the hand, whose delicate appearance, palm downward, fingers curved slightly, lent a mocking irony to the scene.

'Oh Lord, Doctor,' whispered Farthway as he drew near me. 'I've seen many a horrid thing, and scores of corpses too, but this is truly frightful.'

I had struck another match, and still we stared.

'Well, there's little doubt as to whom the hand belongs,' I said. 'Poor Betsy's apprehensions have proven justified, I fear. How did the wretch come to be up there? I cannot help wondering how the dog...'

'I remember seeing a gentle slope of rock on the other side. If we go round this way, we'll run into it.'

Again in darkness, it took my eyes some time to grow accustomed to the dim light. At length, we came upon a wide crevice in the rock, through which ran a ramp-like path of gently-sloping rock. This we trudged up without difficulty, yet neither of us was eager to reach the far precipice, aware of the grisly scene which awaited us. As we neared the edge, I could see the blurred movement of the terrier as he skipped round the dark object that lay outstretched on the pale surface of the rock. I was amazed, drawing nearer, at the huge size of the object – it appeared several times larger than a man. The projection was perhaps nine feet wide, and the prone object took up a full half of the width.

'It is huge, Farthway. Was this fellow a giant?'

But before he attempted to answer my question, he was already at the body, kneeling over it. I was somewhat surprised to hear him utter a long sigh of grief. Could this cocky lad be a softer sort underneath? Was the bluff and bluster merely a show? Or, perhaps in a more sinister vein, was this sigh some contrived part of his personality, put on for my benefit? To be sure, this fellow was an enigma – far different from the frank and simple gamekeeper one usually finds in the English countryside. Capable as he was, I was a long way from putting my total trust in him.

'Strike a match, Doctor,' said he, his voice full of gravity, 'and you shall see his true size.'

I did so and, leaning over, saw a sight that fairly took my breath away. Farthway too, iron-nerved as he was, gave a gasp, followed by a low moan. The dog lay down in silence beside the remains of his master, his head resting wearily on his paws. The reader will understand the double shock that smote me when I explain that my overestimation of the man's size was due to seeing what I thought was a huge dark object. What I was actually seeing, in the half light, was a body amidst a dark sea of blood: blood as I have never seen it, and pray God never shall see again for the sake of my sanity. It spread out from the corpse in pools and rivulets. It had stained the paws and legs of the dog. It was everywhere, in ghastly profusion. The man lay face downward at the very far edge of the rock. His hands were flung outwards from the body, the one, as the reader knows, protruding even over the edge. From the behaviour of the dog and the large moustache, it was obvious that the man was Charles Compson. He appeared to have fallen violently forward as if having tripped while running at top speed.

But the shock and revulsion that smote like a hammer blow and fairly set me reeling off the rocky projection, was the manner of the man's death.

'Good God in Heaven,' I gasped, 'the giant rat!' For upon looking at his neck and back for only an instant, all the horror of the death chamber of the *Matilda Briggs* came racing back through my soul like an express train. Looking round me at the silent forest in a frenzy of apprehension, I realized I had come upon the confluence of two great tragedies.

The episode of the *Matilda Briggs* and the trial of the Allistairs were in some nefarious way connected. The centre of all the seemingly disparate events – the vortex, as it were – was not Limehouse, nor even London, but the deep and forbidding forests of the Valley of the Severn.

Even as I spoke the dreaded words to Farthway's astonished and confused face, I could picture in my mind's eye the fugitive pursued by the monster. Totally spent, did he seek this outcropping of rock as a final haven from the beast? Stumbling through the forest – the creature at his heels making God knows what horrid sound – did he stumble across the small hillock, and, in desperation, scale it in the hope that the thing would be unable to reach him? I was recalled from these ghastly speculations by Farthway, who was shaking my shoulder.

'There! You've burnt your fingers with that match, sir – what about a rat? What rat could do this?'

But I waved him off.

'Tell me, Farthway, from what you see before you, how did this poor wretch meet his end?'

'He was running from something – that much is clear. He ran up this slope hoping that whatever was chasing him would not follow. But he *was* followed, and brought down and worried to death right on this spot. A boar could do this perhaps, but only if wounded – or mad –'

Working our way back down the narrow incline, we found ourselves once again at the edge of the trees. I peered back at the slanting monolith with a shudder. Were it not for the little dog, how many months or years would pass before anyone would have discovered the grisly object on its summit? Hidden from the road in the midst of deep woods, surrounded for miles by wild Shropshire hills and forests, it was indeed a lonely spot to die.

'Here's the spot to look if it's tracks you are searching for,' said Farthway.

Only a few moment's search was needed before we were both kneeling down next to a clear set of enormous tracks. We examined them at length using several matches in the process. Farthway, for all his experience and expertise, was plainly confused.

'I've seen these tracks only once before,' he said finally. 'It was on the hard-packed soil of the forest path near Henry's Hollow. I saw only one print clearly. It had three toes, but I assumed it to be a deformity of sorts, and that the other footprints would appear in the normal cloven patterns of a forest pig, had I been able to see them. Clearly though, it is evident that all the feet of this animal are different from a boar. In fact, they are different from any animal I have ever seen on three continents.'

'I see that some feet bear three toes, but others appear to bear five. Is this possible?'

Farthway assumed a puzzled expression.

'It is possible because we have seen it, sir. But other than that, it is the most extraordinary thing I've seen in years.'

'There are two beasts, then?'

He shook his head.

'It would appear so. But I've never seen the likes of any of this before. The tracks, too, are huge — much bigger than any boar could be. What sort of animal is this?'

'Ah! The more I see evidence of it, the more bizarre and fearsome it becomes! Come, Farthway, we've a long walk back, and must then ride to town again to summon the authorities. Thank God Holmes arrives tomorrow —'

'He is coming tomorrow?' he asked quickly.

'Yes, he wired —' I stopped at mid-sentence and stared at the man. 'How do you know of Holmes?'

'What do you mean? He is a friend of yours?' he answered nervously.

'You responded as if you'd heard of him. Yet, I have been most careful not to mention him in any company save the Allistairs. Now how came you to hear of him? Answer up straightaway now, or it'll go hard with you!'

He remained silent for some time, obviously undergoing some kind of inner struggle between telling me all and holding back.

'I have nothing more to tell you, Doctor,' he said at last. 'I'm afraid that if things go hard with me at Strathcombe, then so be it.'

Considering the ability of the abductors to plant spies in the Allistair household, and apparently come and go about the place as they pleased, this stance by Farthway set me very ill at ease indeed.

'I urge you to reconsider. Your silence will be interpreted as an admission of being in league —'

'Such an interpretation would be unwarranted and foolish. I am in league with no one. Furthermore, I am most anxious for the well being of all the Allistairs — hence my concern for both of you earlier this evening when I'd found you had visited the Hollow. Now please, you must not question further, Doctor. As you have said, there is much to do and little time.'

So saying, he turned and struck out in the direction of the road. I was about to follow, but remembered the one who had brought us to the eerie place. I retraced my steps to the top of the stony precipice. There was poor Clancy, just as we'd left him. I urged him to come away from the dire spot, but no amount of calling would suffice. When I attempted to pick him up, he growled and snapped at me. So I left him there at his dead master's side, his head on his paws in grief. I descended the rock, and started the long, cold walk back to Strathcombe with a man whom, for several reasons, I did not wholly trust.

Never before, in all my years with Sherlock Holmes, had events rushed so ominously and inexorably towards some dark and puzzling *finale*. And never before was I so alone.

Ten

THE VORTEX

I cannot convey in words the relief that coursed through my soul when, shortly after three on the following day, I heard the rattle of the landau in the drive and spied the angular face of Sherlock Holmes, who was perched upon the rear seat.

I was, however, much surprised that he should choose so public an arrival. Surely this formal approach to Strathcombe in broad daylight flew in the face of the warning to the Allistairs that they should seek no help. It seemed to me that he was tempting fate, but so glad was I at his arrival that I decided not to raise the issue. Holmes had come, and I could breathe a bit easier.

'Well, well, Watson,' he observed as he climbed the terrace steps, 'Brundage tells me that things have been cooking here at Strathcombe since your arrival –'

'Boiling over is more the word – dash it, man, it's good to see you!' I blurted as I wrung his hand. 'Brundage has told you about last night's occurrences?'

'The death of young Compson? Most unfortunate. And how's the girl?'

'Off to her relatives. It was all I could do to keep her sanity. But Holmes, I must mention the manner of the man's death –'

'Worried to death?'

'Precisely. An exact duplicate of the McGuinness murder, but how did you guess?'

'Let us just say that for some time I've suspected the abduction of Alice Allistair and the giant rat of Sumatra were connected. No doubt this surprises you. You are also probably surprised that I am showing myself in this rather bold fashion, since the abductors have decreed that Lord and Lady Allistair should act alone. I have my reasons for this too, but shan't explain them now.'

'As you wish...'

'Now you haven't, I hope, mentioned anything of the rat to the Allistairs –'

'Absolutely not; you needn't fear on that score.'

'Good.'

'Lord Allistair is waiting in his study. There is something of the utmost importance we must discuss.'

After a warm greeting from Lord Allistair, and a cup of tea, Sherlock Holmes listened attentively to our story of the message within a message. He sat at the felt gaming table, turning the piece of newsprint round and round in his hand. He even inspected it under his pocket lens.

'Turn up the lamp, would you, Watson?'

'What do you make of it?'

'I would say first of all that your optimism is well founded. If this is indeed Alice's hand, then your daughter is presumably alive and well. The matter of the coded message is, however, more difficult. To all appearances, I would agree with you, Lord Allistair, that this was written – or rather pricked – by your daughter. By running your fingers over the pinpricks, you can feel the bumps are on the front side. Thus, the needle or pin was plied from the back. This was done with extraordinary skill, and just the sort of talent a seamstress would develop. I congratulate you on a fine bit of deduction.'

Lord Allistair beamed with pleasure as he refilled his cup. Surely, Holmes' arrival had a miraculous effect on the man.

'Furthermore, since the natural mode of executing such a message would have been to stick the paper from the front, we can assume that Alice was being closely watched and was forced to resort to the awkward tactic of punching out the holes from underneath. In this manner, if the paper were resting in her lap, her hand, plying the needle, would be hidden from view beneath the paper.'

Lord Allistair could contain himself no longer. He rose from his chair and paced frantically about.

'You see? You see what a clever girl she is? Ah, there's none like her in all the kingdom, I tell you!'

Holmes smiled, paused, and continued.

'Perhaps this also explains why she confined the message to the single short article. If she moved her hand about, it would attract attention.'

'Now as to the message itself. Can you decipher it?'

'I'm afraid, gentlemen,' he said after a cursory glance, 'that I cannot tell you what it says.'

'But Holmes,' I protested, 'surely you can decipher it if you spend the time and effort. You have solved far more difficult puzzles and codes than this in the past. The Dancing Men and the Musgrave Ritual certainly were more taxing.'

'Well, this one is quite difficult, I'm afraid,' he said, and idly tucked the paper away into his breast coat pocket.

'Holmes! This is most unlike you. With your love of the mysterious and complex, this cavalier attitude is surprising indeed. When you say you can't tell us – do you mean you can't – or won't?'

'I mean… well, hello, Lady Allistair, this is indeed a pleasure.'

She greeted him cordially, but unfortunately she had relapsed, after her brief reprieve from anxiety, into another fit of depression. This was occasioned by the death of Charles Compson. While she didn't know the man, Betsy's grief was contagious. Furthermore, the violent manner of his dying had sent new ripples of dread through her.

As I saw her enter the study, I couldn't help thinking that, glad as she was at Holmes' arrival, she was still worried lest our presence in some way endanger her daughter. Sympathetic as I was to her dilemma, my total faith in Holmes' prowess and judgement assured me that the present course of action was the only one. Holmes saw her to a fireside seat, drew a chair near to her and, as I had so often observed in the past, displayed a most sympathetic and reassuring bearing towards her.

'There now, Lady Allistair. It's been most difficult for you, and for such a long time too. I have two distinct feelings: first, I am confident your daughter is safe. Secondly, I have a strong feeling that the trial, hard as it has been, is drawing to a close.'

His words had the desired effect, and it wasn't long before she managed to regain her composure. I could see that Holmes had no intention of returning to the subject of the coded message whilst she was in the room. So, confounded though I was with Holmes' casual attitude towards it, I decided to let the matter drop – at least for the time being.

'And now,' concluded Holmes after his cordial welcome, 'I'm afraid there's some grisly business to attend to. Watson, did I hear you mention that you'd informed the authorities about Mr Compson?'

'Yes. Directly Farthway and I arrived here last night I sent Wiscomb to town with the news. I've no doubt the local inspector is at the scene at this very moment.'

Holmes' face darkened.

'Then we'd best be off, and in a rush too – you know very well what the "local inspector" is capable of doing to even the most rudimentary evidence. Would you care to come along, Lord Allistair? No? Well, perhaps it's best if you remain here. Now, Watson, let's find this Farthway fellow before we depart; he should be of some assistance.'

We found him in his cottage, hovering over a curious-looking lamp on a table that stood before a bow window. I noticed that the window looked directly towards the house and driveway.

He and Holmes shook hands cordially, although I fancied I saw a shade of suspicion or cunning cross his face. He agreed at once to go with us, and promptly pulled on his riding boots. The walls of the tiny cottage were covered with various hunting trophies, mostly heads of fox masks and stags. On a dresser against the far wall lay an officer's sabre, the scabbard of which was brilliant silver bound in gold. Near it stood the tall shako of the Black Watch. I could not help being impressed. As we turned to go, I again noticed the lamp.

'Holmes,' I said, 'isn't that a semaphore lamp? I seem to recall seeing one like it earlier – you remember, aboard the steamship *Rob Roy*, in connection with the adventure of the Curious Boatman –'

'Yes, it's a semaphore lamp,' replied the gamekeeper hurriedly. 'I took it off a derelict in Bantry Bay and keep it as a souvenir. Should we be off?'

Holmes flicked the brass lever on the lamp's side and the metal shutters snapped open and shut with a brisk clacking sound.

'Quite a signalling device, eh, Watson?' remarked Holmes as we left the cottage. 'Now we're to take a carriage – ah, there it is waiting at the foot of the drive.'

I shan't bother you, dear reader, with all the details of our grim expedition. Suffice it to say that we located the fatal site once again, but only because we spotted the small terrier Clancy at the roadside. I thought at first he'd sensibly given up his lonely wake, but when we reached the outcropping of rock and climbed it, the corpse was gone. I heard Holmes curse sharply under his breath.

'Now, Holmes, surely we can't expect the constables to leave the body out in so desolate a place as this — decency dictates that it be gathered up for proper burial —'

With a grunt of disappointment, he whipped out his pocket lens and set to work scouring the rock and its surroundings. He seemed to find nothing of interest save the great bloodstain, which he examined closely. He descended the rock and walked thrice around it until he stopped near the forest's edge. I could hear him mutter an exclamation.

'The animal, whatever its identity, is enormous. Have you seen these?'

'Yes, last night in the dark. Do you know the identity of the animal? Is it indeed a rat?'

'I'll repeat what I said in the carriage with Lestrade a fortnight ago, Watson: it could be some strange animal not yet known by civilized man. I think that possible. Certainly, we now know, by a multitude of means, that it is an *animal* — no puppet or optical trick as we suspected upon hearing Sampson's tale. Mr Farthway, judging from the diameter of these prints, and from the depth of the impression, how much would you guess this animal weighs?'

'Between five and six hundred pounds at least.'

'And I, no novice on the subject of footprints, would concur. With a beast like that at his heels, we can see why young Compson was so anxious to climb this rock.'

The journey back to the house was swift. Farthway sat in the driver's box whilst Holmes and I sat in the landau's rear seat, smoking and talking quietly. I made it plain to Holmes early on that I viewed Farthway with some suspicion, and related his background, along with other recent events which had formed this unsavoury opinion in my mind.

'And I might as well add, Holmes, that I didn't like the look of that signalling lamp he has in his cottage. They can be seen for miles, can they not?'

'Really, Watson,' said Holmes impatiently as smoke burst from between his lips in short puffs, 'you're acting like the town gossip —'

'But he also *knew* you were arriving this morning — yet I'd not so much as mentioned your name, nor had Lord Allistair for that matter — how came he to this knowledge?'

Holmes visibly started at this revelation. He fixed his eyes on the back of the gamekeeper, only a few feet from us, who blithely minded the reins without the slightest show of suspicion or concern. Obviously, he could not hear a word we said, for we were talking *sotto voce* and the clatter of the horse and coach obliterated every trace of our conversation.

'Well, that is interesting. I shall remember to have a private talk with Mr Farthway directly we reach the house.'

'Come to think of it, there's something else I remember too,' said I, as I leaned forward and asked, in a loud voice, 'I say, Farthway, who of the household staff informed you of our journey to Henry's Hollow yesterday?'

I had evidently caught him off guard. The question seemed to both puzzle and annoy him.

'I, ah, cannot recall exactly, sir.'

'You cannot recall?' I persisted, 'that is strange, considering it was only yesterday. When you recall, will you let me know?'

I sat back in the carriage and chuckled to myself.

'Neither Lord Allistair nor I breathed a word of our ride to Henry's Hollow to anyone,' I said. 'This fellow has a lot of information he has no business having. I say — oh, well here's the house behind those trees. See the chimney stack? I suppose the two of us and Lord Allistair should have a lengthy, private chat.'

'Capital, Watson. Let's begin after dinner.'

And so we did. Lord Allistair had Brundage build the fire up and, as we sat before it with our brandy, he closed the door and bolted it.

'Doctor Watson is correct, Mr Holmes. Neither of us mentioned our little expedition. How came Farthway to know of it, and your arrival here as well? I must confess this makes me uneasy. We are in violation of the instructions. Considering the manner in which they've been known to deal with those that cross them – I'm thinking of this poor Compson fellow – I am beginning to fear the worst.'

'While I fully understand your concern, Lord Allistair, I am afraid we're bound to our present course of action. If I were to depart now it would raise as many suspicions as my arrival. Furthermore, to dismiss Farthway, as you and Watson seem intent upon doing, would only rouse his anger if he is one of the confederates, or diminish our friends if indeed he is loyal.'

This point impressed us both. Based on my long association with him, my inclination was to follow Holmes' judgement. We decided to wait it out.

'And now, let me hear more about this place called Henry's Hollow.'

We described the place at length, and I mentioned the traces of woodsmoke I had smelted there. Holmes plied us with many questions – how large was the hollow? What of the hillside caverns, how many were there, and how large? Did we see any other traces of recent habitation in the strange place? Would it be possible to conceal horses there, or possibly a cart? Lord Allistair answered all of these as best he could, and we concluded our session after he drew a rough sketch of the place for Holmes to keep. It showed the relation of the Hollow to Strathcombe with regard to distance, direction, and forest paths, and indicated points of interest in the Hollow as well.

'If you don't mind my saying so, Holmes,' I remarked as we went upstairs for the night several hours later, 'you seem to have lost some of your old zeal.'

'Really?' he replied with irritation, 'what makes you say that?'

'Did you have that private conference with Farthway?'

'Yes, right after our meeting in His Lordship's study. While the two of you played billiards, I visited his cottage again. We had a lengthy discussion. Here Watson, come into my room for a minute.'

I followed him into a room similar to the one I occupied. This one, however, looked out directly over Farthway's cottage. Holmes seated himself and relighted his pipe.

'It's not like you, Holmes, to cast puzzles aside as you did the coded message. Furthermore my observations of Farthway seem to have been quite accurate, even valuable, yet you seem to take his proximity to, nay, *involvement in*, this business almost casually –'

'Do I? Really, I hadn't thought so. It is just that I am more careful, less emotionally charged than others of my acquaintance.'

Sensing this barb was aimed at me, I rose from my chair and began pacing up and down the room before the window. Through its ancient glass I could see that twilight was fading.

'Did you observe the Allistairs at supper tonight? I've never seen two gloomier people. Obviously, our presence here is reassuring to a certain degree, but deeply troubling to them in another. Holmes, we must *do* something!'

He rose also and placed a steadying hand on my shoulder.

'Good old Watson, always the man of action! Always drawn at full-bow to spring forth to render assistance. But we must wait till the ransom demand is delivered. To do anything else at this juncture would be imprudent, even disastrous. No doubt the tension is telling on you, as it is on all of us. Has it really been just ten days since we found Jenard's body? It seems like an age...'

'What have you learned of Farthway?'

'Ah! First, he was informed of your visit to the Hollow by poor Betsy, who overheard you discussing the jaunt shortly before she entered Lord Allistair's study.'

'That could be true,' I admitted at last, 'or it could be otherwise.'

'Still, we must accept it for now. To stir things up here, with regard to Farthway or anyone else, could have dire consequences. We *must* play the waiting game, Watson. Our success in the case, and the welfare of Alice Allistair, depends on it. But wait, I can perhaps set your mind at ease a bit – is the door bolted?'

I went over and bolted it, then returned to my chair. Holmes drew his close to mine.

'As you know, it is often my custom not to reveal all I know about certain cases until my theories can be borne out by events. Now in this case, I have for some time suspected a link between the kidnapping of Alice Allistair and the bloody events connected with the *Matilda Briggs*. The reasons for this are many, but suffice it to say that, so far, my suspicions have proved correct.'

He went over to the window.

'As for what will soon transpire out in that wilderness, I have my theories too. But it is a deadly business, and if we are to have a prayer of success, you – and Lord Allistair as well – must follow the kidnapper's instructions exactly and without question. Will you do this?'

'You know very well my faith in you, Holmes. Yes, I give you my assurance that Lord Allistair will comply as well.'

'Excellent. Then get to bed. I'm sure that tomorrow we'll need all the strength we can muster. Goodnight.'

It would be incontrovertibly demonstrated the following day how true his warning would be. As I left his quarters, I heard a clap of thunder overhead.

I retired soon afterwards, pausing beforehand at my window to sweep my eyes over the dark landscape. A light rain had followed the thunder – the type of drizzling shower that may last for days on end. Drawing the covers about me, I listened to the rain upon the windows, and soon drifted off.

I awoke in the dead of night. A sound in the hallway – perhaps a stealthy tread – had set me bolt upright. The sound was ever so faint, but I had not been sleeping soundly, and so was sensitive to the slightest disturbance. After drawing on my trousers, I went to the dresser. I opened the face of my watch and felt the hands. It was shortly after three. Without a sound, I entered the hallway and cocked my ears. All was quiet. I stood motionless in the dark for several minutes, but could hear nothing. Assuming it was only my nervous imagination, I turned to re-enter my room. But as a last-minute thought, I decided to look in on Holmes. A very light sleeper himself, perhaps he had also heard the noise.

I rapped softly on his door and waited. Hearing no reply, I opened his door and approached the bed. Imagine my surprise and distress at finding him gone! Moreover, his bed had not been slept in. Had Holmes himself been kidnapped, or lured away on a false errand? I let out a low curse. Was there no relief from this anxiety? How ironic, thought I, that just as Holmes arrives and things seem on an even keel at last, he disappears at the hour of greatest need!

But I reconsidered a moment. Reflecting on my friend's unique constitution and strange regimen, I decided it was quite possible he'd gone for a midnight walk. I succeeded in fooling myself in this way for a few minutes. Then two things shook me back to reality. One was Holmes' earlier urging of the need for plenty of sleep. The second thing was an event which sent me reeling with apprehension. Standing near the window I chanced to be glancing out over the grounds. Suddenly the curtains in the cottage window beneath flew open; a dull glow fanned out from the window on to the ground. In the dim light, I could see a pair of hands upon the brass signalling lamp I had seen earlier. In the next instant, there shot forth from the cottage a beam of incredible brilliance. As bright as the headlight on a locomotive engine, it cut through the night like a white knife as far as the eye could see. The next instant, all was black again, and my eyes were seeing streaks and spots in the beam's absence. Thrice more it flashed, then there was a long pause.

As soundlessly as possible, I threw up the sash, thrust out my head, and peered in the direction the beam had pointed. Winking in the distance, at the very edge of the great forest, was another light – far less brilliant, but plainly visible. When it had finished its message, the light below me shot forth again. I noticed it was made even more visible by the drizzle that caught itself in the glare. After several flashes in quick succession, the lamp ceased; the curtains were redrawn. As I turned to dash from the bedroom, I heard the slamming of the cottage door and the rush of feet on the gravel drive.

Then this explained Holmes' absence! He'd obviously seen the flashing signal from his bedroom and left the house to investigate. Disappointed that he'd left without me, I paused only long enough to snatch up my revolver before plunging down the staircase.

I left by the front door. Barefoot, I slipped silently down the terrace steps and round the drive to Farthway's cottage. The door was unlocked, and the cottage was empty. The gamekeeper's bed too, was undisturbed. Then Holmes had heeded my suspicions; he had stayed up waiting for Farthway to signal his confederates.

The odour of hot metal sent me over to the window. I flicked the lamp's lever, but it had been extinguished. A thought struck me: should I relight the lamp and set it flashing? A false signal might foil their plans.

On the other hand, any misleading on my part might endanger Lord Allistair's daughter, so I left the cottage, closing the door behind me.

Ambling down the drive in the dead of night, I felt as dejected as an orphan. Obviously, Holmes had left in pursuit of Farthway – no doubt it was his tread I'd heard in the hallway. But why had he gone alone? Why, after all the adventures we had shared, had he chosen to complete this one without me? Did he fear for my safety? Did he think me unfit? I was disappointed, and more than a little hurt, by his actions.

Since sleep was out of the question, I continued to walk the grounds. The old timbered lodge, scarcely visible, loomed up ominously through the trees. I stopped at the stables; they were silent save for the drunken snoring of Wiscomb. I entered, and walking past the stalls, heard the swish of horsetails and thumping of hooves. The animals snorted at me, but became calm when I spoke to them. There seemed to be no horses missing. So the chase, wherever it was occurring, was on foot.

I returned to the terrace where I sat on the balustrade for almost an hour. But nothing happened. There were no sounds except the usual night-time ones: the sighing of the great trees overhead, the hooting of owls and din of crickets. The rain continued to mist downwards. With a chill, I realized I was clad in nothing except my trousers and nightshirt, and longed for the warmth of bed. I made my way wearily back to my room and, after a lengthy bout of conjecture and worry, fell asleep.

I awakened with a start. A shadowy figure was kneeling at my bedside.

'Hsssst! Watson! Up man, up!'

It was Holmes, dressed in a dripping waterproof. His face bore the keen look I have long associated with impending action.

'Holmes, thank God you're safe! But where the devil were you last night, and why didn't you rouse me?'

My voice must have shown irritation, for he gripped my shoulder earnestly.

'Steady, old fellow. There's no time to explain it now. Take my word that what was done was done in your best interest –'

'Did you catch Farthway? Where –'

'There, there!' he interjected sternly. 'Now you mustn't ask, really you mustn't! Farthway is gone and I've returned safe. Now there's the end of it. We must concentrate on the matter at hand: *the demand has arrived.* The money is to be carried by you and Lord Allistair –'

'By *me*?' I said, getting groggily out of bed. 'Surely there is some mistake. No one in these parts knows of me.'

'You aren't mentioned by name – but come! Everyone's downstairs waiting.'

With that, he departed, and it was only after several minutes that the full import of his words struck me. I must confess I had not planned on being the actual courier of the money. A *confidant*, yes, but an actual *participant* in the exchange! That I hadn't counted on. Furthermore, the choice of Lord Allistair as courier also puzzled me. I could of course understand the villains wanting his wealth, but requesting his personal delivery of it was nonsensical. Upon reflection, I realize that I should have been suspicious at the outset, as events were later to prove. My heart thumping madly in anticipation, I went downstairs into the great hallway.

It was a tense scene that greeted me there. Lord Allistair, a non-smoker, was pacing wildly to and fro in the hallway puffing frantically on one of Holmes' cigarettes. His wife was seated on the leather bench, still as a wax figurine save for her hands, which trembled in her lap as she wrung them. Brundage stood with the tea tray near the door. The breakfast upon it was untouched, even unnoticed. Holmes, exuding torrents of smoke, muttered to himself as he peered through the lattice windows. For the first time I noticed his appearance. His trouser legs were torn and muddy, especially about the knees. His face was lined with tiny cuts and scratches. Obviously, his night-time chase had taken him through the woods and thickets. The fine rain beat on the windows with scarcely a sound. The silence was broken only by the hall clock, which struck the hour of seven.

Holmes approached solemnly and thrust a note into my hand. Like the first note from the kidnappers, this one was composed of letters pasted upon a notesheet. It read:

LORD ALLISTAIR – You shall carry the required sum to the oak ring. You shall be accompanied by the man who rode there with you earlier and no one else. You shall come unarmed. My manservant holds a knife to your daughter's throat. You imperil her life if you fail.

The last portion of the note was particularly ominous – made even more so by the absence of any written message from Alice.

'So there you have it,' said Holmes dryly.

Lord Allistair, called from his intense reverie by the sound of Holmes' voice, came forward to greet me.

'How are you this morning, Doctor? Eh? Well, I'm a bit shaken too, I'll admit. The note seems clear enough; we're to return to Henry's Hollow. It's strange, though, that they should have included you –'

'They've seen us together no doubt. I shall be happy to go with you and shall try to be a stabilizing influence.'

'I can't help thinking... perhaps the coded message was meant for you after all...'

'We haven't the time now to puzzle over it.'

'You must remember this, Doctor: you're not bound to go. If you'd rather not –'

'Nonsense, Lord Allistair! I am bound to go, and in more ways than one, not the least of which is my affection for you and your family. Let us be off then. You have the money I presume...'

He pointed to a pair of leather saddle pouches into which the notes had been transferred. These I slung over my shoulders after donning my heavy coat. Upon seeing us make ready, Lady Allistair sprang from her bench and clung to Lord Allistair in a fit of worry.

'Oh dear God!' she cried. 'What if I'm to lose you both?'

We comforted her as best we could. Then Holmes and I left them alone for a few minutes while we talked on the terrace outside. How different Strathcombe looked early on that drizzly morning compared to the peaceful, sun-washed retreat of two evenings earlier! The terrace stones were slick and shiny with rain. The wind stung our cheeks and ears. It was dark.

'There, I don't like the look of that!'

Holmes pointed towards the stream that ran through the meadow and willow clumps. A heavy mist was rising from the wet bottom-lands of the valley. An ominous pale grey colour, it crept towards the woods on either side.

'Where was the note found?' I asked, to change the subject.

'Tied to this very door-knocker, wrapped in oiled paper. Brundage discovered it less than an hour ago. It was evidently left during the night. Ah! I hear His Lordship coming. Quick, Watson, listen carefully to what I have to say –'

He grabbed me by the shoulders and peered intently into my face.

'You must know, dear fellow, that you are embarking upon a dangerous errand. Not only dangerous, but possibly fatal, despite all that I can, and *will* do to help you. Do you understand?'

'I do. And I accept the risk. What will you be doing in the interim?'

'I cannot say. First, because to reveal my plans to you might jeopardize everyone's safety. Secondly, though I have a few notions as to what will transpire, I am not yet fully certain. Will you trust my judgement?'

'Implicitly. As I always have.'

'Then Godspeed to you, friend. If all works well, we shall by tonight have freed Alice Allistair and caught the villains who have taken her and murdered others. Shhh! Not a word!'

Lord Allistair strode on to the terrace looking remarkably composed. But whether it was composure or contained vehemence, I couldn't say.

'Whatever the outcome, gentlemen,' he said grimly as we walked to the stables, 'the conclusion is at hand. Thank God for that at least.'

Wiscomb had our mounts ready. They pawed the gravel as he held the reins. I flung the pouches over the flanks of Lord Allistair's horse, and mounted my own. Although none of the staff save Brundage and his wife were aware of the ransom demand, Wiscomb could sense the import of the moment.

'God bless you, sir,' he said softly as he helped Lord Allistair into his saddle.

'Thank you, Wiscomb. You are to go to the house now and remain there; Brundage has strict instructions for everyone, Farthway included.'

'Farthway, sir? Farthway has gone.'

Lord Allistair turned sharply in disbelief.

'Gone! Gone where?'

'I don't know, sir. He's not in his quarters.'

I glared at Holmes and shook my head slightly. This certainly was not an auspicious beginning. But Holmes met my stern glance with a blank, resigned expression.

'Well, we shan't worry over him,' said His Lordship, and we started off down the drive together. As we headed towards the mist in the valley, I looked back at Holmes, who raised his hand in farewell.

It is at this point that the memories of the horrific occurrences at Henry's Hollow cause my pen to shake, my brow to grow damp. It is many, many years later that I write these words, and though the recollections of the trial should have faded and dimmed with time, yet they seem in some perverse way to grow more vivid.

We made our way into the drifting mist. As we ascended the opposite side of the valley, it seemed to cling and follow us into the forest. It swirled amongst the tree trunks. It crawled and floated up the slopes; it flowed languidly down into the dells and hollows of the woods.

If the forest seemed gloomy on our previous trip, it was fearsome now. The nearest trees were easily seen – the oaks with their rich brown bark, the beeches with their blue-grey metallic sheen – but after only a few yards, even the most massive of the trunks were faint. Beyond them lay a pale grey curtain that was impenetrable.

As unnerving as the mist was the utter silence of the woods. No jays shrieked and cackled. No songbirds trilled. The only sounds were the thump of hooves and faint patter of rain upon the leaves.

After twenty minutes we paused while Lord Allistair examined the path.

'It's much more difficult to find one's way in the fog,' said he. 'In normal daylight I have landmarks enough to guide me – but now it's a labyrinth. Pray to God we're on the right path and haven't missed a turn. What a tragedy to lose my daughter because we cannot find the place!'

'No need to worry yet, Lord Allistair. See that curious bent tree there? I remember that from the day before yesterday – it came just before you showed me the Keep from a small clearing –'

'Yes, I do remember it. You've a keen eye, Doctor. Henry's Hollow lies not far ahead.'

After several moments (it seemed like hours) we stopped on the path. Through the mist, I could barely recognize the strange symmetry of the oak ring some yards ahead. We waited for a shout, a whistle. None came. Proceeding still further, going as slowly as possible, we at last arrived at the rim of oaks. Peering down, one could see only the uppermost branches of the trees in the hollow, for they were above the low-lying mist. Beneath us the grey earth fell gently away into the swirling vapour. There came to my ears a faint rustling sound.

'Stand to!' a voice called.

Not twenty feet away, a shadowy hooded figure emerged from behind a trunk and approached us.

'Don't move,' the figure cautioned, and strode catlike by us back to the trail over which we had passed and disappeared.

This behaviour only served to heighten my anxiety. But after a few minutes, I divined the reason for it. I turned my head to Lord Allistair and whispered.

'He's listening on the path to be sure there are no others.'

He nodded in agreement. How fortunate that we had obeyed the instructions! Once again, I couldn't help but wonder at the careful planning and painstaking execution of the diabolical plot. There was certainly, at the centre of this evil web, a man of monstrous cunning and deliberation.

The figure returned and strode silently round us. He was dressed in black from head to toe and carried a pistol. The hood covered his entire head, and as can be imagined, increased the chimerical quality of his appearance.

'Open your coats.'

We obeyed, and the figure seemed satisfied that we were unarmed. He beckoned us to follow him and led us down into the hollow. As we guided our mounts down the slope, the air grew heavy with the thick, dank smell of matted vegetation and wet earth. There was another odour, very faint, that was almost musky. Our guide stepped behind a tree and emerged carrying a lantern, which he held aloft as he walked before us. The mist formed a delicate halo round the lamp, which I assumed was being used as a signal since it was utterly useless to guide us.

We passed the chimney tree which marked the approximate centre of the hollow. We were then proceeding to the far end of it – the portion that Lord Allistair had not shown me.

We proceeded one behind the other along a faint track that wound between the trees. As we made a turn in this path, a breeze coming from the far end of the hollow sprang up and smote us head on.

Our horses stopped in their tracks.

There were a few seconds of silence. Then Lord Allistair's horse snorted twice, the thick streams of vapour shooting from its nostrils. It whinnied sharply, its head bobbing up and down. My horse stretched its neck forward and brought its nose up. It grunted, stamped its feet, and began to back up. The breeze freshened still more, and Lord Allistair's horse wheeled and bucked. He fought to stay in the saddle, and deftly brought the animal towards me. It rolled its eyes so that the whites showed.

Alarmed, our guide ran back to us and, clutching at the horse's bridle, gave the order to dismount. Puzzled, Lord Allistair complied, and I followed. As instructed, we tied the animals together to a small tree and proceeded on foot, Lord Allistair carrying the saddle pouches. I looked back to see them huddled together, flank to flank. They stamped their feet and pawed the earth, and their ears pointed in our direction, turning and twitching.

I need not relate the effect of this incident upon me. Suffice it to say that the previous incidents of this sort of behaviour on the part of the horses and dogs gave me an inkling of what could be waiting for us at the far end of the hollow. My knees turned weak, and I felt a tingling in my limbs. So as not to alarm my companion, I managed to control the terror that was beginning to well up inside of me.

We came at last to the far end of Henry's Hollow. I heard the sound of falling water. During my initial visit to the place, I assumed that it was elliptical in shape and similar on all sides. I was in error, however, because although roughly the shape I had imagined, the far side of the hollow was not a sloping, dish-shaped depression but a deep gorge, bounded by a perpendicular cliff of layered limestone.

This precipice rose some thirty feet, and was topped by an oak ridge as was the rest of the rim. Upon reaching this sheer wall, we turned to the left and descended a steep path that led us to a small clearing in the shadow of the cliff. From the rocky wall spurted a miniature cascade, the sound of which had been audible for some distance. The clearing was covered with ferns and moss. I imagined the sun never shone in this place, so tucked away was it in the dankest, gloomiest part of the hollow. At the far end of the clearing I saw a glow from a campfire. In all probability, this place was the source of the smoke I'd detected earlier. The mist in the clearing was as thick as the heaviest London fog. From the splashing sound of water, I surmised that the tiny waterfall fed a pool at the base of the cliff. From this pool the mist seemed to waft up in thick clouds.

We made our way into the clearing. After a few steps, I could see the campfire. Stretched out next to it was a pair of shiny boots – the firelight flickered off them. As the wraith-like cloud of mist was borne away, I could see the man who lounged by the firelight. The wide-brimmed hat, drooping moustache, dark complexion and earrings were unmistakable. It was the gypsy who'd followed us the day of our arrival. We drew still closer, and the dark-shrouded figure who had guided us to the dismal lair stepped close to the seated gypsy and whispered into his ear. The gypsy, in turn, whispered back.

'Bring the money forward,' said the hooded figure in a low, measured monotone. The two men examined the contents of the pouch. The several minutes. Although they did not count all of it, they seemed satisfied that the ransom was complete.

'My daughter!' shouted Lord Allistair. I could see the perspiration on his brow — the throbbing arteries of his neck and forehead. He had clearly waited long enough. 'Where is my daughter?'

The gypsy drew a revolver from his loose coat and pointed it at Lord Allistair's breast. His companion did the same, and pointed his gun at me. The gypsy made a sign, and his companion commenced speaking.

'Your daughter is safe. You shall see her for a few minutes when I have her brought forward. Now listen carefully to what I have to say: you have apparently kept your word. You have come as instructed with the required amount of money. That is good. You shall see in a few seconds that we have kept our word: your daughter is safe. Not only is she safe, but she has not been harmed in any way.

'But there remains for you, Lord Allistair, one final task which you must accomplish before we release your daughter to you. Failure to complete this task will result in her death —'

'What is it — in the name of Heaven! And why was I not advised of this remaining duty earlier?'

The figure paused and, in an explanatory tone, continued.

'In order to secure our safe passage from this country, we need additional hostages.'

'I refuse.'

The gypsy beckoned to his companion, who bent over close to receive more instructions. I thought it odd that the gypsy, obviously the leader of the two, did no talking. The possibility struck me though, that there could be a language problem. In any event, the hooded figure continued as spokesman.

'If you refuse, we cannot guarantee the safety of your daughter. You must know that we will keep the hostages only long enough to escape.

They will be released unharmed shortly thereafter.'

'How can I be assured of this?'

'You must trust us to keep our word, as we have done thus far. Look here...'

With this, he cried out in a language I had never heard before – nor since, for that matter. Almost immediately, two dim figures appeared in the mist behind the fire. All we could see of them was their silhouettes, but one appeared to be of medium height, the other short and crooked.

'Come forward slowly,' said the hooded figure, and Lord Allistair and I approached the two men and the fire. After a few steps, it was apparent that the pool fed by the waterfall lay directly behind the campfire. The two figures were standing on the opposite bank.

'Father!' cried an anguished voice, and at the same instant there strode into the firelight a spectacle that I shall never forget. I remembered the portraits of Alice Allistair; there was one at the Bayswater residence, and another at Strathcombe. She was stunning in her loveliness – yet the sad creature that stood waving in the mist before us bore little if any resemblance to her pictures. Her features drawn as if in incredible pain and anguish, she appeared to have been crying for weeks on end. Her bosom heaved and shook, and she had the captured, frightened expression on her face that I had observed before only on the faces of the inmates of prisons and asylums. One glance at her told me of the torture and confinement she had endured these two months, yet I was certain it was even far worse than I had imagined. Lord Allistair dropped to his knees with a low cry.

'Oh Father –' she began, but was cut short by the other figure that leapt forward from the grey fog. It was remarkable for its ugliness. He was a hunchbacked Malay – no doubt the same one Sampson had mentioned. His appearance was hideous: a thick, greasy face, an ugly, twisted gash for a mouth, a nose like a blob of glazier's putty. The whole face was enclosed in skin the colour of boot leather, and topped by a muslin turban, stained with grease and dirt. The small eyes danced in his gnomelike head. The stunted arms twitched, and the thick lips trembled in excited babbling.

But these observations were secondary. The object that held our attention was clutched in the wretch's right fist, and directed at the throat of the lovely girl. It was a dagger, and one glance at its blade, glinting in the firelight, was enough. Recalling the ghastly wounds inflicted upon Raymond Jenard, I was convinced that but a few strokes of this weapon were capable of rending flesh in the most gruesome manner. The blade was a foot long, and wound its way to and fro from hilt to tip in a zig-zag fashion, like the path of a crawling snake. I heard a gasp from Lord Allistair, and turned to see him leap forward towards his captive daughter.

'Halt! No further!' shouted the gypsy, bringing his revolver up and cocking the hammer as he did so.

Lord Allistair paused, then drew back. The gypsy glanced at me for an instant, then turned away. But it was too late, he had cried out, and in perfect English. Furthermore, the voice was faintly familiar. I had heard it before – somewhere.

'Are you all right, Alice?'

'Yes, Father. Oh, thank Heaven you've come! I –' but the poor girl, choked with sobs, was unable to continue.

Heartened by the appearance of his daughter, Lord Allistair considered for a moment, then spoke.

'Who are the hostages?'

The hooded figure pointed in my direction.

'This man, and the man who arrived yesterday,' said he.

'I cannot do this. These men are my guests. As a gentleman I cannot –'

'For God's sake man, *do it*!' I shouted. 'They want the two of us only to make certain a general alarm isn't raised until they're safely away. Is this not so?'

Both men nodded.

Lord Allistair looked at his weeping daughter, then at me.

'You must understand, Doctor, how torn I am —'

'Nonsense! Go! Fetch him at once! You must hurry — we've come this far — there's no stopping now. They have kept their word; therefore I don't fear for myself. Now there's the end of it: you must be off!'

He turned towards the kidnappers.

'How shall Alice be returned to me?'

'One of us will follow you back to the house with her,' said the hooded figure in a carefully rehearsed speech, 'we shall be far behind you, and hidden. When we see that the second hostage is well upon his way here, we shall release your daughter in the vicinity of the house. She will find her way home from there.'

'Very well,' said Lord Allistair after some reflection.

'But mind,' continued the masked man, 'any divergence from the pre-arranged plan will spell her death.'

'This is most repugnant to me,' said Lord Allistair. 'But I see I have little choice in the matter.'

'I shall guide you to your horse. But first, I must fasten your companion to the tree with these.'

While the gypsy held his pistol on Lord Allistair, the other approached, carrying a pair of heavy iron shackles of the type used on prison ships. Realizing total co-operation was the only sensible course, I complied readily as he bade me sit on the ground, my back against a small beech tree. He then drew my arms behind me round the tree and shackled my wrists together. Being bound in this fashion made me most uncomfortable in many ways. However, sensing that my predicament was most painful to Lord Allistair, I avoided his glance and pretended to make light of the matter as he left the clearing, led by the hooded guide.

Just before they disappeared into the grey vapour, he turned and looked at his daughter.

'Never fear, dearest,' he said hoarsely, 'all will be well.'

And then, with a glance at me, added, 'I am terribly sorry, Doctor... you must –'

'Nonsense,' I quipped, as jovially as possible, 'the sooner you complete your errand, the sooner we're together again. Now off you go!'

They departed, and a short while later the guide returned. After an exchange of nods with the gypsy, he led Alice Allistair from the clearing. I noticed as they passed me that she was sobbing softly, and that her hands were bound behind her. She whirled in an instant, her eyes fixed upon me with a look of guilt, and dread. She cried out:

'Oh, Doctor Watson! I tried–'

But she could not finish; a hand was clapped over her face, and she was half-led, half-dragged, from the clearing. Enraged, I swore an oath, straining at my bonds. But it was useless. Confined as I was, I could not even rise to my feet. Ominous thoughts raced through my brain. Then the coded message *was* sent by Alice Allistair, and it *was* meant for me! I remembered Holmes' casual dismissal of the message, and cursed him under my breath. How could he have been so careless, so foolish? But I was interrupted from these thoughts by a peal of laughter. Turning my head, I saw that an enormous change had overcome the gypsy.

No longer lounging idly by the fire, he was convulsed with laughter. The laughter was not normal. It was explosive – maniacal. He shrieked, he giggled, he sobbed with laughter. He lolled on the ground; his arms and legs twitched.

The hunchback, seeing this fit overtake his master, ran from the clearing and returned instantly, bearing a tin cup. The gypsy gulped down its contents, which I assumed to be spirits of some sort, and grew calmer. He stood up, paced about, and mopped his brow with a colourful handkerchief. Then he approached and, stopping not ten feet away, leaned towards me.

'You must excuse the outburst, Doctor Watson, but I've waited so long...'

An icy chill pierced my chest at these words. The voice caught, and stayed in my ears. It was a voice I knew, and was associated with unpleasantness.

The gypsy drew still nearer.

'You know my voice? Come, come, Doctor, can't you recall it? I am sure your clever friend Sherlock Holmes would remember in an instant...'

But he was taken again by a fit of laughter. Wailing, he caught at his side until it subsided. As he made a tremendous effort to control himself, I observed the unmistakable symptoms: the trembling in the extremities, the perspiring, the wild-eyed stare, the raving, convulsive laughter. It was quite apparent: *the man was mad.*

'Who am I, Doctor Watson? Eh? I see by your puzzled look that you don't recollect. Do you need some help?'

With this, he drew up to me and, in an instant, had torn off the gypsy disguise. What I saw caused things to weave and whirl about, then grow dim. I was speechless with awe: the face looking into mine had come forth from the grave.

'Impossible!' I gasped. 'You are dead!'

Again, a change came over the man. The raving maniac was replaced by the cold, calculating machine I had so often observed in earlier times.

'No, Doctor,' he said in a voice that was barely audible, 'no, I am not dead. Though people have thought so for some time.'

I listened spellbound, the terror growing in me.

'My presumed death made my escape easier,' he went on soothingly, 'and still protects me. The only reason I shall reveal all to you is because I have the assurance – nay the *certainty* – that neither you nor Sherlock Holmes will live to see tomorrow's sun.'

Eleven

Cp

THE BEAST IN HENRY'S HOLLOW

'Stapleton! So you are the villain behind this nefarious scheme!'

'Ah, but you may as well know my name: Rodger Baskerville! Though I have travelled under many different guises, that is my true name. And Baskerville Hall my true residence!'

'That is debatable, to say the least.'

He struck me across the face. Then, as if alarmed by his lack of self-control, he caught his fist up and held it to his breast. He rocked to and fro on his haunches, his head flung back, eyes half-closed.

'I am excitable lately,' he groaned. 'The strain, the strain has been *intolerable*. If you knew of the planning, the waiting... Ah! But it shall be over soon. Oh, Doctor Watson! Although I have reason to despise you and your foul friend, I admit that the death you are to suffer is a *horrid* one!'

A fluid panic overtook me and turned my limbs to water. My hair stood on end.

'What's this? Do I detect, the look of fear upon your face, eh?'

He rolled his head backwards and, staring straight up into the grey sky, shrieked with laughter.

'Oh this is delicious. Truly delicious! Already the long wait is well worth it.'

The fit seized him again, and he was convulsed. Finally, he managed to calm himself, and proceeded in the soft, soothing voice that so characterized the Stapleton of my acquaintance.

'I trust you are impressed with the planning and execution of this venture – you should be. It is the product of intense thought and firm discipline. You should know at the outset, Doctor Watson, that I have also planned your death. Your death, and the death of Sherlock Holmes. In a sense I regret killing you, since you are obviously a dupe and a simpleton, and kept by our "friend" only because you are a toy to feed his pride. However, Sherlock Holmes has wronged me deeply, and must be punished. Part of his punishment is death, but the other part–'

And here he paused for emphasis.

'– is watching *you* die before him.'

'You beast!' I cried. 'You are mad!'

'*Stop it!* Stop it, Doctor!' he screamed. 'Now we'll have no more of such talk, do you hear?'

He stared down at me in a fit of rage. I remained silent, and after another pause, he continued in a low voice.

'I am excitable, true. But who wouldn't be as he sees the genius of his plan unfolding? Who wouldn't be agitated as the hour of sweet revenge draws closer?'

He paused to light a cigarette. The hollow was entirely silent save for the splashing of the tiny waterfall behind me.

'Ah, I bask in the euphoria of it! At this very moment Sherlock Holmes, supposedly the finest mind in Europe, gropes his way through the fog, unaware that he comes to meet his death! And as the lamb strays towards the wolf, I shall tell you a story. Would you like that?

Yes, of course you would! We have almost an hour, and no doubt you are anxious to hear of my brilliant evasion from the Grimpen mire...'

It is a mark of the madman to indulge in fantasies and grandiose delusions. So Baskerville regarded his every thought and action as divinely inspired. But I noticed his eyes wander and glaze slightly as he fell into his narrative. The liquor was taking effect – aided, no doubt, by the nervous exhaustion that was clearly overtaking him. It is ennervating to rave and shriek. Also, now that the battle was won, the passion that had kept him going at fever pitch for the past weeks was quickly fading. My only hope of escape, however faint, was to keep him talking – to feed his delusions. In this way, I hoped, he would be enfeebled by the time Holmes arrived. What would happen then was in the hands of fate.

'Yes, I'd be delighted to hear your story. And pray, don't leave out a word. I must admit you've won, Baskerville. You are a devilishly clever chap –'

'Indeed I am! And so, let's have no more talk of...'

He looked furtively sideways and continued in a whisper.

'... *madness*...'

'It was sheer genius the way you eluded capture on the moors. Everyone thought you'd perished in the mire –'

'Idiot! Did it never occur to you that I had an escape route planned well beforehand? Hah! Holmes was fortunate enough to see through my little scheme, but even he was too muddle-headed to foresee the possibility that I had prepared for everything. Well! As to what happened –'

Drawing yet closer, he sat cross-legged, facing me, on the dank earth – the mist swirling in spirals about him. A languid expression on his face, he began his tale. Seeing that he sat nearby, I made one supreme effort to break free my shackles with the hope of swinging my arm round and catching him on the temple with the chain.

'Don't waste your energy, Doctor. It's useless, I assure you. Those chains can hold a Shire horse – now, ah yes, the flight from the moor...'

'We found Sir Henry's boot at the edge of the path. We assumed you dropped it in flight, then sank into the bog –'

'You assumed that because I *wished* you to assume it; I *planned* for it. When I heard the pistol shots through the fog, I knew the hound was dead and my plan had been discovered. I left my house and ran to the old tin mine at the centre of the bog, dropping the boot on the way deliberately. Once at the mine, however, I picked up a haversack I had hidden there for just such an eventuality – for as loutish as your friend Sherlock Holmes is, I had respect for his tenacity.'

'How decent of you –' I interjected sarcastically, then winced in expectation of another blow. But engrossed in the tale that extolled his prowess, he ignored my comment.

'The haversack contained a blanket and tins of food, enough for several days. Now the brilliance of my planning, Doctor Watson, was in the forging of *another path*, unknown even to my wife, which led from the tin mine out on to the moor in the opposite direction. Had your friend been more careful, less flushed with his apparent success, he would have noticed it. But as fate would have it, he did not, and assumed I was dead.

'By the time you arrived at the abandoned mine, I was miles away. Tramping the countryside by night and sleeping in rocky crevices during the day, I made good progress. On the third day, I took a chance and entered a small village. I bought a newspaper and was delighted to discover that I was dead. You've no idea, Doctor Watson, how easy it is to get away when it's widely supposed that you are lying at the bottom of a bog. I made my way northward, heading for Yorkshire since I know that country well. But on the way I entered the valley of the Severn, and there I fell in with old King Zoltan and his gypsy tribe. They were a generous people, and asked no questions. I adopted their dress and habits, and joined their caravan as it wound its way through the hillsides and forests. Having been raised in Costa Rica and the son of a native mother, I was naturally congenial to their fiery temperament and romantic ways. King Zoltan adopted me as his son, and so my disguise was complete; my escape from England assured.'

The mist was thinning, and more of the clearing was now visible. At its far end, beyond the shallow pool, was a wall of rock. In this wall was a small cave, the entrance of which was a dark crevice. From this narrow fissure I saw the Malay emerge. He hobbled from it on his stunted legs and made his way to the fire, which he built up. This task completed, he scurried back to the burrow in the cliffside, gathering the folds of his filthy robe about him. I watched as Baskerville stretched his legs, and, leaning casually back on one elbow, continued.

'Perhaps you already know that this ring of oaks, and the hollow within, is a favourite stopping place for gypsies. Into this very place our caravan entered in the early winter of '89, just a few weeks after my flight from the moors. We camped here for the winter, living off the game we shot or captured in these forests. During our stay we frequently saw shooting parties as they ventured forth from Strathcombe. I was impressed with the wealth of the estate. When I heard that the owner was none other than Peter Allistair, I was shocked to the core, and overjoyed too, for I had long sought to repay him for his insolence —'

'Lord Allistair? What did —'

'Never mind,' said Baskerville with a wave of the wrist, 'it happened long ago, before even the hound, but I could never forgive him for ruining me. I had planned to kill him some dark night, but realized the risk was great, and the punishment too swift…'

I sadly recalled the ten weeks of anguish suffered by Lord Allistair, and was only too well aware of the effectiveness of Baskerville's torture. But what had Lord Allistair done to deserve this? Clearly it was not in his character deliberately to wrong any man. My thoughts were interrupted as the man before me continued his gruesome tale.

'But as fate would have it, I had no time for vengeance. In the spring, the old king died. His people carried the body to the bottom of one of these grisly caves and buried him. When I learned that the band was to head south, I decided to depart. With a purse full of gold, a gift from King Zoltan, I continued northwards until I came to Liverpool. There I signed on a ship bound for America.

'It was during the voyage to America, Doctor Watson, that the memories of my frustration crept to the foreground. For weeks, I could think of nothing save the humiliating defeat I suffered at the hands of Sherlock Holmes. Such a brilliant plan, and foiled by an amateur meddler! It was then that the seed of my hatred germinated and began to grow. It grew with each passing day. And as weeks flowed into months, it became –'

'A passion,' I interjected. He glanced at me nervously.

'You could call it that,' he admitted, 'and why not! What normal man, deprived of his rightful inheritance after months of careful planning, wouldn't seek revenge? However, I knew it was best to stay out of England for several years to give added credence to my death, and to let events fade into the past.

'After landing in America I worked my way across that continent, finally arriving in San Francisco. There I signed aboard a Russian sealer, and spent the next fifteen months in the Bering Sea. In that frozen waste, there was little to think about save my hatred for Sherlock Holmes and the revenge I sought. My next ship took me to Santiago, where I met the man who is now carrying Alice Allistair to –'

His tale was interrupted by a sound. It came from the crevice in the rock wall. It was a sound I had never heard before, and it froze the very blood in my veins. It was an animal sound, and began in a series of snuffling grunts, then rose to a deep growl. Finally, it resolved itself into a piercing squeal that echoed off the craggy walls of the ravine in hideous cacphony.

'Good God!'

Looking back, I can scarcely remember saying those words, for my entire soul was seized with a fear so intense that speech was difficult, and thinking almost impossible. The memories swam in my tormented mind: the mutilated body of Captain McGuinness – the gory remains of Compson –

I struggled frantically to escape the bonds. I lunged my body forward a half-dozen times until my limbs ached, my wrists bled. My heart thumped madly, so that my entire chest shook. My stomach had the formless, quivering sensation that comes only with the deepest dread.

'There, there, Doctor Watson! You'll injure yourself! You *shall* be injured, I can assure you,' he added darkly, 'but all in good time. Now you must sit and listen to my story – there's a good chap. Wangi!'

The heathen shuffled from the mouth of the cave and approached. He held a strange object in his hand. It was a wooden rod with an iron hook fixed to its end. I recognized the object: it was a mahout's goad, used to drive elephant. The hook was red at the tip.

'So our friend is misbehaving? He is impatient, eh, Wangi?'

The wretch grinned and babbled, revealing a loathsome mouth of broken and stained teeth. He struck the goad against the ground repeatedly, convulsed with guttural laughter.

'Ah, he is hungry, no doubt! Here Wangi – see how our poor hostage trembles in every limb. No, Doctor, the beast is entirely captive until we release it. He shan't emerge from his lair until Mr Holmes arrives to take his place beside you...'

The misshapen servant hobbled back into the cave. Almost immediately there came a dull thumping sound, and then another animal scream – this one yet longer and louder than the previous one. Though entirely strange (and therefore, all the more terrifying) to my ears, it resembled elements of other animal sounds: the snuffling which began the eerie cries resembled the snorting of a horse; the growling was deep and pervasive, like that of a tiger. The grotesque squeal that terminated the cry resembled the sound a pig makes as its throat is cut. It was made still more fearsome by the fact that it issued from a tunnel of rock, which amplified it – then resounded from the cliff walls in a shattering cadence.

As the sound faded from the hollow, so my sight and senses drifted away. I was propelled into a sea of swirling darkness.

In my swoon, which was short-lived, I dreamed I was drowning. This was no doubt due to the fact that, upon waking, I could scarcely breathe for all the spirits Baskerville had poured down my throat in efforts to revive his victim. I gagged and choked on the harsh rum. Nevertheless, it brought me round.

'There now, Doctor. Your friend approaches and time grows short. How am I to complete my marvellous tale if you won't stay awake?'

I nodded my head in weak resignation and he continued.

'It was early in '93 when I met Jones in Santiago. He had jumped ship from the *Meeradler*, a Prussian nitrate barque, and they were scouring the docks for him. Accustomed to pursuit, I helped him elude the officers. We struck up an immediate friendship, and consequently decided to sign on the *Dunmore* bound for Bombay. As I have mentioned previously, Doctor Watson, my desire for revenge was beginning to occupy a large portion of my thoughts. The long journey to India was no exception. It was my original plan to sail from India aboard a ship bound for London. Once in port, I could easily arrange a way to kill your friend and disappear, as I had so successfully done before. But as fate would have it, another opportunity presented itself in Bombay in the person of Alice Allistair, who was on a holiday there – no doubt you know all this – with her companion. Quite naturally, the local newspapers reserved ample space on their pages for coverage of her visit to Delhi and Bombay. It was thus through the newspapers, and gossip at fashionable tea rooms, that Jones and I were kept abreast of her every appointment and destination.

'I related to Jones my exploits with Zoltan's gypsy band, and my first-hand knowledge of the Allistair fortune. Together, we planned a daring and brilliant abduction of the Allistair girl which you no doubt read about –'

'All England read about it. It has been one of the most infamous crimes in recent years.'

'As I stated previously, I had a personal reason for wanting to abduct this particular girl: Peter Allistair had wronged me long ago. And so, by kidnapping his daughter, I could extract not only a fortune from him… but pain as well…'

Here he lost himself in a maniacal chuckle, and I reflected upon Lord Allistair's earlier suspicion that the terrible suffering inflicted upon him and his wife was deliberate and personal.

'What has he done to you?' I cried. 'What could he have possibly done that would warrant such atrocious behaviour on your part?'

'That does not concern you. Suffice it to say that he deserved punishment. The look upon his face today tells me he has indeed suffered – and so my rewards are doubled. But time grows short; I'll return to my narrative. We decoyed Miss Allistair's companion, a certain Miss Haskins, on a false errand. With her disposed of temporarily, we then thrust the lady into a palanquin and then, several streets later, into a delivery cart. The cleverness of the plan lay in remaining in the city, rather than attempting cross-country flight. We hid in a ramshackle working-class section of the city, hard by the Fort. Typically, the city and environs swarmed with British troops and Sepoys. Typically again, they looked everywhere but near the Fort! There we remained safe for over a week until the uproar subsided.

'Here also, Doctor, I may as well make a confession: genius that I am, I had miscalculated the effect of Lady Alice's abduction upon the military and populace at large. Obviously, it makes no sense to take a hostage in India for ransoming in Britain. It was my *original* intention to obtain the ransom money in India through an intermediary. In this way, of course, the whole business would have been completed in a matter of days.'

'You've no idea,' I interjected, 'the misery you've caused! You may kill me, perhaps even Sherlock Holmes as well, but I swear to you – you shall pay for all you've done!'

'That could not be helped. And it's *you*, my friend, who shall pay, not I. In a matter of hours, Jones and I shall be on our way to Liverpool, where we'll catch a ship for Rio de Janeiro, there to spend the remainder of our lives in luxury…'

'And Wangi?'

'As for our humpbacked friend, he has served us well. However, he is noticeable, to say the least. Very much so. His presence would hamper our leaving…'

He placed his hand on the pistol butt that projected from his belt.

'I'm afraid this is poor Wangi's last day on earth – ah! To warn him is useless – he speaks no English, as you've noticed. Now, to return to our adventures…'

I received his plan with incredulity. Obviously the unfortunate wretch, misshapen and heathen though he was, had been of enormous help, yet he was to be killed and cast aside without remorse.

The progression of his insanity had clearly made Baskerville a beast. Where there had been intelligence, there was now only animal cunning. Always a cold man, even the last vestiges of civilized behaviour had now fallen away, leaving a stark, vicious brute who killed as mechanically as a viper.

'Our miscalculation made one thing clear: we could not hope to ransom the lady in India. Bombay had been sealed as tight as a drum, which was easy, considering it is situated on an island. Troops were everywhere – they swarmed in the streets and on the roads; trains and ships were searched; all bridges were watched; the alarm had been raised.

'Now, as you may have heard, the abductors were decribed as natives: Jones and I deliberately disguised ourselves as Hindis. With the teaming millions of these fellows overflowing the city and countryside, and not a hair's difference between them, it's no wonder the authorities were frustrated. But as a pair of English journeymen who ambled about Bombay, we attracted no notice whatsoever. Lady Alice remained humanely, but safely, confined in our quarters.

'When we realized that it was necessary to obtain the ransom outside the country, the problem of exit presented itself. As I mentioned, to attempt to smuggle Lady Alice from the port of Bombay was out of the question. However, we observed in the course of our many ramblings through the city that trains to the interior and eastern ports weren't carefully inspected. It was a simple matter therefore, to obtain tickets for the two of us to Madras, with provision for the carriage of a large ship's trunk –'

'Monsters!' I cried. 'To imprison her –'

'Quite so, Doctor. It was distasteful. I can assure you, though, we had no other option. Trapped as we were in Bombay, surrounded by troops and search parties, we had only three choices. The first was to free the girl and flee, in which case she could describe and identify us. This course of action was suicidal. The second option was to flee with the girl to another port city, as we did. The third choice was to kill her. This was most odious; besides which, it made ransoming impossible. So we selected the second alternative. Lady Alice was drugged to a deep sleep and placed in the trunk, carefully altered to allow for ventilation. This was the only instance we were obliged to resort to the use of drugs. As you saw for yourself, she has been well treated these twelve weeks.'

He paused for another smoke. So entranced was I at this casual narration of horrendous deeds that, for the moment at least, I forgot my plight and the strange cries from the cavern.

'Our darkest moment was the loading of the trunk on to the baggage carriage. If they'd opened it, we'd have hanged for sure. But our appearance as well-to-do British citizens, and a handsome sum handed to the baggage clerk, was enough and we were off. The journey to Madras takes just over four and twenty hours. We rocked over the rails, and the countryside shot past us: great oceans of red earth dotted with scrub and thorn trees, bullock carts, buffalo, and camels. And mostly, of course, hordes of brown men wrapped in robes, with wizened faces and bony limbs.

'Once arrived in that steamy port city, we again found humble lodgings and set the young lady free from her confinement. She had weathered the journey extremely well and recovered almost immediately, except of course, for the long bouts of weeping... The next few days were spent along the waterfront searching for a vessel bound for London. We found none, and were about to set off for Calcutta, when we spotted an Arab dhow making her way towards the quay. She was a coastal trader – one of thousands in the Indian Ocean. They roam about, taking on and discharging crew and cargo as they bounce from port to port along the coastlines of Africa and Asia.

'She came up to the quay and made fast. Larger than most dhow coasters, her decks were piled high with cargo: hides, copra, spices, hemp, coconuts. Her crew came from every corner of the globe: Arabs, Malays, Negroes, Hindis, Chinese. We knew that these men, if such they could be called, were a desperate lot. For the right price, they would do our bidding and ask no questions.

'The captain was a fierce Arab named Harun Sarouk. He sat on the sun-drenched deck while his heathen crew tended the huge sail. He puffed on his hookah, cross-legged on a pile of hemp while his humpbacked Malay servant, the same one who's in the cavern yonder, fanned him with a palm frond. The boat had come from Zanzibar by way of Ceylon. It would depart in two days for Batavia. Sarouk would take us, and our passenger, if we paid him well.

'We set sail two nights later, and the trade winds took us eastward with great speed. After six days, we stopped at Kutaradja, at the head of the island of Sumatra, for the natives there had a wondrous animal that they'd captured in the jungle...'

He let his voice trail off to a whisper, and reclined with a smirk upon his face. My eyes moved to the fissure in the rock. It was dark and silent.

'... a most wondrous and horrifying monster: a *giant rat*!'

Again, I was recalled to horror, and my face became damp with perspiration; my limbs shook.

'It sounds incredible, does it not?' he taunted me in a soft voice, 'yet it is real, and, as you may have seen, quite capable of gnawing a man to death...'

Once again, I made a frantic attempt to break free. All my efforts were futile and only revealed that I had strained my muscles and done great damage to the scar tissue of my old bullet wound. The deep throbbing in my shoulder told me that it would never be the same.

However, since I had not long to live, what did it matter? Baskerville watched my struggles idly. He reached for a long stick and, turning on his elbow, poked the dying fire. He turned back to me with a leer.

'You thought the hound fierce? You were afraid of it? Then I must tell you, Doctor, that compared with the creature you will see emerge from that cavern, the hound was a toy, a *play thing*!' He began to quake in his passion, but was interrupted by Wangi, who had emerged from the burrow and sat squatting at the edge of the clearing.

'Hssst!'

Baskerville turned towards the savage, who drew his grotesque dagger from the folds of his robe. The warning sound came again from between his thick, gnarled lips, and he leaned forward, pointing upwards.

I heard behind me, and to my left, the faint sound of rustling leaves. A twig snapped, and the measured cadence of footfalls came to my ears. The Malay weaved in a crouch, holding his dagger in an upraised fist. But the greater change came over Baskerville, who visibly shook with anticipation. The strain was showing. Eyes bulging, he snatched the pistol from his belt and drew back the hammer. The footfalls grew nearer. I strained to turn my head, but try as I might, I was unable to look behind me at the approaching figure.

'Fly, Holmes! Fly!' I shouted at the top of my lungs. 'He means to kill us both!'

In a rage, Baskerville pointed his weapon at my breast. I closed my eyes, mumbling a snatch of prayer. But the bullet never came. When I opened my eyes, I saw that he had resumed his former stance: eyes staring madly into the mist in the direction of the footsteps, pistol held in both his trembling hands.

'Come forward, Sherlock Holmes!' he shouted triumphantly. 'Come! Come join your friend...'

The sounds grew closer, and at last I glimpsed the familiar slender figure through the swirling grey vapour. The silhouette advanced slowly, with incredible composure and deliberation. The sight filled me with remorse. I was aware, as Holmes surely must have been, of the risks involved with his profession. But to see him brought low by such a beast as Baskerville – it was too poignant. The figure halted, and I heard the calm voice ring out.

'I shall go no further until my friend is released.'

'Then, Mr Holmes, you shall die where you stand,' said Baskerville in a quavering voice, 'and your friend shall die slowly...'

After a pause, Holmes advanced into the clearing.

'Dammit, man, have you no sense! Turn and fly, I beg you!' I shouted, my voice hoarse with the effort. 'There's no saving me, Holmes, and Miss Alice is delivered safe. Turn and be off!'

'If you fly,' warned Baskerville, 'Alice Allistair shall die a lingering and lonely death. Mark my word! She is by now tightly bound in the bottom of Strathcombe's lime kiln. She is helpless and silent, I can assure you. If you do not comply, her parents shall never learn of her whereabouts. However, if you accompany us as hostages, we shall leave instructions here to effect her rescue. What say you, Mr Holmes? Do your friends live... or die?'

Before I could again cry out a warning to my companion, I saw from the corner of my eye a pair of dusky hands whirling about. Barely half an instant later, I felt the suffocating sensation of a heavy cloth fastened tightly about my lower face. So intent was I in watching Holmes' approach, I'd failed to notice Wangi sneaking round behind me. In a flash, I was silenced. Then it occurred to me that Holmes must have arrived unexpectedly early; I was to have been gagged before so as not to warn him of Baskerville's gruesome revenge.

'Your friend has no trust in me, Holmes. But you are a fairly intelligent man. I am sure you will do what's right...'

'I obviously have no alternative...' said Holmes in a resigned tone.

I shook my head to and fro till my head ached and my ears rang. I kicked and screamed, but all that issued was a muffled moan. Baskerville had planned his revenge as only a twisted, tortured soul was capable. Seeing my dear friend led to his slaughter was more than I could bear. I fought to hold back sobs of rage and frustration.

'I'm terribly sorry, Watson,' he said softly and advanced towards Baskerville, who held the pistol pointed at his heart. Never taking his eyes from Holmes, he stepped backward and caught up another pair of manacles. Wangi crept behind Holmes, dagger in hand.

'As soon as Jones arrives, we'll fasten you to that tree yonder. Then, when we've prepared our flight, you shall join us. When we're safe from this vicinity, you shall be released...'

'I know your history too well, Baskerville,' Holmes interjected, 'to doubt for a moment that you desire my death. I am under no illusions as to what you plan for me. But I ask you, in the name of all that's decent, to free my friend...'

He had come to the hollow then, knowing he was to die, in a valiant sacrifice for me. He had come with the same aplomb, the same steadfast resolution, that he had shown as he walked the narrow ledge of the Riechenbach Falls to meet Moriarty. His words tore at my breast. When all was said and done – in the final hour – there was no truer soul, no more gallant companion, than Sherlock Holmes. Baskerville's trembling quickened; the manacles he held clanked and rattled from his spasms. He said nothing.

'And where's your friend, Jones?' Holmes enquired slyly. 'Was he not to return post haste? Has he forgotten you? Has he fled?'

'He would be foolish to do so!' blurted Baskerville. 'The ransom is taken! Our flight is set!'

Yet, for all his braggadocio, a wave of uncertainty crossed his face.

His entire body twitched with nervousness. It is said that partners in crime never trust each other. The doubtful flicker on Baskerville's face showed me the saying's truth.

'You are right, Baskerville. I have no desire to see my friends perish at your hand. Keep me, therefore, and free the Doctor...'

The villain approached, shackles in hand.

'I'll set your friend free as soon as you allow us to place these on your wrists. I cannot allow both of you to be free at once...'

To my horror, Holmes was taken in by this promise. He advanced towards Baskerville, arms outstretched.

'Since I'm to die, and your escape is assured, would you consent to satisfying my curiosity?'

'What is it?' snapped Baskerville with a twitch.

'Will you admit to killing Raymond Jenard?'

'Of course!' said he with a wave of the hand. 'He had to die! He discovered that Alice Allistair was aboard...'

'And McGuinness, and Compson?'

'Yes, yes!' he screamed. 'Now...'

Baskerville raised the manacles to Holmes' outstretched hands. With mounting dread, I watched as he placed the first iron band round Holmes' delicate wrist and snapped it shut. The metallic click had a chilling finality. Keeping his pistol out of reach, yet pointed at Holmes' breast, he took the free end of the shackles and led Holmes towards a smallish tree, similar to mine and not ten feet away. Thrash as I might, Holmes paid not the slightest attention to me and allowed himself to be led, timid as a sheep, in the direction of the tree. The deformed Malay crouched behind him with drawn dagger. Clearly his situation was hopeless. Soon he would be joining me, awaiting the emergence of the giant rat from its lair. The irony struck me like a hammer blow: here was a man of brilliance, dedicated to helping those in desperation and destroying evil wherever he found it. This very man was to die an ignoble and hideous death: gnawed and worried to death by a giant rodent! Hopefully, the beast would be so fearsome that we would faint dead away at the sight of it, and so be spared the worst of the agony.

But apparently the strain was too much even for Holmes. Suddenly he clasped his free hand to his chest, made a mild coughing sound, and doubled over. Stunned, Baskerville drew back and gazed in amazement at the slender, bent frame as it wheezed and choked.

The Malay showed confusion in his coarse features, and Baskerville drew close to Holmes and stretched out a hand to steady him.

It happened in an instant. I never cease to be amazed at the sudden bursts of speed and strength my friend is capable of. One moment he was bent double, and apparently on the verge of fainting. The next instant, he had dropped to a low crouch, grabbed the gun in Baskerville's hand, and was beginning the high, wide arc with his right fist. He straightened his body as he swung, and the blow had the force of every muscle in his body. My eyes could not follow it. The blow caught Baskerville on the tip of his jaw.

Holmes' advantage was only momentary, however, in a flash the Malay sprang like a panther from behind. I saw the wicked blade descend and heard my friend's sharp cry. The blade was raised again, and I closed my eyes, for I knew the second wound would be fatal. But before Wangi could drive the dagger home, there came a muffled explosion and puff of blue smoke. The wretch grabbed his middle and fell in a writhing heap upon the ground. The two men rolled over and over, locked in a death grip. The revolver, still smoking, was held in Baskerville's hand. Holmes' long, thin fingers were clasped round his wrist. They struggled fiercely; their breathing grew loud and rapid. As they rolled about, I could see the dark stain on the back of Holmes' coat growing larger as each second passed. Not a heavily built man, it wouldn't be long before his strength left him. Yet still he struggled, and seemed to get the best of Baskerville. There was a sudden flurry of motion, and I saw the glint of the pistol as it flew from Baskerville's hand, aided no doubt by Holmes' iron grip. A small splash told me it had landed in the pool.

At last the men parted, both on the verge of unconsciousness. Baskerville was reeling from the tremendous blow Holmes had dealt him. Holmes, having lost much blood, grew paler by the second. But clearly the villain had the edge, for as time passed, his condition abated, while Holmes' worsened.

Baskerville looked round for help, but it would not come from his gnomelike servant. The Malay, tangled in his white robe, flopped and writhed grotesquely on the earth like a giant flounder out of water. Still clutching at his stomach, he worked his mouth in silent gasps. There was no sound from his lips, only trickles of blood that ran down his chin. I couldn't help but pity the poor wretch. He was dying a macabre, brutish death, one that seemed oddly befitting a man of his cruel and bestial nature.

As a last resort, Baskerville staggered to the side of his fallen accomplice and seized the dagger. Twenty feet away, Holmes stared back. It was the first, and last, time I observed a look of fear on his face. Too weak to run, he had no escape. He glared at the serpentine blade of this kris, the instrument that had gravely wounded him, and was now to kill him. Baskerville lurched forward. Even in his exhausted state, the prospect of final revenge caused his shoulders to shake with laughter. Holmes dropped to his knees. He reached round to grab at his wound. His eyelids flickered.

Ten feet away Baskerville, knife raised, made a final lunge. For an instant Holmes dropped his head, staring at the ground. Then, as Baskerville seemed to hover over him like the Angel of Death, his left hand made two tight circles in the air. The chain whirred. Holmes staggered to his feet, swept his hand wide, and the whirling manacle caught Baskerville on the ear with all the force of a mace and chain. He dropped senseless and Holmes, pale as a ghost, hobbled over to where I sat chained to the tree. He tore the gag from my face, clapped his hand to my shoulder.

'Watson!' he panted. 'Can you ever forgive me...'

'Holmes! Behind you!'

Baskerville was moving. With all the persistence of Hydra, he refused to succumb. He crawled towards the fissure in the rock. Holmes, realizing the danger immediately, rose to his feet in pursuit. But after two steps he fell, and could not rise.

'... I have not the strength...' he said weakly.

Baskerville disappeared into the cave. Wangi lay motionless. Holmes stirred his legs slowly, like a child awakening from deep slumber. The mist was rising. Now a great deal of the high rock wall was visible. I could see almost to its summit. The hole in the cliffside glared at me like a monstrous eye socket. All was silent. Perhaps Baskerville had fainted...

Then it began: a series of thumps, then the animal cry. Behind the snuffling growls, I could hear a crazed cackle as Baskerville goaded the beast into a frenzy. The reader may think that by this time I was inured to horror. However the opposite was the case: I was in a state of complete emotional collapse. As the raucous cries bellowed from the cavern, my vision grew dim. All things grew dark and blurry, save for that thing upon which my eyes were riveted: the mouth of the cave.

Holmes slowly raised himself up on his elbows and stared likewise. He tried to bring his knees under him in an attempt to stand, but it was useless; the strength had oozed from him. His fingers clutched the earth and pawed it idly.

'... I am so... tired, Watson...'

Baskerville cried out twice. But his shouts were soon obscured by a series of sharp squeals. All was silent for a moment. Then the guttural grunting and snuffling was heard again. The sound seemed to change: it grew less sonorous, higher. The beast was drawing near to the entrance of the cave. I heard too the scraping of feet on earth and the crunching of small stones.

In an instant, I was looking at it. It took my breath away, for never have I seen a sight so foul, so horrid, as that face which peered from its burrow. The huge nose twitched, the rat ears turned in small jerks. The small eyes rolled. Holmes groaned in horror and disbelief. It was immense. The head was almost two feet long. It grunted and growled. Sniffing the air, it came to focus upon the prostrate form of my friend. No doubt it smelled his blood. Then, horror of horrors! It squealed in rage, popping its jaws and revealing enormous incisor teeth!

Holmes, the colour drained from his face, stared transfixed at the monster. It lunged forward, yet something held it back. It was then that I noticed the hawser round its neck. It was as thick as a man's wrist. The animal snapped its head back and tore at the rope. It paused for a moment to glare in our direction, and I saw the cable was half-gnawed through. In a moment, it would be free.

'Goodbye, Holmes...' I said with an air of resignation.

The monster lunged again. With a crack, the cable broke. It bounded into the clearing, a gigantic grey-black creature. It paused for a moment, then ran at Holmes, head down, jaws open.

'Holmes! Holmes! Dear God!' I remember shrieking. But my senses again grew dim. In the swirling darkness that descended around me, I could yet see the huge monster – maddened no doubt by the smell of blood – grasp Holmes' shoulder with its huge teeth and shake him. The tiny eyes rolled in frenzy, and the rat let forth a guttural squeal of rage.

I also heard, dimly and as if from a great distance, Holmes cry out in pain. The next instant he was hurled over on to his back. He flung his fists desperately at the huge head and gnashing teeth, but they had little effect. He would not last more than half a minute. Overcome with fear and sorrow, I fainted dead away.

Twelve

RECOVERY

I was brought around by an enormous crash that resounded through the hollow and seemed to shake the very earth under me. I opened my eyes to see Holmes miraculously still alive, pawing feebly at the monster, which suddenly jerked upright and spun in a tight circle, biting at its own flank. Shortly thereafter, the creature seemed to be mysteriously propelled backwards by an invisible jolt, and the next instant came a second explosion. In the ringing silence that followed, I heard the metallic sound of a breech working. There came, too, the sound of footsteps above me. A shower of pebbles fell into the pool. I looked up and could see through the mist the outline of a figure at the cliff's edge. Could it be Jones?

There came a dull thump as the animal was spun about and flung down, then a third and final crash. It twitched twice, then lay still. A small hole in its side poured forth great rivulets of blood. I then had an inkling of who the figure on the cliffside was. But when I again looked up, it was gone.

For perhaps a minute, there was no sound except the waterfall.

Baskerville was somewhere in the dark recesses of the cave either dead or maimed, for it was apparent by his cries that the rat had attacked him. Wangi was beyond help. My immediate concern was for Holmes.

I cannot describe my relief when I saw him thrash about, heard him curse, and saw him draw himself up into a sitting position.

'Ah Watson, how utterly foolish of me! I should never have undertaken this plan under –'

He paused to groan and reach for his shoulder.

'– under these conditions...'

'What plan? Do you –'

But I was interrupted by a small man scurrying into the clearing with blinding speed. He rushed to Holmes' side and knelt over him. Dressed in a macintosh and felt hat, I could not recognize him until I heard the familiar, intense voice.

'Are you all right, man?'

'I might live, but no thanks to you, Lestrade,' said Holmes dryly. 'I'll keep – unfasten Watson and use the shackles to secure our friend in the cave.' He inclined his head in the proper direction.

Lestrade extracted a huge ring of keys from his coat pocket and was at my side in no time.

'Ah, standard Naval issue, these. I have a key right here – have you free in no time, old man...'

I fairly bubbled over with questions. How long had he been nearby? Who was the figure on the cliff? Did Holmes arrange it all beforehand? My questions were unanswered, however, because as soon as I was released Lestrade dashed to the mouth of the cave and disappeared.

Upon being freed, my first duty was to tend to Holmes' wound. I took off his coat and shirt. Fortunately, Wangi had dealt him a glancing blow; the blade had entered the right shoulder directly from above – parallel to the spine. But it had been deflected outwards by the shoulder blade. Consequently, a good deal of muscle tissue had been severed (which accounted for the heavy bleeding) but no organs were damaged. I made a crude pressure bandage and sling from his shirt. Holmes was able to stand, but just barely.

'By Jove, look, Holmes!' I said, pointing up the hillside.

Ian Farthway entered the clearing carrying his rifle. He walked straight to the dead animal and kicked it twice. Satisfied, he joined us, his face full of apology.

'You needn't bother to explain, Farthway,' said Holmes. 'The heavy mist made things impossible. I shall never forgive myself for placing Watson in this predicament!'

'You were stationed up there all along?'

'Yes, Doctor. Unfortunately, the mist made all of you invisible. I was unable to get a clear shot until the beast was almost upon you —'

'Holmes! What is this thing?' I enquired as I walked unsteadily towards the animal that lay frozen in death. Holmes, leaning on Farthway, followed slowly. The animal was strange indeed. While its head looked like a rat's, save for the size, the body resembled a pig. Were it not for the men it had killed and the horrific start it had given us, one could almost say it had a comical appearance.

Holmes stood between us; we held him up.

'There's your giant rat, Watson: *Tapirus Indicus*. The Sumatran tapir, a nocturnal pachyderm whose nearest living relative is the horse. See here...'

He knelt at the side of the strange beast and pulled up the fleshy snout, revealing huge yellow teeth.

'In tooth structure, it is almost identical to the horse. Note these incisor teeth, Watson, which you so astutely identified aboard the *Matilda Briggs* by the wounds they left.'

'Then it must be vegetarian. Why did it attack humans?'

'We cannot be sure. In nature it is a shy beast. It feeds at night along jungle river banks, avoiding people altogether. But in the hands of a warped personality like Baskerville, Heaven knows what it could become...'

'He seems to have a talent for training diabolical creatures. This animal then killed out of rage, not for food. But why did Baskerville bring it with him? What was the purpose served?'

'I shall tell all at length, Watson. It's the very least I owe you, having endangered your life and sanity. However, I am still slightly fuzzy...'

He grew suddenly heavy in our arms, and we set him gently on the ground. A cry for assistance came from the cavern, and Farthway hurried off to help.

'Once again my apologies, dear fellow. When I warned you of the possible danger involved, I had no idea...'

'I understand. Now let me fetch some water.'

'I had of course arranged for double coverage for you,' he continued between sips. 'Farthway above you and Lestrade in the hollow. As luck would have it, neither could help. Whilst Farthway was foiled by the mist, Lestrade probably had trouble with Jones −'

'You didn't interfere!'

'Oh yes we did. But here's Lestrade himself to tell us. Well, Lestrade, you have our friend in tow?'

The two men carried Baskerville into the clearing and laid him down. He was in a light coma. He moaned and shook as a child does in a nightmare. That word seemed an apt description of what his life had become. His wounds, which I examined, were minor, but the head injuries Holmes had given him could have severe consequences. But considering the condition of the man's brain, I doubted they could have anything but beneficial effects. I looked down and shook my head slowly.

'He'll never stand trial.'

'Why so?' asked Farthway. 'We all heard his confession. Mr Holmes asked him the questions deliberately –'

'Much as we'd like to see him hang, no physician or judge of any competence would rule him fit for trial or sentencing. The man's in the final stages of insanity. No doubt he's been suffering for years, but the strain and anticipation of this episode sent him over the edge.'

'My opinion, while non-professional, concurs with yours,' said Holmes. 'He's bound for Bedlam, not Dartmoor...'

Baskerville began to stir and moan. Lestrade, always the professional, slipped a pair of handcuffs on his wrists.

'I shall send for a wagon in town,' he said, 'but first we must track down Sampson –'

'No need, there he is yonder. And look at the cargo strung on his back!'

The boatswain, with his rolling sailor's gait, strode easily down the hollow with Jones flung across his shoulder like a sea bag. Reaching us, he dumped the man unceremoniously upon the ground like a load of rubbish. The man didn't move. He'd been beaten severely round the head, and a glance at John Sampson's flayed knuckles revealed the source of his injuries. Sampson did not speak, but continued to glower at the two unconscious villians who lay sprawled on the earth, only a few feet from the grotesque monster.

Remembering the Malay, I bent over him, and was immediately conscious of a human stench that was more noxious than the animal one. As I suspected, he was dead.

'What has happened to Alice Allistair?'

'All is well, Watson. Lestrade and Sampson intercepted Jones and the young lady directly they left the hollow. There was a bit of a chase, which explains Lestrade's absence from our predicament. The girl is now safely in Strathcombe, engaged in a joyful reunion with her parents.'

And so our sad and ragged procession wound its way out of the dreary place, leaving behind the two bodies: one of a misshapen brown man whom fate had cast far from his homeland, to die in a dank pit at the hands of the white men he served; the other, a strange and timid creature of the jungle streams who, in the hands of a madman filled with hate, had become a ferocious killer.

The trek through the forest tired us more than we anticipated, and it was a relief indeed to see Brundage waiting at the meadow's edge with a carriage and team. Baskerville's limp form was deposited on the floor, to be followed by Jones. Holmes, who had taxed himself far more than he realized, fainted with the attempt to climb aboard. We laid him on the front seat whilst I, supported by Lestrade, rode in the back. While I had lost no blood, I must admit that I was badly shaken, and the ride to Strathcombe is hazy in my memory.

As he was borne through the great hall, Holmes awoke momentarily to witness the fruits of his endeavour: the heartwarming spectacle of Lord and Lady Allistair, in a state of complete relief and rapture, embracing their daughter on the sofa. Holmes' lip trembled, and for the only time I can ever recall, I observed his eyes fill, and a tear across his cheek.

We were half-carried upstairs, and spent the better part of a fortnight recovering. With the help of Meg's rich stock broth, mutton chops, and stews, washed down with quarts of Ludlow ale, we recovered quickly. After slightly more than a week upon our backs, we were once again ready to venture out of doors.

Thirteen

THE POOL

I awoke. The willow boughs sighed above me. The stream chuckled over rocks and along the moss-covered banks. A titmouse pranced amongst the roots of the trees, pausing now and then to whistle. Hearing a sonorous clamour borne from afar by the wind, I turned my head to see a long skein of geese winging its way over the horizon.

'Drat!' cried a voice.

I rolled over on the grass and back into the sunshine. The sun had shifted while I slept. The warmth felt delicious on my back.

'Oh blast!' came the voice again, and I heard a great splashing commotion.

'Watson, my casting arm appears to be ruined. That heathen devil Wangi! I must say the world is none the poorer for his departure...'

'Exercise is the best thing, Holmes. That and staying in the sun. My, it's uncommonly warm for October!'

I raised myself up on my elbows and watched my companion working his fly rod in the midst of the pool. Painful as the operation was, he displayed extraordinary skill. The line swung to and fro by long

213

loops. It rolled and swung about in great circles, with a delicate hissing sound. In a final stroke, he laid the line down upon the swirling water, and the tiny coloured float drifted gaily past a boulder. Instantly, there came a great flurry of splashing water, and I caught a glimpse of the brilliant iridescence of the trout as it struck at the fly.

'Ha! There's number three, and a big fellow! It's a pity Lord Allistair doesn't make more use of his trout pool – but perhaps more fortunate for me.'

While he played the fish, I reached over the bank and drew the bottle of Barsac from its resting place in the shallows. Its sweet, heady aroma was overpowering as I drew the cork and filled the glasses.

Holmes scooped his prize up in the landing net and struggled ashore. After cleaning the fish with a skill and precision that would have done credit to any surgeon, he filled the body cavity with damp moss and placed it on a cool rock next to the others he had caught.

I drew out my watch. It was one fifteen, and the garden party was to begin at two.

'Now, Holmes, you promised. We've just enough time for you to keep it.'

'Very well, dear fellow,' he sighed as he seated himself on the bank and took a sip, 'I shall tell you all.'

'It seems incredible to me that you knew not only the identity of the kidnapper, but his plan as well. It's as if you read his very thoughts...'

'I dare say I did, almost. But there's no sorcery involved, simply keen observation and careful deduction. But where to begin? Well, the beginning will do, eh? Now Watson, it's always been my practice, in examining any crime, to separate the singular features from the ordinary ones. For it is the unique, the grotesque elements of a case that lead to its solution. No doubt I've mentioned many times before that the most difficult cases are those that lack these distinguishing features.

'Now let us consider the case of the giant rat of Sumatra in this light. As you may recall, my curiosity was pricked at the outset by the strange disposal, or shall we say "non-disposal" of Jenard's body. This flaunting of the murder deed was incomprehensible to me, at least early on. But this I knew and so stated to you: those who killed Jenard knew of me; the fact that he was put to death a street from our lodgings was certainly more than coincidental. So we have the throwing down of the body, which was really a flinging down of the gauntlet by Baskerville: an invitation to do battle. You know enough of the man's character and personality to see how this brazen act would be not unnatural for him.'

I nodded my head in agreement.

'Secondly, the fact that whoever killed Jenard knew of me meant that *I* was involved somehow, directly or indirectly, with the deed.

'With Sampson's tale, my curiosity was sharpened still further, as no doubt yours was also. Considering the date of Alice Allistair's disappearance, and that part of the globe in which the *Matilda Briggs* was sailing, could not there be some connection? It was a remote possibility, but still a possibility.

'And now would be as good a time as any to explore the question of *why* Baskerville took the bother and expense — to say nothing of the *risk* — of buying and transporting the animal itself, the giant rat, halfway round the world.'

'He was intrigued by animals. He also had an infamous talent for transforming even gentle ones into killers,' I said.

'Yes, but there's a deeper reason behind his initial decision to buy the beast and stow it aboard the *Briggs*, Watson. Shortly after listening to Sampson's fantastic story, I did some reading up on rats at the British Museum. To my astonishment, I discovered that although people in general have always loathed them, the most passionate hatred of rats is displayed by sailors. This exists throughout all written history, from the time of Odysseus to the present. This is perhaps magnified by the fact, simple and unavoidable, that there is no *escape* from rats at sea. Man and beast are locked together in the ship and must share each other's company, no matter how unpleasant. But I digress...

'Baskerville, and we must *never* underestimate his cleverness, realized that the tapir he saw on the beaches of Sumatra resembled a huge rat, especially its head. If he could only secure this animal aboard ship and give the crew the *impression* that it was a giant rat...'

'They would be terrified!' I cried. 'They would avoid that part of the ship altogether!'

'Precisely. You see, Baskerville was keenly aware that it would be difficult, if not impossible, to keep his hostage in the after hold for six weeks unnoticed. She might cry out. Jones or Wangi might leave a door ajar, and she would be seen. Furthermore, how to explain the food that must be brought to her? You see, Watson, how the presence of this "giant rat" was a perfect mask for the real crime?'

I nodded my head slowly. Surely, to quote an old phrase, there was 'method in his madness'.

'When did you determine the beast was a tapir, and how did you come to know this?'

'I was nearly certain of the animal's identity early on by a process of elimination. I knew the animal was huge, and resembled a rat, in the head at least. After some research I struck upon the Sumatran tapir. For a time I admit I was put off the scent by the complete unanimity of the authorities on the tapir that it is a placid and nocturnal herbivore. But I have since found evidence that the recent catastrophic explosion of Krakatoa, an island off the Sumatran coast, has had extraordinary effects upon the habits and behaviour of many animal species throughout the area. The tapir is not found in captivity, so it's no wonder that superstitious sailors took it for a giant rat. Since Baskerville was anxious that the head be seen, but not the body, we can assume that he indeed wished everyone aboard the *Briggs* to think there was such a beast on board.'

'Then why was it taken aboard in secrecy?'

'As you've probably suspected, Alice Allistair was in the crate along with the rat. Not in the same compartment, of course, because they had partitioned it. But she was swung aboard with the monster, and confined in the same dingy hold with it for the entire voyage. You recall Winkler's mention of Jones "sneaking food aft"? Remember the food was in two bundles, one thrice the other's size?'

'Of course, the large bundle for the animal, the small one for Alice. Lord, to be shut up with that beast for eight weeks, the horror, the cruelty of it!'

'Quite so. She was no doubt in terror every second of the long voyage. It is remarkable she still has her wits. Surely a girl of lesser character and will would have succumbed long ago –'

'She is not yet fully recovered,' I said in a professional tone.

'I can see that. Well, to return to our investigation. Upon visiting the *Matilda Briggs*, I uncovered two pieces of evidence which gave further credence to my embryonic theory: the candle stub and the message in candle smoke. Simply stated, both together told me that someone posing as Jenard – but definitely *not* Jenard – was giving us a clue as to the nature of the real crime behind the so-called giant rat. In a hasty, almost childish, bit of verse –'

'All is stairs and passageways where the rat sleeps, his treasure keeps –'

'Yes, now it's painfully obvious that the first three words, minus the middle and final "s", spell Allistair –'

'By Jove, it never occurred to me!'

'Well it did to me,' he remarked with some scorn. 'In any event, the message gave a good deal of weight to my supposition that Alice Allistair was, or had been, aboard the vessel. The crucial point is that someone was attempting to give the impression that Jenard had written the words as a warning to the world. Both yourself and Lestrade interpreted the words this way. However, we knew by the candle butt that Jenard couldn't have written them. Why then was the message written at all?'

Holmes paused to refill his glass.

'Barsac, the sweetest of the Sauternes... it's almost cloying...'

'Dash it, Holmes! Get on with the story!'

'Someone wished to cast me on to the scent of the Allistair kidnapping, yet wished to do so as Jenard.

'You see, if Jenard had intended to give warning of the rat, why not do so plainly? Clearly, the cryptic warning was meant to arouse my interest, for whoever wrote it was certain I'd decipher it. Evidently that person knew me well. In short, Watson, I suspected a trap, an ensnarement aimed at *me*.'

'You knew it was Baskerville?'

'No. I didn't even suspect it could be him until after our luncheon at the Binnacle. You'll recall that both Scanlon and Thomas mentioned "Reverend Ripley's" fascination with petrels and plankton...'

'Yes. I thought it curious you were so interested in that...'

'Details, Watson. *Details!* Of course you remember Baskerville's naturalistic bent, especially his fondness for collecting butterflies. Well, I had an inkling it could be him, since who else should wish to ensnare me? Moriarty is dead for several years, and others who have vowed my death are behind bars. I sent a wire to Exeter, and the reply I got was "no absolute proof". No one, then, had found Baskerville's body. He *could* still be alive. Considering the general cunning of the man, I went on this assumption. It would be natural for him to plan an escape if things went wrong. Besides, who could be a likelier candidate to train a giant rat than the man who had trained the giant hound?'

'The pieces certainly fit,' said I.

'But where *was* this rat? It was not still aboard the *Briggs*. Had it been killed and dumped into Blackwall Reach, or somehow smuggled into London? When our trail led to the livery stable, and we there discovered that a large wagon had been bought, my suspicions grew that the animal had been slipped ashore. Remember the gold coins paid to the smith? They were Indian. Thus another link was established between the abduction of Alice Allistair from Bombay and the *Matilda Briggs*.

'The filing of the iron fence, the splotch of grease upon the quay, the frenzied behaviour of the hounds – all these told me of the loading of the rat on to the wagon in the early hours of the morning.'

'But how did the rat – the tapir – get from the ship to the quay?'

'The tapir is an aquatic animal, similar in this respect to the hippopotamus. It was a simple matter, after the tapir had finished with McGuinness, to open the lumber port, drive the beast down into the water – there being only a six-foot drop – and guide it to shore as it swam alongside the *Briggs*' dinghy.'

'Then they loaded it into the wagon,' I said, 'at the low point of the quay, made their way through the fence, replaced the cut section, and headed along the side streets...'

'But you remember, Watson, when we strolled about with the dogs, that I mentioned the "upstream events", things that appeared implausible. The first was, as we've discussed, the disposal of Jenard's body. But you also might recall the fact that Nip and Tuck showed us that the *three of us had been followed* to the Binnacle from the *Briggs*.'

'I remember. You stated that this was not normal behaviour for a criminal – to pursue the pursuers...'

'No, not normal for the average criminal. But when I considered the effrontery that this criminal was displaying, I was convinced it was Baskerville; it could be nobody else.'

'This brashness seems a hallmark of his,' I admitted. 'I remember in the earlier case he even impersonated you...'

'... but *why* did Baskerville follow us, perhaps even into the inn, if not to determine for himself that I had taken the bait, that I had become so engrossed in the case that I would follow it *anywhere*?'

'Ah, and from this point you *knew* it was a trap!'

'Certainly. Hence my apprehension, and warnings to you not to leave our flat unarmed.'

'And what were Baskerville and his henchmen doing in the interim?'

'After determining that I was indeed on the case, as hooked, you might say, as those three trout, he departed the city in the wagon, leaving Jones behind –'

'For what purpose?'

'To deliver the ransom note to the Allistairs' residence, for one. Also to keep an eye on the both of us and report developments to Baskerville, who was settling himself into Henry's Hollow, preparing for the ransoming and our execution...'

I shuddered.

'It was Jones, of course, who followed me at Paddington. I remained in London, by the way, only long enough to give the *impression* I was remaining in the city. Actually, of course, I lost him soon thereafter and later in the day returned to the station where I caught the 2:45 to Shrewsbury –'

'You were out *here* then?'

'My dear Watson, where else would I be? Back at our flat playing my fiddle whilst you faced the danger alone? I made Shrewsbury my headquarters. Any wires you sent to me in London were re-routed by Lestrade's men back to me, thence to you via the city office –'

'Then this explains the delay in messages,' said I. 'Were you ever in the Rutlidge telegraph office?'

'Yes, now that you mention it. On the night of your arrival —'

'And were you not dressed as a gypsy?'

'Quite so, good for you, Watson! Yes, it was quite a game of cat and mouse with Baskerville. You see, I knew I had to be on the scene to get the necessary information. Yet, if any of them discovered me near Strathcombe when I was supposed to be in London, the game would have been up in an instant — I was forced to be extremely furtive, and adopted the gypsy dress...'

'I can understand your secrecy with Baskerville,' I said in a hurt tone, 'but why was *I* not informed?'

'Simple: neither you nor Lord Allistair is a good actor, Watson. This is because deceit is not in your natures. To apprise you of my plans would have rendered them useless. Your actions would have given us away in an instant. Baskerville would either fly or kill the girl. It has been a nerve-racking business. But I was hereabouts as much as I dared, keeping a lookout. Incidently, it might interest you to know that it was *I* who was watching you from the Keep. Never at any time were you more than a mile from us —'

'*Us?*'

'Either Farthway or myself. We kept in constant touch, even after my "official arrival" at the lodge. This explains the semaphore lamp too. A capital idea of Farthway's, don't you think? His cottage being directly below my room, and the lamp pointing towards the forest, it was thus a simple matter for Lestrade, Farthway, and me to be in constant communication...'

'This grows wearying,' said I, reaching for the bottle. 'So Farthway was your cohort, and our guardian. This explains his odd behaviour —'

'Yes, his early morning jaunts, his knowledge of your visit to the Hollow — for he followed you there and back — and his irritation that you'd exposed yourself to danger.'

'... I must apologize to him... I take it then, you sought him out early on, before even our arrival here.'

'Yes indeed, for I heard of his courage and reliability – not to mention the marksmanship to which we owe our lives.'

'Ah. And you wisely summoned Lestrade and Sampson too. The boatswain behaved most admirably – doubtless because he was driven to avenge his dead friend.'

'But despite the help I had, I was unable, unfortunately, to prevent the death of this Compson fellow –'

'You couldn't be everywhere at once. Now tell me the particulars about what occurred the night before our ordeal.'

'Our night-time errand, as you may have surmised by now, was a last-minute reconnaissance of the enemy's camp. I was fairly certain the exchange would take place in the Hollow, but a final check was necessary to make sure. We did creep close enough to see the campfire, and the manacles set out in readiness.'

'Why did you not seize them all then?'

'Are you forgetting the girl? No, we could not attempt anything by force with her confined in the cavern –'

'Yes, quite so. But how did you guess the note was to be delivered at dawn?'

'I knew Baskerville would try to spring his trap as soon as possible after the quarry was within range. Because of this, I deliberately made my "arrival" as obvious as possible. Brundage met me at the train, unaware that I had merely taken it down the line a stop – in the dead of night – and back again to Shrewsbury at lunchtime. No doubt one of the confederates saw my arrival as well and passed the word.

'It was no surprise to learn that the ransom note was delivered within hours of my arrival. Once Baskerville learned I was on the scene, he acted at once.'

'It did strike me as curious that you arrived in so noticeable a fashion, almost in defiance of the warning note.'

'The caution to the Allistairs not to seek assistance was clever of Baskerville. For, much as he wished me to come out here, he realized that any note he sent without the standard warning would lack authenticity. He went on the assumption that if my curiosity were sufficiently aroused, I'd come anyway.'

'So you came openly to show him his lure had worked.'

'Yes, I wanted to indulge his sense of his own genius and cunning: to make him feel he'd outwitted me. This, incidently, was another reason I didn't leave London directly, but played the waiting game.'

I paused momentarily to wipe my brow.

'Your explanations have proved most illuminating. But I still have a number of questions. What about the fire in Jenard's lodgings? And were you ever able to decipher the coded message sent to us on the ransom note?'

'I'll answer these questions as we walk up to the house. We mustn't be late for the garden party.'

Holmes packed his fish into the creel, slung his rod over his shoulder, and we walked up the sloping meadow towards Strathcombe.

'Before Lestrade carted him off, I had a long talk with Jones. He was most co-operative. It won't save him from the rope, I'm afraid, but he'll swing into eternity in a somewhat better frame of mind. The story Baskerville related to you before my arrival at the Hollow is accurate. The kidnappers smuggled the girl from India in the manner described. By the way, Watson, I was aware of their flight across India. My questions to the British Railways offices proved fruitful.

'Once they had Alice aboard the *Matilda Briggs* and bound for home their problems seemed over. McGuinness bent to their will, and they had the giant rat to protect their secret. Shortly before arriving in

London, however, one crewman, Raymond Jenard, discovered the *real* secret in the after hold. We'll never know how he found out, for he didn't even have the chance to tell his good friend John Sampson about the captive lady, Sampson being engaged elsewhere.

'Jenard, upon going ashore, vowed to notify the authorities. However, he decided to grab a pint at a waterfront tavern beforehand. There, he asked the barkeeper for advice. This barkeeper knows me well – I am bound by oath not to mention his name or the name of his establishment to anyone – and recommended that Jenard walk across town to see me. Is this clear so far?'

'Perfectly.'

'But as fate would have it, Jones was lounging over a mug in that same establishment, not ten feet away and hidden behind a pillar. He heard the barkeeper say, "Yes, lad, my friend Sherlock Holmes is the one to seek. You'll find him at 221B Baker Street – he's the one to tell about the captive lady..."

'Instantly Jones crouched down in his chair to hide from the departing Jenard, who failed to see him. Just before he reached the door, he turned and said, "Even if I am unable to reach this man, I have it all written down in my diary –" patting his sea bag as he says this. As soon as Jenard was on his way, Jones sped to inform Baskerville that Lady Alice had been discovered.'

Here Holmes paused to catch his breath. Though his wound had practically healed, the injury manifested itself in early fatigue.

'Leaving Alice bound in one of the cabins – they didn't worry about the crew since they'd fled the ship – they went to Jenard's rooms where they expected to intercept him. But he'd already left, headed for our flat. His sea bag was there, but not the diary. They assumed he had the diary with him. But what if he'd hidden it in the flat? Surely Jenard, knowing the true secret of the *Matilda Briggs*, must die. Eventually, the authorities would search his rooms. What if the diary were hidden there? It is at this point that a spark of Baskerville's madness boiled to the surface. Since they hadn't time to search the rooms for a diary that *might* be there, he decided to set them afire. And so, in a rage of frustration, without regard or even a warning to the other inhabitants of the building, the paraffin lamps, and spare containers also, were emptied on to the rugs, furniture, and curtains –'

'You needn't complete the story,' I interjected. 'You and I know too well the outcome…'

We stood in silence for a moment, pondering the horror and wanton brutality of it.

'Before the flames had scarcely begun to flicker, the three of them were in a hansom racing for Baker Street, all eyes peeled for Jenard. They tracked him down only a few blocks from his destination, and lured him into the clothier's doorway. This was accomplished by Baskerville, who, in a disguised voice, called for help. As might be expected, Jenard responded to the call as any decent citizen would. Once inside the doorway, the three of them set upon him. The use of the chloroformed rag – another tie with Baskerville and his butterflies, by the way – ensured a quick and silent end to Raymond Jenard.

'It is interesting to note, Watson, that had they followed their original plan and merely left Jenard's body on the rooftop, they would probably have succeeded.

'But standing there on the rooftop peering down at Jenard's body, something happened in Baskerville's twisted brain. As is characteristic of a fine mind gone awry, Baskerville fancied himself a genius. He perceived a way to accomplish *two* ends at the same time: the recovery of the ransom money *and* revenge against me.'

'Of course!' I said. 'He then deliberately mutilated the body and, at the right moment, threw it down on to the kerb to entice your curiosity –'

'Quite. He was throwing down the bait, and a gauntlet of challenge as well. Of course, you and I know the ultimate irony: I had *already* been summoned secretly into the affair by Lord Allistair himself. Had Baskerville discovered this, he would have been driven over the brink much sooner, I'm sure. Setting the trap for me was Baskerville's nemesis, for he allowed me to establish the links that led to his identification. Had I *not* known it was Baskerville at the centre of the web, I'm certain I would have advised Lord Allistair to pay the money and be done with it. They, at least, Baskerville and Jones, would no doubt be *en route* to South America at this very moment.

'He carried his evil one step too far, and so was undone.'

'After fleeing down the rear ladder they returned to the *Briggs*. It was always their intention to do away with McGuinness. But now the plan changed somewhat and became bolder. Now the "rat", which was to have been killed and dumped unceremoniously into the Reach, was to do the deed.

'Just before the weird party quit the ship in the midnight darkness, Baskerville was seized with yet another idea: a warning message, supposedly penned by Jenard, that would connect the kidnapping and the mysterious giant rat of Sumatra. Thus, he crept forward in the darkness and, with the candle butt we discovered, wrote the bit of simple verse that was to guarantee my entrance into the case.'

'And from that moment on, it had Baskerville's mark on it in every detail. Now for the final question: the message done in pinpricks.'

'Pshaw! Don't tell me you haven't yet deciphered it –'

'I regret I do not possess your powers, Holmes,' I said sarcastically. 'I am merely mortal.'

'There, there, old fellow,' he chuckled. 'I remembered to bring the message with me. Here it is in my fly book.'

He opened the fleece-lined pouch and, from amidst scores of tiny feathered hooks, drew forth the message as copied by Lord Allistair and myself. He seated himself on the grass and spread the paper before him:

> LONDON – The Home Office today announced a joint production agreement signed with Belgium. It involves the manufacture of internal combustion engines.

'A simple code, although by saying that, I'm not in any way detracting from Lady Alice's cleverness – not to mention courage – in sending it to you. Your basic supposition that the dots point out letters of words is correct. Your error was in failing to recognize that, due to the brevity of the article, Lady Alice was forced to run through it several times to spell the message. Thus, a word may carry through into a different dot structure.'

'I'm afraid I don't follow you.'

'In other words, the differing dot placements do not indicate separate words, but the number of times Lady Alice "ran through" the article to find letters…'

I scratched my head in bewilderment.

'Here, let me show you,' said he with a touch of impatience.

'Your first word, counting the single dot on top as the "starter", was ATRA, is that not so?'

I nodded.

'You then assumed the second word to be spelled by the single dot underneath, which yields WARE. The other words were PISSETBE and JOHN. Since only John is a word, the others are then parts of words. In short, they are parts of a message *strung together*. If we string these in a line, we get this: ATRAWAREPISSETBEJOHN.'

'I can make nothing of it. Dash it, man, it's not as simple as you say!'

'I forgot to mention that you made *two* errors in attempting to decode this. The second was assuming that the next word was formed by the single dot underneath, rather than the double one on top. Following this template, we interchange the WARE and PISSETBE, to get the following: ATRAPISSETBEWAREJOHN.'

I stared vacantly at it for a few seconds before the message jumped forth: A TRAP IS SET BEWARE JOHN.

'What an ass I am!' I cried.

Holmes made no comment.

'I certainly owe Alice my deepest appreciation. She is clever indeed to have thought up this cryptogram at a moment's notice. I take it you knew the message all along.'

'Yes. But of course to tell you of Baskerville's trap would have altered your behaviour; he could sense trouble in an instant. No, indeed. For my plan to work, which it did just *barely* I'm ashamed to say, it was necessary for you to be in the dark on all counts. I have never regretted anything more in my life, Watson, than putting you through that trial in the Hollow. You are visibly greyer in the temples, if you haven't noticed. I can scarcely look my old friend in the face without a twinge of guilt.'

I stared at the ground for a moment before replying, for my throat had caught that curious tightening ache that comes in times of deep emotion.

'There... there was absolutely no other way...' I managed at last. 'We all did our best.'

We finished the walk in silence, since any additional words would only have subtracted from the moment. When we entered the stone gate, however, and the long linen-covered tables were visible at the end of the great lawn, Holmes resumed.

'On the bright side, of course, there's Lord Allistair's generosity towards us.'

'*Generosity?* My dear Holmes, rich as the man is, his gifts border on the foolhardy!'

As he threw his head back in laughter though, I could not help but recall the dark side of the adventure's conclusion. It was a sad and tragic spectacle, and will haunt my memories till the end of my days. I can still call up the picture in vivid detail: Rodger Baskerville strapped to a leather pallet, soaked through with sweat as he thrashed his head and shrieked. In his ravings he'd bitten through his tongue, and his cheeks were flecked with red froth. As they slid the pallet into the van he began to call Holmes' name. They drew the steel door shut and locked it, and the wagon began its tortuous journey down the road. But even as it drew further and further away, I could still hear issuing from the tiny barred window in the steel door the ringing voice of the lunatic: '*Holmes – no walls shall hold me!*'

'There, there, Watson, try to think more pleasant thoughts! His suffering has probably diminished with time.'

'You've read my thoughts!'

'No. I've read your face. You were staring down that bend in the road where we last saw the asylum carriage. Your face bore a look of hatred, then, as might be expected of a physician and man of your character: pity.'

'Perhaps it should have borne the look of fear as well. You recall his boast of escaping. If any man could devise a means of escaping the stoutest walls, it is he.'

'True. But happiness in life consists largely of refusing to worry about matters over which one has no control.'

We had by this time reached the low stone fence that surrounded the immediate lawns of the estate. As we turned and entered at the gate, we could see, at the far edge of the green expanse, several long banquet tables covered in gleaming linen. A score or so of servants hurried to and fro, bearing silver trays and steaming dishes. A line of carriages stood in the drive, with more arriving by the minute. We seated ourselves on a stone bench, and presently saw coming towards us a handsome and heartwarming sight.

'Ah Watson, it takes no great brain power to fathom the reason for Farthway's presence at Strathcombe, does it now?'

'Certainly not,' I replied. 'Well, I'm terribly happy for the both of them.'

Arm in arm, Alice Allistair and Ian Farthway made their way slowly towards us. The lady's step was still a bit unsteady, but Farthway's, strong arms and noble bearing were a tremendous reassurance. The tender glances they exchanged were further evidence of a bond that had existed for some time and showed no sign of diminishing.

Alice Allistair was fast on the mend – as each day passed she had grown more and more to resemble the lovely creature I had seen in the family portraits. With help from all of us, she seated herself on the bench.

With genuine gratitude and admiration, I wrung her hand in thanks for her clever coded message. She brushed off the string of compliments with becoming modesty and folded her hands in her lap.

'Now, Ian, you mustn't scold me,' she said in mock anger, 'I've been waiting to tell these gentlemen all they wish to know – no *please*, all of you, I implore you, you must let me speak. To keep this tale locked in my bosom is to let it gnaw at my soul. I must, and shall, tell you all.'

And so the young lady, hand in hand with the man who had done so much to secure her release, related the weird and horrible tale of her abduction, which was alike in every detail to the one I was forced to hear while bound to the tree in Henry's Hollow. Her journey had grown more frightful as time progressed, for the captivity in Bombay, while unpleasant, was devoid of horror. Likewise the confinement aboard the train and trip across the Indian Ocean in the Arab trader.

'The terror did not begin until we landed in Sumatra, Mr Holmes.

There Baskerville and Jones had a long meeting which I overheard. To my amazement and horror, I learned I was to be quartered with a mad beast the natives had trapped in the jungle!'

Here she paused to compose herself and receive a reassuring glance from Farthway.

'It was not long before I discovered that it was a tapir, a usually shy animal that lives on a diet of river plants. But it seems that this animal was exceptional – perhaps a descendant of some vicious strain, for it had killed several natives who were bathing in the river.'

'This has occurred with hippopotamuses too,' interjected Farthway, 'there have been rogue hippos that have killed scores of people out of sheer malice, though they are also vegetarian and usually shy...'

'Then I can assure you, Ian, this animal was a rogue. His savage temper was not improved, I might add, by being trapped in a staked pit and lashed in a crate. Add to this the weeks of cruelty and abuse from Wangi...'

Holmes and I exchanged glances. Being forced to endure eight weeks in close proximity to this creature, it was no wonder she had been in a distraught state.

'But why,' I asked her to change the subject, 'did Jones and Baskerville appear in Batavia without you – with the Malay instead?'

'They explained the necessity of this to me before they departed. Recalling the difficulties of sneaking me from Bombay, they were not eager to repeat the experience in the port of Batavia – for the Dutch are notorious for their stringent cargo procedures –'

'So I had suspected,' observed Holmes. 'There was a great risk that you would be discovered, Lady Alice – particularly since they would be forced to enter *and* leave the port in order to place you on the *Briggs*. No, they were clever indeed to arrange for the midnight rendezvous up the coast. In this way, the port authorities could be circumvented altogether and the transfer made –'

'– the only remaining witnesses were the crew, whom they drugged with liquor...' I added.

'It was all carefully arranged,' explained Alice, her eyes growing damp. 'I was left in the care of that savage group of men – with only the promise of gold as a pledge of my safety...'

'What a dreadful man!' I said.

'For their part, they took the wretch Wangi along as a guide and hostage both –'

'Hardly an equal exchange –' snorted Farthway.

'The three of them made their way in a small *proa* southwards. We were to follow in a few days to a prearranged meeting place down the coast. They had little difficulty in locating a ship departing for England. Having bent Captain James McGuinness to their will by threats and bribes, they were in complete command of the *Briggs* from the instant she left the docks of Batavia...'

'You needn't continue your painful narrative, Lady Alice,' said Holmes rising. 'The rendezvous and the transferring of cargo we know of through John Sampson. The voyage, with all of its pain and horror, we can only imagine. Now here come your parents out on to the terrace. Do let's go up.'

We walked up the garden path to greet the Allistairs, who had just strode down the terrace steps. Certainly the spirit rules the body, for with the return of Alice and the lifting of the enormous emotional burden shared for so long, they appeared years younger.

'I suppose the only thing that still puzzles me,' mused Lord Allistair as he settled his wife into a garden chair and sat down next to her, 'is the personal desire for vengeance against me on Baskerville's part. Did you by chance ever discover his motive?' he asked his daughter.

'No, not specifically. He only said you'd wronged him years ago...'

His Lordship knitted his brows in concentration.

'I cannot recall it,' he said finally.

'He wouldn't tell me, though I asked him,' said I. 'I suppose we'll never know.'

A gentle cough came from Holmes' direction. All eyes focused on his gaunt form, slung nonchalantly in the wicker chair.

'It is just possible, Lord Allistair,' said he in a soft voice, 'that you have overlooked an event which occurred twelve years ago...'

Lord Allistair sipped at his port, the same quizzical expression on his face.

'That would have been in eighty-two. Ah, I see it now! It was in eighty-two that Cavendish was murdered in Phoenix Park – surely this has something to do with Home Rule and Parnell –'

'No, sir. It is more personal. In eighteen-eighty-two your son Peter was nine years old...'

Instantly, the puzzlement left Lord Allistair's face.

'Mr Holmes, may I see you alone for a moment?'

'Of course. But perhaps you wish to let the matter drop altogether.'

After a momentary struggle within himself, Lord Allistair faced his wife with a candid and frank expression.

'Elizabeth, there is something you must know that up until now I have not told you –'

Farthway and I rose to go, and I was dumbstruck by Holmes' arrogance and callousness by remaining seated.

'Please gentlemen, stay!' said Lord Allistair, raising his hand. 'You, Doctor, especially, have the right to know the events that led to the endangering of your life. Now, dearest, you needn't look so alarmed – what I am about to reveal I am ashamed of, but it is not something that would come between us.

'Now, Mr Holmes, there is more than one side to this story, but having seen you work, if only briefly, I am assuming you are in command of all the facts –'

'That would be a safe assumption, Lord Allistair.'

'Then let me begin by telling all of you,' and he swept his arm in a circle as he spoke, 'that while innocent of the crime itself, I am guilty of protecting the guilty party, and so am guilty as an accomplice.'

We stared with incredulity at him. Was this man, who had so distinguished himself in the public service, about to tarnish his glittering career?

'In the year mentioned, my son Peter began his second year at the Malton School in Yorkshire, which was run by a man named Vandeleur – are we not thinking along the same lines, Mr Holmes?'

'Yes, sir, we are. And by the way, I cannot tell you how delighted I am that you're –'

'Making it public at last? Hah! It should have been done years ago, in an honest and forthright manner. I owe you yet another debt, sir, in bringing this to my attention. Thank you for your offer to keep the matter quiet; but upon even a moment's reflection, I can see that if my word's to mean anything, I must tell all –'

'As I knew you would –'

'Well then, a little way into the term, you can imagine my surprise when I was informed by the headmaster – this Vandeleur fellow – that my son had cheated in his exams.'

There was a short silence as we absorbed this detail. I saw Lady Allistair wince.

'Since I was unable to leave London at the time – the Irish crisis I mentioned was at its height – I wrote to Peter and asked him if the charge were true. He answered that it was. I was of course mortified to learn the charge was true – but gladdened that Peter had voluntarily confessed. Well, as most of you can surmise, the cheating incident would mean that Peter's chances of attending Harrow, or any other

decent school, were shot. I was distressed that such a foolish incident –
and I say *incident* because Peter is a generally honest fellow – that such
an incident should ruin his life.'

He paused to sip his port, and, in a reflective tone, continued.

'But just as I resigned myself to it, there came a letter from Vandeleur,
informing me that, for a certain sum of money, he would keep the
matter quiet...'

'I say! The leopard doesn't change his spots, eh Holmes?' I said, for
I remembered 'Vandeleur' well.

'Well I, of course, was revolted by this offer, tempting though it was.
But what sort of man would make such an offer? Not a man who should
run a boys' school, I concluded. Therefore, I engaged a professional
acquaintance of mine in the area to look into the school. Were there
any irregularities? How was the place financed? This sort of thing. In
less than a fortnight, he'd uncovered enough malpractices – I needn't
elaborate – to send Vandeleur to jail for a long, long time. You see, I
wasn't the first person he'd tried to wring...'

'And so you, through your agent, approached him with your
evidence,' said Lady Allistair.

'That is correct. Realizing he was caught in his own web, the man
fled, the matter of the cheating was forgotten, and nothing of the
incident has surfaced until now. I deeply apologize, dearest, and to all
of you as well, for having kept it secret.'

'I remember your explaining this part of Baskerville's past to me,'
said I. 'This then led to your questions about young Peter and his
schooling at the Allistairs' London residence.'

'Yes. When I heard of the Yorkshire school, the last piece in the
puzzle had fallen into place. For as driven by money as Baskerville
was, he was driven even more by hatred and revenge. Well, the
time has come to put aside all unpleasant things. Let us talk of the

future. Mr Farthway, am I given to understand that you'll shake off this rustic life and return to London with the Allistairs? Ah, and you'll be seeing quite a bit of a certain young lady, yes? Well, that is good news. It should interest all of you that John Sampson has been promoted by the Oriental Trading Company to be first mate aboard the *Matilda Briggs.*'

'Splendid!' we cried, and raised our glasses.

'I'm afraid we must retire to the Hall to greet our guests,' said His Lordship rising. 'You're free to join us, or amuse yourselves in any way you please until luncheon. Come, dearest, up we go.'

We hadn't long to wait, that was obvious. The servants, at an ever-increasing pace, filled the long tables with an array of food that staggered the imagination: partridges in plum chutney, skewered rack of lamb, cold cracked lobster, asparagus in lemon sauce, chilled turbot, fresh baked breads and pies – the list was endless. All this was to be accompanied by three white wines and four reds, iced cider, local beer and ale, and an array of fine brandies.

'What shall we all do then?' asked Alice. 'We've only a little while. Shall we go – oh Beryl! There's my dear Beryl – come, Ian, you must meet her, you really must!'

So saying, she led him into the house, leaving the two of us alone on the terrace.

'Well, there'll be another tearful reunion. I'm sure Miss Haskins' recovery is almost complete. I can see the holiday in Brighton did her a world of good. No, let's not go in, Watson. Nice as they are, I'm sure that most of the people don't have much to say that's of interest to me.'

'I agree. What shall we do then?'

'Ah, look yonder, under that Chinese elm. Is that not a croquet field?'

'So it is, how about a match?'

So after a few minutes of practice, during which the air was filled with the gentle clacking of wooden spheres and mallets, Holmes approached the home stake.

'Watson, I shall take the yellow, and you the red… so. Now then, old fellow, shall we toss for first hit?'

POSTSCRIPT

Over the strong objections of my modest friend Doctor John Watson, I have taken the liberty of inserting this brief note at the conclusion of the adventure that has come to be known as The Giant Rat of Sumatra.

As mentioned in passing in the last chapter of this manuscript both Watson and I were given cheques by Lord Allistair upon the safe return of his daughter. The sum shall not be named, but suffice it to say that it made the earlier cheque given to me by the Duke of Holdernesse[*] seem paltry indeed. I invested my share in a variety of ways, some of which, I am loath to admit, hardly reflect the acumen portrayed in so many of Watson's stories.

What I wish to make public in this postscript (again, over the protestations of my friend) is the investment Watson made with the lion's share of his gift.

If you enter the halls of a great London hospital and amble about, before long you'll come to a small wing, newer than the rest, devoted

---

[*] Given to Holmes at the close of *The Adventure of the Priory School.*

exclusively to the treatment of children suffering from burns. A small brass plaque, affixed to the wall at the entrance, reads 'Dedicated to the memory of Abbie Wellings, who died in the fire of 15 September 1894'. The person responsible for the construction and maintenance of this facility is John H. Watson, MD. In addition to providing the major part of the funds required, Watson also prevailed upon a large number of friends, myself included, for donations. I confess that of all my investments, this particular one allows me the soundest sleep, and pays the most bountiful dividends.

I make this statement because, after years of having my praises sung, I feel it is long overdue to repay in kind. Good old Watson!

S.H.
Sussex, 1912

NOTES

This book was begun in late spring of 1970. It has been, from the time of its conception, a serious attempt to continue the Sherlockian saga much as Sir Arthur Conan Doyle would have written it were he alive today. It is *not* an attempt, comical or otherwise, to show that Sherlock Holmes was what he wasn't, or wasn't what he was.

Besides the sage itself, other sources consulted in preparation of this book include William Baring-Gould's *Annotated Sherlock Holmes*, John Dickson Carr's *The Life of Sir Arthur Conan Doyle*, Dickson Carr's and Adrian Conan Doyle's *The Exploits of Sherlock Holmes*, and other works by Christopher Morley, Vincent Starrett, and others too numerous to mention here. Standard reference works include the OED, *Encyclopaedia Britannica*, *The Times Atlas*, and period maps of London and environs furnished by the Guildhall Library of the British Museum and Stanford Maps Ltd. A number of inconsistencies with the saga remain in the book. Those I am aware of remain because I feel that deleting them would interfere with the plot or detract from the mood or story line.

Those I am unaware of will no doubt be unearthed by Sherlockian enthusiasts in short order.

I am grateful to Julian Shuckburgh of W. H. Allen, Publishers, for his thoughtful comments and suggestions with regard to this edition. I also owe a tremendous debt to my brother John for his expertise and early encouragement.

The notes that follow will I hope provide the reader with some background information of interest. No attempt is made to cover each and every point in question, nor are the notes keyed to the text by footnotes, since I think they detract from the appearance and flow of the prose.

R.L.B.
Concord, Massachusetts, 1976

CHAPTER ONE

PAGE 11 *'... the point of departure was therefore St Thomas"*

We are assuming here that ambulances would only be dispatched from the larger hospitals. If this is the case, then the two hospitals named (Charing Cross and St Thomas') are appropriate. However, there were many hospitals closer to 221B, including various 'lying in' hospitals that no doubt dispatched carriages.

PAGE 11 *'... we were walking south down Baker Street towards Portman Square.'*

Fine, but if the body is discovered south of the flat, and the hospital lies also to the south, how then could the ambulance 'dash beneath' the window at 221B?

CHAPTER TWO

PAGE 28 *'Holmes... settled himself before the crackling fireplace.'*

The fireplace at 221B was designed primarily for coal, yet there are instances in the canon that refer to logs being burnt in it. Besides, what's the use of a fireplace that doesn't crackle?

PAGE 32 *'Instead of proceeding along the usual route... We were running along the coast of Sumatra.'*

Just ten years earlier (in 1883), the volcanic island of Krakatoa literally 'blew its top' in the Straits of Sunda. The explosion was probably the greatest in the history of the world – even more tremendous than our nuclear blasts. The sound was purportedly heard hundreds of miles away.

PAGE 34 *'But then I heard it: the clanking of the aft windlass...'*

The windlass is a large winch, secured by a huge wheel with a notched edge. The pawls are actually ratchets that fall into the notches, thus preventing the drum from reversing. But usually the windlass is located forward, on the foredeck, not aft. We must assume that the *Briggs*, being a cargo vessel, had several windlasses for the loading and unloading of cargo.

CHAPTER THREE

PAGE 42 *'On the diminutive side, we have our miniature ponies of the Shetland Isles...'*
Holmes is in error, of course. While Darwin's assertions are true, the Shetland pony is the result of deliberate selective breeding. Its small size was desirable for working in the mine tunnels.

CHAPTER FIVE

PAGE 77 *'Yes, Watson, if you would be so kind, get me four ounces of navy-cut.'*
According to the majority of references, Holmes generally smoked 'shag', an inexpensive tobacco that was strong and harsh. However, like most pipe smokers, he probably liked to switch tobaccos now and then. Navy-cut, invented by a sailor, is a tobacco blend obtained by twisting leaves of tobacco into a cable, then slicing into thin sections. The result is a strong, slow burning smoke of pungency that Holmes would certainly have enjoyed.

CHAPTER SEVEN

PAGE 121 *'According to legend, Henry had the forge made to re-temper his sword. With it, he vowed to kill Owen Glendower...'*
Henry IV and Glendower were, of course, real people, but the 'legend' of Henry's Hollow is entirely fantasy, as is the Hollow itself.

CHAPTER EIGHT

PAGE 128 *'The most obvious explanation is, of course, that the pinpricks point out the letters in the article either directly above or below them...'*
This 'code' was invented – or at least implemented – by Sir Arthur himself. During the First World War it was used to communicate news to British

prisoners of war. A book would be sent to the prisoner with the pinpricks commencing at a pre-arranged point. By selecting the letters indicated, the prisoner could then be truthfully apprised of the war's progress.

CHAPTER NINE

PAGE 147 *'... I tell you this because I harbour in my soul some resentment for those who've never done an honest day's work.'*
'Are you referring to me?' I bristled.
Why is Watson so defensive? Could it be that he harbours some doubts about his career? Why is it he seems to have so much free time? But are we not thankful for his lagging practice? Do we not offer prayers up daily for it? On another note, aren't we also thankful that the young Southsea physician (DoctorDoyle) found himself idle and so began *Study in Scarlet?*

CHAPTER TEN

PAGE 159 *'The Dancing Men and the Musgrave Ritual certainly were more taxing.'*
The Dancing Men would be puzzling indeed to Holmes in 1894, since he did not even solve the case until 1898!

PAGE 167 *'I quickly opened the face of my watch and felt the hands.'*
How else is Watson to tell the time in the dark? Luminous dials weren't invented yet. Note his watch is not a hunter's watch with metal face that must be opened to read the time, but rather has a plain glass crystal that could be raised to insert the winding key. We know Watson's watch had a winding key because it is clearly described at the opening of *The Sign of the Four*, when Watson gives Holmes the timepiece to examine to test the validity of the deductive method.

To tell the time in the dark, all Watson had to do is prise up the glass crystal, and orienting the '12' by feeling for the projecting stem, then feel the two hands. It was no doubt a delicate task, but one which could easily enough be mastered with sufficient practice.

CHAPTER ELEVEN

PAGE 197 *'The captain was a fierce Arab named Harun Sarouk...'*
This name is as nonsensical as those Doyle gave to the Agra confederates in *The Sign of the Four*. Harun is an Arab name. Sarouk, as many readers may know, is a type of Persian carpet.

CHAPTER TWELVE

PAGE 209 *'There's your giant rat, Watson: Tapirus Indicus.'*
Of all the elements in this story, the identity of the giant rat is the most controversial. Many readers have told me that the choice of the Sumatran tapir as the villain is unwise. The animal, they say, is timid and herbivorous and would never attack man.

While this is true, I would remind them that the hippo, also timid (usually) and herbivorous, has killed thousands of people along the rivers of Africa. Furthermore, using Holmes' own method of applying the principle of Occam's Razor, I ask them: *what then, can the animal be?* Even the biggest rats cannot exceed two feet in length. Baring-Gould mentions *Rhizomys sumatrenis* in his *Annotated Sherlock Holmes*: the great Sumatran bamboo rat. But even this monster grows to only a foot and a half in length – hardly 'giant' enough to be fearsome.

I needed an animal as fierce as Baskerville's hound, and an animal that was truly *giant*. The tapir is logical because it somewhat resembles a rodent, is truly giant, and has the proper dentition. Moreover, its range is restricted to Sumatra and the surrounding islands.

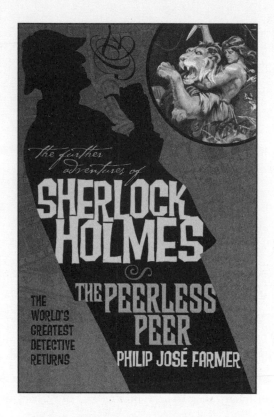

THE FURTHER ADVENTURES
OF SHERLOCK HOLMES

THE PEERLESS PEER

Philip José Farmer

During the Second World War, Mycroft Holmes dispatches his brother
Sherlock and Dr. Watson to recover a stolen formula. During their
perilous journey, they are captured by a German zeppelin. Subsequently
forced to abandon ship, the pair parachute into the dark African
jungle where they encounter the lord of the jungle himself…

ISBN: 9780857681201

AVAILABLE JUNE 2011

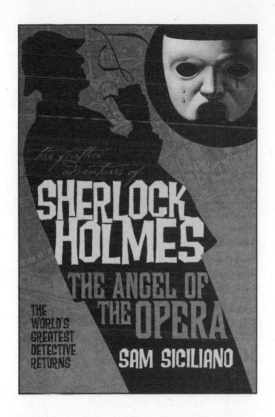

THE FURTHER ADVENTURES
OF SHERLOCK HOLMES
THE ANGEL OF THE OPERA

Sam Siciliano

the famous Opera House. Once there, he is challenged to discover the true
motivations and secrets of the notorious phantom, who rules its depths
with passion and defiance.

ISBN: 9781848568617

AVAILABLE NOW!

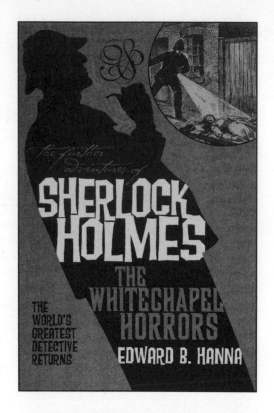

THE FURTHER ADVENTURES
OF SHERLOCK HOLMES

DR JEKYLL AND MR HOLMES

Loren D. Estleman

When Sir Danvers Carew is brutally murdered, the Queen herself calls on
Sherlock Holmes to investigate. In the course of his enquiries, the esteemed
detective is struck by the strange link between the highly respectable Dr.
Henry Jekyll and the immoral, debauched Edward Hyde...

ISBN: 9781848567474

AVAILABLE NOW!

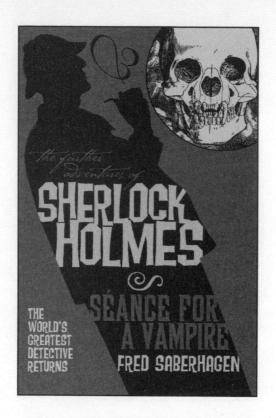

THE FURTHER ADVENTURES
OF SHERLOCK HOLMES
SÉANCE FOR A VAMPIRE

Fred Saberhagen

Wealthy British aristocrat Ambrose Altamont hires Sherlock Holmes to
expose two suspect psychics. During the ensuing séance, Altamont's
deceased daughter reappears as a vampire—and Holmes vanishes.
Watson has no choice but to summon the only one who might be able to
help — Holmes's vampire cousin, Prince Dracula.
ISBN: 9781848566774

AVAILABLE NOW!

THE FURTHER ADVENTURES
OF SHERLOCK HOLMES
THE SEVENTH BULLET

Daniel D. Victor

Sherlock Holmes and Dr. Watson travel to New York City to
investigate the assassination of true-life muckraker and author
David Graham Phillips is assassinated. They soon find themselves
caught in a web of deceit, violence and political intrigue, which
only the great Sherlock Holmes can unravel.
ISBN: 9781848566767

AVAILABLE NOW!

THE FURTHER ADVENTURES
OF SHERLOCK HOLMES

THE MAN FROM HELL

Barrie Roberts

In 1886, wealthy philanthropist Lord Backwater is found beaten
to death on the grounds of his estate. Sherlock Holmes and Dr.
Watson must pit their wits against a ruthless new enemy...
ISBN. 9781848565081

AVAILABLE NOW!

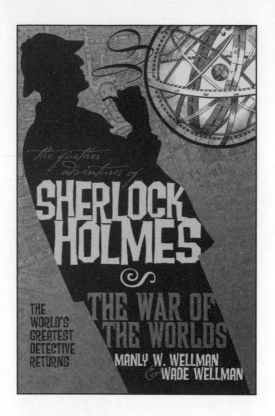

THE FURTHER ADVENTURES
OF SHERLOCK HOLMES
THE WAR OF THE WORLDS

Manley W. Wellman & Wade Wellman

Sherlock Holmes, Professor Challenger and Dr. Watson meet
their match when the streets of London are left decimated by
a prolonged alien attack. Who could be responsible for such
destruction? Sherlock Holmes is about to find out...
ISBN: 9781848564916

AVAILABLE NOW!